Christmas Stories from Georgia

Christmas Stories from Georgia

Edited by

DOROTHY DODGE ROBBINS

and KENNETH ROBBINS

UNIVERSITY PRESS OF MISSISSIPPI / *JACKSON*

www.upress.state.ms.us

The University Press of Mississippi is a member of the
Association of American University Presses.

"Christmas Eve at Johnson's Drugs N Goods"; "Yule Tides and Water Buffalo";
"A Christmas Gift for General Sherman"; "Once a Thief"; "The Education of Edie Mac";
"The Brown- and Blue-Eyed Santa Claus"; "A Conscript's Christmas"; "We Are Looking
at You, Agnes"; "Healing the Sick"; "A Holliday Tale"; and the excerpt from *Gone With
the Wind* are works of fiction. Names, characters, incidents, and places are fictitious or
are used fictitiously. The characters are products of the authors' imaginations and do not
represent any actual persons.

First edition 2005

"Little Things Mean a Lot to Little Ones" by Lewis Grizzard, reprinted by
permission of Debra Grizzard; selection from *Gone With the Wind* by Margaret
Mitchell, copyright © 1936 by Macmillan Publishing Company, a division of Macmillan,
Inc., copyright renewed © 1964 by Stephens Mitchell and Trust Company of Georgia
as executors of Margaret Mitchell Marsh, reprinted by permission of William Morris
Agency, Inc. on behalf of the author; "Christmas Eve at Johnson's Drugs N Goods"
by Toni Cade Bambara, from *The Sea Birds Are Still Alive* by Toni Cade Bambara,
copyright © 1974, 1976, 1977 by Toni Cade Babara, used by permission of Random
House, Inc.; "Memory of a Large Christmas" by Lillian Smith, reprinted by permission
of The Lillian E. Smith Foundation, Inc.; "We Are Looking at You, Agnes" by Erskine
Caldwell, copyright © 1931 by Erskine Caldwell, reprinted by permission of Virgina
Caldwell Hibbs and McIntosh & Otis, Inc.; selection from *Christmas Gift* by Ferrol
Sams, Longstreet Press, © 1989 by Ferrol Sams, reprinted by permission; "A Conscript's
Christmas" by Joel Chandler Harris, from *The Century*, vol. 41, issue 2 (Dec 1890);
selection from *The Silent Stars Go By* by Philip Lee Williams courtesy of Hill Street Press,
© 1998 by Philip Lee Williams.

Library of Congress Cataloging-in-Publication Data

Christmas stories from Georgia / edited by Dorothy Dodge Robbins and Kenneth
Robbins.—1st ed.
   p. cm.
  ISBN 1-57806-795-2 (alk. paper)
  1. Georgia—Social life and customs—Fiction. 2. Short stories, American—Georgia.
3. Christmas—Georgia—Fiction. 4. American fiction—Georgia. 5. Christmas stories,
American. I. Robbins, Dorothy Dodge. II. Robbins, Kenn.

  PS558.G4C49 2005
  813'.0108334—dc22   2005007409

British Library Cataloging-in-Publication Data available

For our siblings, with whom we shared
many delightful Christmases:
John, Michael, David, Susanna, Sarah,
Robert, Andrew, Barry, Judith,
and the late beloved Jim

Contents

CONTENTS

Introduction

DOROTHY DODGE ROBBINS

*It is a good time to feel happy, for there is
something about Christmas that seems like a recess
from a long year of work, and toil, and tribulation.*

—Bill Arp

For Georgians, Christmas has, historically and culturally, been a well-deserved and much anticipated breather from the often monotonous and arduous labors of daily life. The busy season begrudgingly affords Georgians time to partake of the recuperative spiritual, familial, and festive traditions by which they depart one year and enter another. The twelve days of Christmas provide a shared time frame for these holiday tales and memoirs by established and emerging writers, even as the stories themselves traverse several centuries of Georgia's literary heritage. From the rhododendron-rimmed Blue Ridge Mountains to the azalea-lined boulevards of Savannah, the landscapes described by these writers are exclusively Georgian, and the events, the characters, and the Christmas rituals depicted herein reflect that particular sensibility.

The Christmas season has long been associated with innocent faith in a benevolent Saint Nicholas and a gentle birth in Bethlehem. As across the world, so too in Georgia;

and yet, the land and the customs of its diverse population uniquely shape the contours of these beliefs. Memories of childhood Christmases prevail in this collection with descriptions of family gatherings, some peaceful in keeping with the spirit of the season, some turbulent in defiance of it. Fondly does Philip Lee Williams recall entering the piney woods on foot with his father and brother to harvest the perfect cedar in a selection from *The Silent Stars Go By*. In Jason Taylor's "Yule Tides and Water Buffalo," a rooftop topple reaffirms two skeptical brothers' belief in a beneficent, if clumsy, Santa. The excerpt from *Christmas Gift!*, by Ferrol Sams, gamely tries to reconcile discarded Sears, Roebuck boxes with images of a North Pole workshop, doubt with belief, and innocence with loss. But when the fallen angel returns home for the holidays in Erskine Caldwell's "We Are Looking at You, Agnes," no one wants to acknowledge her presence, let alone wish her a merry Christmas.

Christmas as marked by disenfranchised or marginalized members of society may lack the sheen, grandeur, and price tag of established middle-class rituals, but perhaps these alternative celebrations reflect more accurately the ironies and beauties of the season. For some people there is no Saint Nick with his bountiful sack. They must become Santa, for the sake of others less fortunate or equally misfortunate, and despite their own perceived damnation or salvation. This hard realization is conveyed poignantly in Janice Daugharty's "Once a Thief," Jim Hendricks's "A Holliday Tale," and Laura Dabundo's "The Brown- and Blue-Eyed Santa Claus." Lillian Smith's account of her own Depression-era Christmas, a day when convicted felons from the local chain gang were welcomed at the feast despite her family's reduced circumstances, recalls the biblical proverb describing the lion lying down with the lamb. Her title accurately dubs it—"Memory of a Large Christmas."

Certainly a one-size Christmas does not suit all participants in this collection. Disillusioned by her father's holiday absence and overwhelmed by the crass commercialism of both products and consumers in the store where she works part-time, a young woman considers a different option—Kwanza—in Toni Cade Bambara's "Christmas Eve at Johnson's Drugs N Goods." The transformative nature of the season is acknowledged as well in other selections. "The Education of Edie Mac" by Jack Slay, Jr., chronicles one Christmas season in the life of an adolescent whose tone-deaf trumpeting conjures visions of his deceased older brother. On the night of the annual holiday parade, this ghost of Christmas past wakes to guide his kid brother out of marching band and into manhood. Finally, Karen Schwind's "Healing the Sick" leaves little doubt that the laying on of hands is doubly powerful during the season of light.

Indelibly, history leaves its imprint on a people and their literature. The American Civil War provides context for three of the fictional stories in this collection. In each the observance of Christmas offers a brief and uneasy reprieve from the brutalities of war, but cannot efface the characters' knowledge of its dogged continuance. "A Conscript's Christmas" is spent in cat-and-mouse pursuit along the rugged, snow-swept trails of the Blue Ridge Mountains. Commander and deserter exchange roles in this topsy-turvy classic by Joel Chandler Harris. Ken Robbins's "A Christmas Gift for General Sherman" is one the Yankee commander can neither refuse nor exchange as he meets his tactical match in Celestine Bell of Savannah. And Scarlett O'Hara, icon of indomitable southern womanhood, woos her beloved

Ashley Wilkes, home on a brief holiday furlough, even as events of war threaten to engulf them both in this climactic chapter from Margaret Mitchell's Pulitzer Prize–winning *Gone With the Wind*.

The renowned Georgian wit and its accompanying wisdom make their presence known at intervals throughout this holiday anthology, but dominate two particular pieces. Lewis Grizzard explains why empty boxes hold the greatest appeal to the youngest of children, surpassing in interest the often complicated gadgets they house, as he lauds the humble slinky in "Little Things Mean a Lot to Little Ones." Wise men become crash test dummies and dinosaurs mingle with barnyard animals in "Nativity Scenes." Raymond Atkins provides a genealogy of biblical proportion, listing surviving and new members of his ill-fated, yet providential, child-friendly, if not childproof, crèches.

This holiday season, predictably full in scope and brief in days, may you find within the pages of this Georgia literary Christmas a sense of renewal and respite, a measure of solace and even happiness.

Christmas Stories from Georgia

Memory of a
Large Christmas

LILLIAN SMITH

Everything about our family was big: there were nine of us and our mother and father and a cousin or two, and Little Grandma when it was her turn to stay with us, and Big Grandma when it was hers, and there were three bird dogs and four cats and their kittens and once a small alligator and a pet coon. And the house took them all in. And still there were empty corners and stairways and pantries, and maybe the winter parlor would have nobody in it, but if it did you could go to the summer parlor, or if you felt too crowded you could slip in the closet under the stairs and crawl on and on until it grew small and low, then you could get down on your stomach and crawl way back where things were quiet and dim, and sometimes you liked that.

But not often. Most of the time you wanted to be with the others racing round the veranda, or huddled up somewhere playing games. It was only when Big Grandma came that we began to scramble for hide-outs, for Big Grandma filled up the whole place. She could scrouge even Christmas.

We dreaded her coming. We'd moan, Oh Mama why! And our mother would look at us, her dark eyes growing darker, darker, then she'd say softly, "Your grandmother is very good with the hog killing."

My big brothers, two, three, four of them would launch a collective protest: old Japers and Desto from the farm could handle the hogs. And Papa was there. Why Big Grandma! She gets in the way, showing the men how hogs should be stuck, calling them to do this and that, and all the time hogs squealing and Grandma getting too close to the knives and the wind blowing smoke every which-away from fires under pots where water is heating for the scraping, oh Mama!

Mother soothed her rebellious sons, "Remember the sausage. Nobody can make sausage as good as your grandmother's; she knows just how to dry the sage and rub and crumble it just right and how much red pepper to put in and she never puts in too much fat." Mother was expert in the fine usages of reiteration, "And she stuffs the skins just right," turning to the Twelve Year Old—"last year you helped her and you loved it."

"I didn't have no sense last year. I was just a kid."

Mother's voice begged. "You love her sausage and hot biscuits, everyone of you"—

"But Mama"—

"You love her sausage, remember."

Yes, we did. But we didn't love Big Grandma. Especially at Christmas.

Christmas began when pecans started falling. The early November rains loosened the nuts from their outer shells and sent them plopping like machine gun bullets on the roof of the veranda. In the night, you'd listen and you'd know IT would soon be here.

IT was *not* Thanksgiving. We skipped that day. At school, there were exercises, yes, and we dressed up like

New England Pilgrims and play-acted Priscilla and Miles Standish and made like we had just landed on Plymouth Rock. But the truth is, the only Plymouth Rocks we saw in our minds were the black and white hens scratching round at the hen house. In those days, the Pilgrims and Thanksgiving did not dent the imaginations of little Southerners, some of whose parents wouldn't concede they had a thing to be thankful for, anyway. It was football that elevated the day into a festival—but that was later than these memories.

We eased over the national holiday without one tummy ache. Turkey? that was Christmas. Pumpkin pie? not for us. Sweet potato pie was Deep South dessert in the fall. We had it once or twice a week. Now and then, Mother varied it with sweet potato pone—rather nice if you don't try it often: raw sweet potato was grated, mixed with cane syrup, milk, eggs and spices and slowly baked, then served with thick unbeaten cream; plain, earthy, caloric and good. But not Christmasy.

Pecans were. Everybody in town had at least one tree. Some had a dozen. No matter. Pecans were prestige. They fitted Christmas.

And so you lay there, listening to the drip drip of rain and plop plop of nuts, feeling something good is going to happen, something good and it won't be long now. And you'd better sneak out early in the morning before your five brothers and three sisters and get you a few pecans and hide them. Strange how those nuts made squirrels out of us. Nothing was more plentiful and yet we hid piles of them all over the place. Of course, when there are nine of you and the cousins, you get in the habit of hiding things.

. . . Christmas pushed us. Overnight the drab stores gushed forth like illuminated fountains with choice imported china dishes, sets of silver, fancy leather wallets and toilet kits, and elegant initialed white linen handkerchiefs for the men and boys, and manicure sets and perfumes and laces and silver toilet sets and sewing baskets for the women and girls, and in the jeweler's store were watches and gold pins and rings and necklaces and everywhere toys and red wagons and fire engines and tin soldiers and gold boxes of candy spangled with red velvet poinsettias, and even in the meat market there were stacks of Roman candles and sparklers and firecrackers. (We southerners were still too sullen to celebrate the Fourth, and saved our fireworks for Christmas.)

Dolls were everywhere: "penny dolls," twenty-dollar dolls, boy dolls and girl dolls, dressed dolls and naked dolls, and French bisque dolls and "china head" dolls were in drugstores, drygoods stores; the hardware store had them, too, tucked in front of the plows, perched on the yellow mule collars, decorating the ends of the snuff shelf.

You went round saying boldly, There's a beautiful doll in Mr. Pennington's store only it hasn't any clothes on, but it would look beautiful in a hemstitched white polkadotted dress with little ribbons. And you said it in time, for you hoped, although you dared not breathe it, that its dress would be made by Miss Ada. You had not quite given up your belief that Santa might have a difficult time without Miss Ada's help. So, playing it safe, you wrote a letter and kneeling on the hearth in your mother's bedroom you watched for the moment when, if you let go, the updraft from the flames would whoosh your message to the North Pole. But, having acquired a smidge of your mother's canniness, you also persuaded the Seventeen-year-old to take another letter to Miss Ada's, in case Santa dropped by. . . .

The more the illuminated fountains gushed, the deeper the nine of us were plunged in financial complexities. For there were so many to buy presents for—not only each other but the grandmas and the cousins and the cook, and the cook's husband and her grandson and the nurse, and Desto and Japers and the washerwoman out at Mt. Pisgah, who came in once a week in her rickety wagon to bring the huge white bundles of washed and ironed clothes; and teacher at school and teacher at Sunday School.

To manage it all, we toted in wood, cleaned lamp chimneys, ran to the meat market for the steak for supper, swept Grandma's room, made our beds without being told, swept the tiled walks that led to the street, washed our mother's handkerchiefs, washed our father's socks, offered to wash his feet after he'd walked home from the office. And sometimes he'd let us, as he sat reading the *Savannah News* or the *Florida Times-Union*. We'd bring a basin and mother's lavender soap and wash his feet and powder them with the Spiro he liked to use, then slip a fresh pair of socks on the moist feet, and bring his carpet slippers. And sometimes, we'd hear him say to Mother, "The children are getting mighty thoughtful." And his blue eyes would twinkle and he'd chuckle and Mother's dark eyes would laugh and they seemed to have such nice secrets—though there were thunder and lightning times, too, and silences that raced your heart, but these you didn't think about at Christmas.

We evolved all kinds of money-making schemes, such as reselling our newspapers and magazines to the neighbors. But our mother stopped that one flat. One brother suggested we sell our summer clothes at a smash bargain in mill town, but Dad stopped that one. We settled for less speculative ventures, the older ones taking jobs in the stores after school hours. We kids earned what we spent. We were not rich people, not as wealth is thought of in the cities. We were just small-town people who lived in an ample and comfortable way. We were given little spending money: a nickel was nice, a dime was big, a quarter rich, a dollar was a dream.

The younger ones skittered along contenting themselves with whatever they could improvise for the grown folks. Once I gave my father a pincushion made of a piece of red velvet from an old hat of Mother's, which I scrunched up and filled with bird seed snitched from the shelf where the canary's food was kept, and centered with a gilt button found on the floor when my brother was home from military school. My father seemed to like it; he told me he'd never had a red velvet pincushion in all his life and had never used pins but he was not too old to learn, and he thought it was fine that I could do something besides rattle my tongue. . . .

Christmas Eve came. All day, Mother and Grandma and the cook and the two oldest sisters worked in the kitchen. Fruit cakes had been made for a month, wrapped in clean white towels and stored in the dark pantry. But the lean pork had to be ground for pork salad, the twenty-eight-pound turkey had to have its head chopped off, and then it must be picked and cleaned and hung high in the passageway between house and dining room, and then, of course, you had to put a turkey feather in your hair and make like you were Indians; then coconuts had to be grated for ambrosia and for the six-layered coconut cake and the eight coconut custard pies, and you helped punch out the eyes of the coconuts; then of course you needed to drink some of the coconut milk, and as you watched the grownups grate the nut meats into vast snowy mounds you nibbled at the pieces too small to be grated—and by that time, you felt sort of dizzy but here came the dray from the depot bringing the barrel of oysters in the shell (they were shipped from Apalachicola), and you watched them cover the barrel with ice, for you can't count on North Florida's winter staying winter. It was time, then, to lick the pan where the filling for the Lord Baltimore cake had been beaten and somebody laid down the caramel pan—but you tried to lick it and couldn't, you felt too glazy-eyed and poked out. And finally, you lay down on the back porch in the warm sun and fell asleep.

When you woke up it was almost dark. The sun had dropped behind the woodhouse. Curls of smoke floated from the chimney of the cook's house in the back yard. Her husband was smoking his pipe on the porch and Town, his grandson, was lounging on the steps reading a book. Town read everything Thirteen and Fifteen read, although he went to school only three months each year, for that was all the school there was for Town to go to. But his two friends taught him what they learned each day and he kept right up with them—although, maybe, they didn't know they were teaching and he didn't know he was learning. They just liked to do everything together so they did it. Now Town's grandfather was speaking to him: you saw Town move inside to lie before the fire and continue his reading; you knew he had been told what your father told you, "It'll ruin your eyes in that light."

In the kitchen they were preparing supper. You didn't want it. You played round with your spoon. Your mother came to your chair, felt your cheek, leaned down and felt your head with her lips to see if you had fever. You liked this so much, sometimes you played sick to get her to do it. She decided you didn't need any Castoria (the family answer to everything wrong with children) but Big Granny called out to say she might as well give you Castor Oil, everybody ought to be given a jigger of Castor Oil on Christmas Eve to make way for Christmas.

Mother did not seem to hear but accelerated stocking-hanging. Twelve were hung. The foresighted had reserved Big Granny's weeks ahead, the laggards made do with Aunt Chloe's (first choice) or Mother's (second choice). The long black stockings hung from the mantel in Mother's bedroom each with a name on it.

Five o'clock, next morning, the little ones were scrambling round the fireplace, feeling in the dark for theirs. Mother, in her bed, did not stir. Father, in the adjoining room, turned over, muttered *my my my*. The rule was, you tiptoed and you whispered and you looked through your stocking but you couldn't touch the big presents lying right before you until you had dressed.

So you took down your knobby stocking and in the light from the fire which someone had thrown kindling on, you dug in. And all the time, there—on a fine new doll rocker—sat the beautiful doll Miss Ada (well, maybe) had dressed but you dared not touch it until you had washed your face and put on your clothes. You stood and stared at it and then you saw a tea-set and you stared at it and the suspense was almost unendurable. But at that moment, a big sister appeared and offered to help you dress quick, and then, suddenly, Mother was in her wrapper and our father was tiptoeing in from his room, making like he didn't know what it was all about. This big act of Absolute Astonishment which he staged each year gave an extra polish to an already shining moment. Where did it all come from! what a fire engine! what a doll! what a tea-set! what soldiers! what a rocking horse—

Finally, we went to breakfast. No verses on this day. We sat down to a table which held the same breakfast every Christmas: before my father's place, in an enormous platter, was a cold gelatiny hog's head which had been boiled with bay leaves and spices, a few pickled pig's feet were with it, and up and down the long table were three big platters of sausage and bowls of grits and plates of biscuits, and butter and syrup.

We waited for Mother. She came in from the kitchen, flushed from last-minute doings, and sat down. Then Fifteen and Thirteen got up again, looking solemn, walked to the corner of the bay window. With a fine flick of the wrist, the fifteen-year-old uncovered the small children's table (the overflow table when company was present). Behold! the future heirlooms. You felt a letdown, having overheard the plans and knowing what might have been there. But the others gaped admiration. The boys had presented the parents with eighteen plates, each with a splendid fish painted on it, and eighteen side dishes for the bones. The oldest then made a presentation speech on the necessity for heirlooms. He said in times of revolutionary unrest heirlooms had a most stabilizing effect, they gave a thrust to one's patriotism (or something to that effect), and he and his brother were making the gift not so much to the parents as to the fourth and fifth generation. And then everybody applauded, for he was a natural—you felt like applauding whenever you saw him.

(Later, you heard your father ask where in the name of heaven did the boys get enough money to buy all those dishes. They must have cost plenty! Mother said they probably did. "But where . . ." and then he did a double-take. "Not . . ." "I'm afraid so," was the reply. In January, when the bills came in, he found the donors had done what

11

he half guessed and Mother's intuition confirmed: they had charged them to his account at the Supply Store.)

After the excitement of the unexpected gift subsided, our father took down the Bible and opened it at the second chapter of St. Luke. Nine pairs of eyes turned toward him as we waited to hear what we had heard every Christmas of our lives:

And it came to pass in those days that there went out a decree from Caesar Augustus, that all the world should be taxed. And Joseph also went . . . unto the city of David, which is called Bethlehem: . . . to be taxed with Mary his espoused wife, being great with child. And the days were accomplished that she should be delivered. And she brought forth her firstborn son, and wrapped him in swaddling clothes, and laid him in a manger. . . . And there were in the same country shepherds abiding in the field, keeping watch over their flock by night. And, lo, the angel of the Lord . . .

As he read in his deep warm voice, we followed the words, knowing them by heart. We knew, too, that to him it was not only the story of the Christ Child but of Every Child, every new beginning, every new chance for peace on earth. When he was done, we bowed our heads: he thanked God for "all the good things which we do not merit" and asked his blessing on all who were suffering and in need in every country in the whole world, and then he asked for courage, courage to have vision, for "without vision the people perish."

The bay window was bright. Fire and cat were purring. Canary was at peace. Mother sat between her two eldest home from college, and her eyes were big and dark and somehow sad and tender, and there was flour on her nose.

A good silence was settling on us. Then the youngest one said, "I fink Thesus was a fine little fellow"—and a sausage perched on top of the pile shivered and rolled off the platter toward him. And everybody laughed and began to eat breakfast.

In the middle of the day we had dinner. But by the time the dinner bell rang and we assembled in the dining room, we had little space left for turkey and Mother's succulent dressing made of nuts and oysters and celery and eggs and bread and turkey "essence," for we had been nibbling all morning on raisins and candy and crystallized fruit and pecans (which were cracked and in bowls, everywhere). The next day, and the next, the results of the cooking and baking that had gone on for days would be more appreciated. After all, there is no better time to eat a piece of coconut pie than after you have been racing round for hours and someone says, Let's have a piece of coconut pie! You stop, everybody goes to the pantry, and you eat a piece of pie, then you get a spoon and scoop out a little cold turkey dressing, then you pick up an olive, then you take a piece of stuffed celery left over from Christmas, and then you dash out to the back yard and climb up on the roof of the woodhouse and call the others to come up there . . .

On Christmas afternoon, we went visiting and our friends came visiting us and sometimes we'd meet half way between our houses. We girls had, of course, to show off our dolls and books and sewing baskets and manicure sets and the big boys had to show off their bicycles and shotguns and the little boys showed off their red wagons and fire engines. But before dark we were home again and a stillness settled down over the house.

And then, after things had been quiet a long time, our father would call out, "Where are the boys? It's about time to get our fireworks organized." But he knew: the boys—and the girls—were on their own beds, each in his own room or corner of a room, looking things over more closely or reading (books by the piles came at Christmas time). And now, each face had become its own, settling in its own private curves, its own secret question marks, its own wisting or wondering lines. Each had crawled into his secret hide-out. Thirteen-year-old in his corner might be playing a new Mozart concerto he had wanted, or polishing his new gun; fifteen-year-old might be reading the new big dictionary which he had especially asked for; the nine-year-old philosopher might be squatting at the window, face like a Buddha, looking deep into eternal matters as was his way. Suddenly one of them would stop, look around as though he had never met the others and turn a cartwheel or two, then they were all turning cartwheels or wrasslin with each other and you'd hear them thumping the floor and rolling off beds and maybe the slats would fall out and the whole bed come tumbling down.

Then our father would call up and say, "I'm waiting, boys!" And there'd be three or four *yessirs* and you'd hear them dashing down the backstairs or the hall stairs and soon you'd hear our father planning the fireworks which would be set off at eight o'clock.

After the Big Illumination, when Roman candles and rockets and cannon crackers were shot off on the front lawn at the proper and dramatic moment by the big boys and Town and our father, while the little ones raced round with sparklers and firewheels and small firecrackers, all the family and sometimes a few stray friends would dash into the dining room for oyster stew, and oysters on the shell and fried oysters; and there'd be a waving of tomato cat-sup and horse-radish bottles and somebody would drop a raw oyster on a rug and a big sister would clean it up . . .

And now everything fades out. And one knows only that there must have been a slow stumbling exhaustion which ended in bed. And finally, the old house was still. And whatever was said was said by the toadfrog underneath the house or by the great pillars which held the house and its children and the parents and Big Grandma or Little Grandma secure on their giant shoulders.

Every Christmas it was like this until the First World War. Then things turned upside down: the new world began to squeeze the old too hard. The world market which the naval stores industry depended upon grew very dizzy indeed; we children of a small inland town heard daily talk of the seas and the ships, the blockade, the Germans and the Russians and the British and strange names and strange places entered our lives and have, of course, stayed there. I heard my father had "over-stretched" himself and I was sure he had; but I was as sure as could be that no matter how much "stretching" he had done he'd never fail to do what he set out to do, and the stretching would turn out to be his magic way of stepping across a wide chasm from where he was to a more exciting place.

But this time, it did not happen quite as I had expected. Our father lost his mills and his turpentine stills, the light plant and ice plant and store and the house that never quite ended—and we moved to our small summer cottage in the mountains. . . .

It was a bit difficult to come down to the size of our small summer cottage after our father's big build-up but we managed it, somehow. He had a way of diverting us from nostalgic moods by arriving home from the little mountain town with two newly purchased feisty black mules, or a Duroc-Jersey sow, or maybe a hundred small apple trees. "What are we going to do with them?" Mother would ask quietly. "Mama, we are going to farm; this is going to be the finest little farm you ever saw. You will raise the prettiest pure-bred pigs in North Georgia and think what this hill will look like with a hundred apple trees in bloom in the spring!"

We were not alone in being poor. Times were hard in the South—much harder for most than for us, as our father often reminded us. Our region was deep in a depression long before the rest of the country felt it—indeed, it had never had real prosperity since the Civil War—only spotty surges of easy money. But even the bank did not know— and it knew plenty—how little money we managed on those years. It got worse instead of better as time passed. And there came a winter when my younger sister and I, who were in Baltimore preparing ourselves to be a great pianist (me) and a great actress (her) felt we were needed at home. We had been supporting ourselves in our schools but even so, we felt the parents needed us.

It was our barter year: Dad would take eggs to town, swap them for flour or cornmeal or coffee, and do it so casually that nobody suspected it was necessary. They thought he was so proud of his wife's Leghorns that he wanted to show their achievements to his friends at the stores. Eggs from the hens, three pigs which he had raised, milk and butter from the cow, beans he grew and dried, and apples from a few old trees already on the property— that was about it. It was enough. For Mother could take cornmeal, mix it with flour, add soda and buttermilk and melted butter, a dab of sugar and salt, and present us with the best hot cakes in the world. Her gravy made of drippings from fried side meat, with flour and milk added and crushed black pepper would have pleased Escoffier or any other great cook. And when things got too dull, my sister and I would hitch up the two feisty mules to the wagon and go for as wild a ride as one wanted over rough clay winter roads.

Nevertheless, the two of us had agreed to skip Christmas. You don't always have to have Christmas, we kept saying to each other. Of course not, the other would answer.

We had forgot our father.

In that year of austerity, he invited the chain gang to have Christmas dinner with us. The prisoners were working the state roads, staying in two shabby red railroad cars on a siding. Our father visited them as he visited "all his neighbors." That night, after he returned from a three-hour visit with the men, we heard him tell Mother about it. She knew what was coming. "Bad place to be living," he said. "Terrible! Not fit for animals much less"—He sighed. "Well, there's more misery in the world than even I know; and a lot of it is unnecessary. That's the wrong part of it, it's unnecessary." He looked in his wife's dark eyes. She waited. "Mama," he said softly, "how about having them out here for Christmas. Wouldn't that be good?" A long silence. Then Mother quietly agreed. Dad walked to town—we had no car—to tell the foreman he would like to have the prisoners and guards come to Christmas dinner.

"All of them?" asked the chain-gang foreman.

"We couldn't hardly leave any of the boys out, could we?"

Close to noon on Christmas Day we saw them coming down the road: forty-eight men in stripes, with their guards. They came up the hill and headed for the house, a few laughing, talking, others grim and suspicious. All had come, white and Negro. We had helped Mother make two caramel cakes and twelve sweet potato pies and a wonderful back-bone-and-rice dish (which Mother, born on the coast, called pilau); and there were hot rolls and Brunswick stew, and a washtub full of apples which our father had polished in front of the fire on Christmas Eve. It would be a splendid dinner, he told Mother who looked a bit wan, probably wondering what we would eat in January.

While we pulled out Mother's best china—piecing out with the famous heirloom fish plates—our father went from man to man shaking hands, and soon they were talking freely with him, and everybody was laughing at his funny—and sometimes on the rare side—stories. And then, there was a hush, and we in the kitchen heard Dad's voice lifted up: "And it came to pass in those days"—

Mother stayed with the oven. The two of us eased to the porch. Dad was standing there, reading from St. Luke. The day was warm and sunny and forty-eight men and their guards were sitting on the grass. Two guards with guns in their hands leaned against trees. Eight of the men were lifers; six of them, in pairs, had their inside legs locked together; ten were killers (one had bashed in his grandma's head), two had robbed banks, three had stolen cars, one had burned down his neighbor's house and barn after an argument, one had raped a girl—all were listening to the old old words.

When my father closed the Bible, he gravely said he hoped their families were having a good Christmas, he hoped all was well "back home." Then he smiled and grew hearty. "Now boys," he said, "eat plenty and have a good time. We're proud to have you today. We would have been a little lonely if you hadn't come. Now let's have a Merry Christmas."

The men laughed. It began with the Negroes, who quickly caught the wonderful absurdity, it spread to the whites and finally all were laughing and muttering Merry Christmas, half deriding, half meaning it, and my father laughed with them for he was never unaware of the absurd which he seemed deliberately, sometimes, to whistle into his life.

They were our guests, and our father moved among them with grace and ease. He was soon asking them about their families, telling them a little about his. One young man talked earnestly in a low voice. I heard my father say, "Son, that's mighty bad. We'll see if we can't do something about it." (Later, he did.)

When Mother said she was ready, our father asked "Son," who was one of the killers, to go help "my wife, won't you with the heavy things." And the young man said he'd be mighty glad to. The one in for raping and another for robbing a bank said they'd be pleased to help, too, and they went in. My sister and I followed, not feeling as casual as we hoped we looked. But when two guards moved toward the door my father peremptorily stopped them with, "The boys will be all right." And "the boys" were. They came back in a few minutes bearing great pots and pans to a serving table we had set up on the porch. My sister and I served the plates. The murderer and his two friends passed them to the men. Afterward, the rapist and two bank robbers and the arsonist said they'd be real pleased to wash up the dishes. But we told them nobody should wash dishes on Christmas—just have a good time.

That evening, after our guests had gone back to their quarters on the railroad siding, we sat by the fire. The parents looked tired. Dad went out for another hickory log to "keep us through the night," laid it in the deep fireplace, scratched the coals, sat down in his chair by the lamp. Mother said she had a letter from the eldest daughter in China—would Papa read it? It was full of cheer as such letters are likely to be. We sat quietly talking of her family, of her work with a religious organization, of China's persisting troubles after the 1911 revolution.

We were quiet after that. Just rested together. Dad glanced through a book or two that his sons had sent him. Then the old look of having something to say to his children settled on his face. He began slowly:

"We've been through some pretty hard times, lately, and I've been proud of my family. Some folks can take prosperity and can't take poverty; some can take being poor and lose their heads when money comes. I want my children to accept it all: the good and the bad, for that is what life is. It can't be wholly good; it won't be wholly bad." He looked at our mother, sitting there, tired but gently involved. "Those men, today—they've made mistakes. Sure. But I have too. Bigger ones maybe than theirs. And you will. You are not likely to commit a crime but you may become blind and refuse to see what you should look at, and that can be worse than a crime. Don't forget that. Never look down on a man. Never. If you can't look him straight in the eyes, then what's wrong is with you." He glanced at the letter from the eldest sister. "The world is changing fast. Folks get hurt and make terrible mistakes at such times. But the one I hope you won't make is to cling to my generation's sins. You'll have plenty of your own, remember. Changing things is mighty risky, but not changing things is worse—that is, if you can think of something better to change to. . . . Mama, believe I'll go to bed. You about ready?"

On the stairs he stopped. "But I don't mean, Sister, you got to get radical." He laughed. His voice dropped to the soft tones he used with his younger children. "We had a good Christmas, didn't we?" He followed our mother up the stairs.

My younger sister and I looked in the fire. What our future would be, we did not know. The curve was too sharp, just here; and sometimes, the dreaming about a curve you can't see round is not a thing you want to talk about. After a long staring in the fire, we succumbed to a little do-you-remember. And soon we were laughing about the fifteen-year-old and Town and the thirteen-year-old and their heirloom year, and the hog killing and the Song of Solomon and the tree shaking and Big Grandma's sausage, the best as our mother used to say that anybody could make, with just enough red pepper and sage . . .

And now the fire in front of us was blurring.

My sister said softly, "It was a large Christmas."

"Which one?"

"All of them," she whispered.

Christmas Eve at Johnson's Drugs N Goods

TONI CADE BAMBARA

I was probably the first to spot them cause I'd been watching the entrance to the store on the lookout for my daddy, knowing that if he didn't show soon, he wouldn't be coming at all. His new family would be expecting him to spend the holidays with them. For the first half of my shift, I'd raced the cleaning cart down the aisles doing a slapdash job on the signs and glass cages, eager to stay in view of the doorway. And look like Johnson's kept getting bigger, swelling, sprawling itself all over the corner lot, just to keep me from the door, to wear me out in the marathon vigil.

In point of fact, Johnson's Drugs N Goods takes up less than one-third of the block. But it's laid out funny in crisscross aisles so you get the feeling like a rat in an endless maze. Plus the ceilings are high and the fluorescents a blazing white. And Mrs. Johnson's got these huge signs sectioning off the spaces—TOBACCO DRUGS HOUSEWARES, etc.— like it was some big-time department store. The thing is, till the two noisy women came in, it felt like a desert under a blazing sun. Piper in Tobacco even had on shades. The new dude in Drugs looked like he was at the end of a wrong-way telescope. I got to feeling like a nomad with a cleaning cart, trekking across the sands with no end in sight, wandering. The overhead lights creating mirages and racing up my heart till I'd realize that wasn't my daddy in the parking lot, just the poster-board Santa Claus. Or that wasn't my daddy in the entrance way, just the Burma Shave man in a frozen stance. Then I'd tried to make out pictures of Daddy getting off the bus at the terminal, or driving a rented car past the Chamber of Commerce building, or sitting jammed-leg in one of them DC point-o-nine brand X planes, coming to see me.

By the time the bus pulled into the lot and the two women in their big-city clothes hit the door, I'd decided Daddy was already at the house waiting for me, knowing that for a mirage too, since Johnson's is right across from the railroad and bus terminals and the house is a dollar-sixty cab away. And I know he wouldn't feature going to the house on the off chance of running into Mama. Or even if he escaped that fate, having to sit in the parlor with his hat in his lap while Aunt Harriet looks him up and down grunting, too busy with the latest crossword puzzle contest to offer the man some supper. And Uncle Henry talking a blue streak bout how he outfoxed the city council or somethin and nary a cold beer in sight for my daddy.

But then the two women came banging into the store and I felt better. Right away the store stopped sprawling, got fixed. And we all got pulled together from our various zones to one focal point—them. Changing up the whole atmosphere of the place fore they even got into the store proper. Before we knew it, we were all smiling, looking halfway like you supposed to on Christmas Eve, even if you do got to work for ole lady Johnson, who don't give you no slack whatever the holiday.

"What the hell does this mean, Ethel?" the one in the fur coat say, talking loud and fast, yanking on the rails that lead the way into the store. "What are we, cattle? Being herded into the blankety-blank store in my fur coat," she grumbles, boosting herself up between the rails, swinging her body along like the kids do in the park.

Me and Piper look at each other and smile. Then Piper moves down to the edge of the counter right under the Tobacco sign so as not to miss nothing. Madeen over in Housewares waved to me to ask what's up and I just shrug. I'm fascinated by the women.

"Look here," the one called Ethel say, drawing the words out lazy slow. "Do you got a token for this sucker?" She's shoving hard against the turnstile folks supposed to exit through. Pushing past and grunting, the turnstile crank cranking like it gonna bust, her Christmas corsage of holly and bells just ajingling and hanging by a thread. Then she gets through and stumbles toward the cigar counter and leans back against it, studying the turnstile hard. It whips back around in place, making scrunching noises like it's been abused.

"You know one thing," she say, dropping her face onto her coat collar so Piper'd know he's being addressed.

"Ma'am?"

"That is one belligerent bad boy, that thing right there."

Piper laughs his prizewinning laugh and starts touching the stacks of gift-wrapped stuff, case the ladies in the market for pipe tobacco or something. Two or three of the customers who'd been falling asleep in the magazines coming to life now, inching forward. Phototropism, I'd call it, if somebody asked me for a word.

The one in the fur coat's coming around now the right way—if you don't count the stiff-elbow rail-walking she was doing—talking about "Oh, my God, I can walk, I can walk, Ethel, praise de lawd."

The two women watching Piper touch the cigars, the humidors, the gift-wrapped boxes. Mostly he's touching himself, cause George Lee Piper love him some George Lee Piper. Can't blame him. Piper be fine.

"You work on commissions, young man?" Fur Coat asking.

"No, ma'am."

The two women look at each other. They look over toward the folks inching forward. They look at me gliding by with the cleaning cart. They look back at each other and shrug.

"So what's his problem?" Ethel says in a stage whisper. "Why he so hot to sell us something?"

"Search me." Fur Coat starts flapping her coat and frisking herself. "You know?" she asking me.

"It's a mystery to me," I say, doing my best to run ole man Samson over. He sneaking around trying to jump Madeen in Housewares. And it is a mystery to me how come Piper always so eager to make a sale. You'd think he had half interest in the place. He says it's because it's his job, and after all, the Johnsons are Black folks. I guess so, I guess so. Me, I just clean the place and stay busy in case Mrs. J is in the prescription booth, peeking out over the top of the glass.

When I look around again, I see that the readers are suddenly very interested in cigars. They crowding around Ethel and Fur Coat. Piper kinda embarrassed by all the attention, though fine as he is, he oughta be used to it. His expression's cool but his hands give him away, sliding around the counter like he shuffling a deck of slippery cards. Fur Coat nudges Ethel and they bend over to watch the hands, doing these chicken-head jerkings. The readers take up positions just like a director was hollering "Places" at em. Piper, never one to disappoint an audience, starts zipping around these invisible walnut shells. Right away Fur Coat whips out a little red change purse and slaps a dollar bill on the counter. Ethel dips deep into her coat pocket, bending her knees and being real comic, then plunks down some change. Ole man Sampson tries to boost up on my cleaning cart to see the shells that ain't there.

"Scuse me, Mr. Sampson," I say, speeding the cart up sudden so that quite naturally he falls off, the dirty dog.

Piper is snapping them imaginary shells around like nobody's business, one of the readers leaning over another's shoulder, staring pop-eyed.

"All right now, everybody step back," Ethel announces. She waves the crowd back and pushes up one coat sleeve, lifts her fists into the air and jerks out one stiff finger from the bunch, and damn if the readers don't lift their heads to behold in amazement this wondrous finger.

"That folks," Fur Coat explains, "is what is known as the indicator finger. The indicator is about to indicate the indicatee."

"Say wha?" Dirty ole man Sampson decides he'd rather sneak up on Madeen than watch the show.

"What's going on over there?" Miz Della asks me. I spray the watch case and make a big thing of wiping it and ignoring her. But then the new dude in Drugs hollers over the same thing.

"Christmas cheer gone to the head. A coupla vaudevillians," I say. He smiles, and Miz Della says "Ohhh" like I was talking to her.

"This one," Ethel says, planting a finger exactly one-quarter of an inch from the countertop.

Piper dumb-shows a lift of the shell, turning his face away as though he can't bear to look and find the elusive pea ain't there and he's gonna have to take the ladies' money. Then his eyes swivel around and sneak a peek and widen, lighting up his whole face in a prizewinning grin.

"You got it," he shouts.

The women grab each other by the coat shoulders and jump each other up and down. And I look toward the back cause I know Mrs. J got to be hearing all this carrying-on, and on payday if Mr. J ain't handing out the checks, she's going to give us some long lecture about decorum and what it means to be on board at Johnson's Drugs N Goods. I wheel over to the glass jars and punch bowls, wanting alibi distance just in case. And also to warn Madeen about Sampson gaining on her. He's ducking down behind the coffeepots, walking squat and shameless.

"Pay us our money, young man," Fur Coat is demanding, rapping her knuckles on the counter.

"We should hate to have to turn the place out, young man."

"It out," echoes Ethel.

The women nod to the crowd and a coupla folks giggle. And Piper tap-taps on the cash register like he shonuff gonna give em they money. I'd rather they turned the place out myself. I want to call my daddy. Only way any of us are going to get home in time to dress for the Christmas dance at the center is for the women to turn it out. Like I say, Piper ain't too clear about the worker's interest versus management's, as the dude in Drugs would say it. So he's light-tapping and quite naturally the cash drawer does not come out. He's yanking some unseen dollar from the not-there drawer and handing it over. Damn if Fur Coat don't snatch it, deal out the bills to herself and her friend and then make a big production out of folding the money flat and jamming it in that little red change purse.

"I wanna thank you," Ethel says, strolling off, swinging her pocketbook so that the crowd got to back up and disperse. Fur Coat spreads her coat and curtsies.

"A pleasure to do business with you ladies," Piper says, tipping his hat, looking kinda disappointed that he didn't sell em something. Tipping his hat the way he tipped the shells, cause you know Mrs. J don't allow no hats indoors. I came to work in slacks one time and she sent me home to change and docked me too. I wear a gele some times just to mess her around, and you can tell she trying to figure out if she'll go for it or not. The woman is crazy. Not Uncle Henry type crazy, but Black property owner type crazy. She thinks this is a museum, which is why folks don't hardly come in here to shop. That's okay cause we all get to know each other well. It's not okay cause it's a drag to look busy. If you look like you ain't buckling under a weight of work, Mrs. J will have you count the Band-Aids in the boxes to make sure the company ain't pulling a fast one. The woman crazy.

Now Uncle Henry type crazy is my kind of crazy. The type crazy to get you a job. He march into the "saloon" as he calls it and tells Leon D that he is not an equal opportunity employer and that he, Alderman Henry Peoples, is going to put some fire to his ass. So soon's summer comes, me and Madeen got us a job at Leon D. Salon. One of them hushed, funeral type shops with skinny models parading around for customers corseted and strangling in their seats, huffin and puffin.

Madeen got fired right off on account of the pound of mascara she wears on each lash and them weird dresses she designs for herself (with less than a yard of cloth each if you ask me). I did my best to hang in there so's me and Madeen'd have hang-around money till Johnson started hiring again. But it was hard getting back and forth from the stockroom to this little kitchen to fix the espresso to the showroom. One minute up to your ass in carpet, the next skidding across white linoleum, the next making all this noise on ceramic tile and people looking around at you and all. Was there for two weeks and just about had it licked by stationing different kind of shoes at each place that I could slip into, but then Leon D stumbled over my bedroom slippers one afternoon.

But to hear Uncle Henry tell it, writing about it all to Daddy, I was working at a promising place making a name for myself. And Aunt Harriet listening to Uncle Henry read the letter, looking me up and down and grunting. She know what kind of name it must be, cause my name in the family is Miss Clumsy. Like if you got a glass-top coffee table with doodads on em, or a hurricane lamp sitting on a mantel anywhere near a door I got to come through, or an antique jar you brought all the way from Venice the time you won the crossword puzzle contest—you can rest assure I'll demolish them by and by. I ain't vicious, I'm just clumsy. It's my gawky stage, Mama says. Aunt Harriet cuts her eye at Mama and grunts.

My daddy advised me on the phone not to mention anything to the Johnsons about this gift of mine for disaster or the fact that I worked at Leon D. Salon. No sense the Johnson's calling up there to check on me and come to find I knocked over a perfume display two times in the same day. Like I say—it's a gift. So when I got to clean the glass jars and punch bowls at Johnson's, I take it slow and pay attention. Then I take up my station relaxed in Fabrics, where the worst that can happen is I upset a box of pins.

Mrs. J is in the prescription booth, and she clears her throat real loud. We all look to the back to read the smoke signals. She ain't paying Fur Coat and Ethel no attention. They over in Cosmetics messing with Miz Della's mind and her customers. Mrs. J got her eye on some young teen-agers browsing around Jewelry. The other eye on Piper. But this does not mean Piper is supposed to check the kids out. It means Madeen is. You got to know how to read Mrs. J to get along.

She always got one eye on Piper. Tries to make it seem like she don't trust him at the cash register. That may be part of the reason now, now that she's worked up this cover story so in her mind. But we all know why she watches Piper, same reason we all do. Cause Piper is so fine you just can't help yourself. Tall and built up, blue-black and smooth, got the nerve to have dimples, and wears this splayed-out push-broom mustache he's always raking in with three fingers. Got a big butt too that makes you wanna hug the customer that asks for the cartoons Piper keeps behind him, two shelfs down. Mercy. And when it's slow, or when Mrs. J comes bustling over for the count, Piper steps from behind the counter and shows his self. You get to see the whole Piper from the shiny boots to the glistening fro and every inch of him fine. Enough to make you holler.

Miz Della in Cosmetics, a sister who's been passing for years but fooling nobody but herself, she always lolligagging over to Tobacco talking bout are there any new samples of those silver-tipped cigars for women. Piper don't even squander energy to bump her off any more. She mostly just ain't even there. At first he would get mad when she used to act hinkty and had these white men picking her up at the store. Then he got sorrowful about it all, saying she was a pitiful person. Now that she's going out with the blond chemist back there, he just wiped her off the map. She tries to mess with him, but Piper ain't heard the news she's been born. Sometimes his act slips, though, cause he does take a lot of unnecessary energy to play up to Madeen whenever Miz Della's hanging around. He's not consistent in his attentions, and that spurs Madeen the dress designer to madness. And Piper really oughta put brakes on that, cause Madeen subject to walk in one day in a fishnet dress and no underwear and then what he goin do about that?

Last year on my birthday my daddy got on us about dressing like hussies to attract the boys. Madeen shrugged it off and went about her business. It hurt my feelings. The onliest reason I was wearing that tight sweater and that skimpy skirt was cause I'd been to the roller rink and that's how we dress. But my daddy didn't even listen and I was really hurt. But then later that night, I come through the living room to make some cocoa and he apologized. He lift up from the couch where he always sleeps when he comes to visit, lifted up and whispered—"Sorry." I could just make him out by the light from the refrigerator.

"Candy," he calls to make sure I heard him. And I don't want to close the frig door cause I know I'll want to remember this scene, figuring it's going to be the last birthday visit cause he fixin to get married and move outta state.

"Sir?"

He pat the couch and I come over and just leave the frig door open so we can see each other. I forgot to put the milk down, so I got this cold milk bottle in my lap, feeling stupid.

"I was a little rough on you earlier," he say, picking something I can't see from my bathrobe. "But you're getting to be a woman now and certain things have to be said. Certain things have to be understood so you can decide what kind of woman you're going to be, ya know?"

31

"Sir," I nod. I'm thinking Aunt Harriet ought to tell me, but then Aunt Harriet prefers to grunt at folks, reserving words for the damn crossword puzzles. And my mama stay on the road so much with the band, when she do come home for a hot minute all she has to tell me is "My slippers're in the back closet" or "Your poor tired Ma'd like some coffee."

He takes my hand and don't even kid me about the milk bottle, just holds my hand for a long time saying nothing, just squeezes it. And I know he feeling bad about moving away and all, but what can he do, he got a life to lead. Just like Mama got her life to lead. Just like I got my life to lead and'll probably leave here myself one day and become an actress or a director. And I know I should tell him it's all right. Sitting there with that milk bottle chilling me through my bathrobe, the light from the refrigerator throwing funny shadows on the wall, I know that years later when I'm in trouble or something, or hear that my daddy died or something like that, I'm going feel real bad that I didn't tell him—it's all right, Daddy, I understand. It ain't like he'd made any promises about making a home for me with him. So it ain't like he's gone back on his word. And if the new wife can't see taking in no half-grown new daughter, hell, I understand that. I can't get the words together, neither can he. So we just squeeze each other's hands. And that'll have to do.

"When I was a young man," he says after while, "there were girls who ran around all made up in sassy clothes. And they were okay to party with, but not the kind you cared for, ya know?" I nod and he pats my hand. But I'm thinking that ain't right, to party with a person you don't care for. How come you can't? I want to ask, but he's talking. And I was raised not to interrupt folk when they talking, especially my daddy. "You and Madeen cause quite a stir down at the barbershop." He tries to laught it, but it comes out scary. "Got to make up your mind now what kind of woman you're going to be. You know what I'm saying?" I nod and he loosens his grip so I can go make my cocoa.

I'm messing around in the kitchenette feeling dishonest. Things I want to say, I haven't said. I look back over toward the couch and know this picture is going to haunt me later. Going to regret the things left unsaid. Like a coward, like a child maybe. I fix my cocoa and keep my silence, but I do remember to put the milk back and close the refrigerator door.

"Candy?"

"Sir?" I'm standing there in the dark, the fridge door closed now and we can't even see each other.

"It's not about looks anyway," he says, and I hear him settling deep into the couch and pulling up the bedclothes. "And it ain't always about attracting some man either . . . not necessarily."

I'm waiting to hear what it is about, the cup shaking in the saucer and me wanting to ask him all over again how it was when he and Mama first met in Central Park, and how it used to be when they lived in Philly and had me and how it was when the two of them were no longer making any sense together but moved down here anyway and then split up. But I could hear that breathing he does just before the snoring starts. So I hustle on down the hall so I won't be listening for it and can't get to sleep.

All night I'm thinking about this woman I'm going to be. I'll look like Mama but don't wanna be no singer. Was named after Grandma Candestine but don't wanna be no fussy old woman with a bunch of kids. Can't see myself turning into Aunt Harriet either, doing crossword puzzles all day long. I look over at Madeen, all sprawled out in her bed, tangled up in the sheets looking like the alcoholic she trying to be these days, sneaking liquor from Uncle Henry's closet. And I know I don't wanna be stumbling down the street with my boobs out and my dress up and my heels cracking off and all. I write for a whole hour in my diary trying to connect with the future me and trying not to hear my daddy snoring.

Fur Coat and Ethel in Housewares talking with Madeen. I know they must be cracking on Miz Della, cause I hear Madeen saying something about equal opportunity. We used to say that Mrs. J was an equal opportunity employer for hiring Miz Della. But then she went and hired real white folks—a blond, crew-cut chemist and a pimply-face kid for the stockroom. If you ask me, that's running equal opportunity in the ground. And running the business underground cause don't nobody round here deal with no white chemist. They used to wrinkly old folks grinding up the herbs and bark and telling them very particular things to do and not to do working the roots. So they keep on going to Mama Drear down past the pond or Doc Jessup in back of the barbershop. Don't do a doctor one bit of good to write out a prescription talking about fill it at Johnson's, cause unless it's an emergency folk stay strictly away from a white root worker, especially if he don't tell you what he doing.

Aunt Harriet in here one day when Mama Drear was too sick to counsel and quite naturally she asks the chemist to explain what all he doing back there with the mortar and pestle and the scooper and the scales. And he say something about rules and regulations, the gist of which was mind your business, lady. Aunt Harriet dug down deep into her crossword-puzzle words and pitched a natural bitch. Called that man a bunch of choicest names. But the line that got me was—"Medication without explanation is obscene." And what she say that for, we ran that in the ground for days. Infatuation without fraternization is obscene. Insemination without obligation is tyranny. Fornication without contraception is obtuse, and so forth and so on. Madeen's best line came out the night we were watching a TV special about welfare. Sterilization without strangulation and hell's damnation is I-owe-you-one-crackers. Look like every situation called for a line like that, and even if it didn't, we made it fit.

Then one Saturday morning we were locked out and we standing around shivering in our sweaters and this old white dude jumps out a pickup truck hysterical, his truck still in gear and backing out the lot. His wife had given their child an overdose of medicine and the kid was out cold. Look like everything he said was grist for the mill.

"She just administered the medicine without even reading the label," he told the chemist, yanking on his jacket so the man couldn't even get out his keys. "She never even considered the fact it might be dangerous, the medicine so old and all." We follow the two down the aisle to the prescription booth, the old white dude talking a mile a minute, saying they tried to keep the kid awake, tried to walk him, but he wouldn't walk. Tried to give him an enema, but he wouldn't stay propped up. Could the chemist suggest something to empty his stomach out and sooth his inflamed ass and what all? And besides he was breathing funny and should he administer mouth-to-mouth resuscitation? The minute he tore out of there and ran down the street to catch up with his truck, we started in.

Administration without consideration is illiterate. Irrigation without resuscitation is evacuation without ambulation is inflammation without information is execution without restitution is. We got downright silly about the whole thing till Mrs. J threatened to fire us all. But we kept it up for a week.

Then the new dude in Drugs who don't never say much stopped the show one afternoon when we were trying to figure out what to call the street riots in the sixties and so forth. He say Revolution without Transformation is Half-assed. Took me a while to ponder that one, a whole day in fact just to work up to it. After while I would listen real hard whenever he opened his mouth, which wasn't often. And I jotted down the titles of the books I'd see him with. And soon's I finish up the stack that's by my bed, I'm hitting the library. He started giving me some of the newspapers he keeps stashed in that blue bag of his we all at first thought was full of funky jockstraps and sneakers. Come to find it's full of carrots and oranges and books and stuff. Madeen say he got a gun in there too. But then Madeen all the time saying something. Like she saying here lately that the chemist's jerking off there behind the poisons and the goopher dust.

The chemist's name is Hubert Tarrly. Madeen tagged him Herbert Tareyton. But the name that stuck was Nazi Youth. Every time I look at him I hear Hitler barking out over the loudspeaker urging the youth to measure up and take over the world. And I can see these stark-eyed gray kids in short pants and suspenders doing jump-ups and scissor kicks and turning they mamas in to the Gestapo for listening to the radio. Chemist looks like he grew up like that, eating knockwurst and beating on Jews, rounding up gypsies, saying *Sieg heil* and shit. Mrs. J said something to him one morning and damn if he didn't click his heels. I like to die. She blushing all over her simple self talking bout that's Southern cavalier style. I could smell the gas. I could see the flaming cross too. Nazi Youth and then some. The dude in Drugs started calling him that too, the dude whose name I can never remember. I always wanna say Ali Baba when I talk about him with my girl friends down at the skating rink or with the older sisters at the arts center. But that ain't right. Either you call a person a name that says what they about or you call em what they call themselves, one or the other.

Now take Fur Coat, for instance. She is clearly about the fur coat. She moving up and down the aisles talking while Ethel in the cloth coat is doing all the work, picking up teapots, checking the price on the dust mops, clicking a bracelet against the punch bowl to see if it ring crystal, hollering to somebody about whether the floor wax need buffing or not. And it's all on account of the fur coat. Her work is something other than that. Like when they were in Cosmetics messing with Miz Della, some white ladies come up talking about what's the latest in face masks. And every time Miz Della pull something out the box, Ethel shake her head and say that brand is crap. Then Fur Coat trots out the sure-fire recipe for the face mask. What she tells the old white ladies is to whip us some egg white to peaks, pour in some honey, some oil of wintergreen, some oil of eucalyptus, the juice of a lemon and a half a teaspoon of arsenic. Now any fool can figure out what lemon juice do to arsenic, or how honey going make the concoction stick, and what all else the oil of this and that'll do to your face. But Fur Coat in her fur coat make you stand still and listen to this madness. Fur Coat an authority in her fur coat. The fur coat is an act of alchemy in itself, as Aunt Harriet would put it.

Just like my mama in her fur coat, same kind too— Persian lamb, bought hot in some riot or other. Mama's coat was part of the Turn the School Out Outfit. Hardly ever came out of the quilted bag cept for that. Wasn't for window-shopping, wasn't for going to rehearsal, wasn't for church teas, was for working her show. She'd flip a flap of that coat back over her hip when she strolled into the classroom to get on the teacher's case bout saying something out of the way about Black folks. Then she'd pick out the exact plank, exact spot she'd take her stand on, then plant one of them black suede pumps from the I. Miller outlet she used to work at. Then she'd lift her chin arrogant proud to start the rap, and all us kids would lean forward and stare at the cameo brooch visible now on the wide-wale wine plush corduroy dress. Then she'd work her show in her outfit. Bam-bam that black suede pocketbook punctuating the points as Mama ticked off the teacher's offenses. And when she got to the good part, and all us kids would strain up off the benches to hear every word so we could play it out in the schoolyard, she'd take both fists and brush that fur coat way back past her hips and she'd challenge the teacher to either change up and apologize or meet her for a showdown at a school-board hearing. And of course ole teacher'd apologize to all us Black kids. Then Mama'd let the coat fall back into place and she'd whip around, the coat draping like queen robes, and march herself out. Mama was baad in her fur coat.

I don't know what-all Fur Coat do in her fur coat but I can tell it's hellafyin whatever it all is. They came into Fabrics and stood around a while trying to see what shit they could get into. All they had in their baskets was a teapot and some light bulbs and some doodads from the special gift department, perfume and whatnot. I waited on a few customers wanting braid and balls of macramé twine, nothing where I could show my stuff. Now if somebody wanted some of the silky, juicy cotton stuff I could get into something fancy, yanking off the yards, measuring it doing a shuffle-stick number, nicking it just so, then ripping the hell out the shit. But didn't nobody ask for that. Fur Coat and Ethel kinda finger some bolts and trade private jokes, then they moved onto Drugs.

"We'd like to see the latest in rubberized fashions for men, young man." Fur Coat is doing a super Lady Granville Whitmore the Third number. "If you would." She bows her head, fluttering her lashes.

Me and Madeen start messing around in the shoe-polish section so's not to miss nothing. I kind of favor Fur Coat, on account of she got my mama's coat on, I guess. On the other hand, I like the way Ethel drawl talk like she too tired and bored to go on. I guess I like em both cause they shopping the right way, having fun and all. And they got plenty of style. I wouldn't mind being like that when I am full-grown.

The dude in Drugs thinks on the request a while, sucking in his lips like he wanna talk to himself on the inside. He's looking up and down the counter, pauses at the plastic rain hats, rejects them, then squints hard at Ethel and Fur Coat. Fur Coat plants a well-heeled foot on the shelf with the tampons and pads and sighs. Something about that sigh I don't like. It's real rather than play snooty. The dude in Drugs always looks a little crumbled, a little rough dry, like he jumped straight out the hamper but not quite straight. But he got stuff to him if you listen rather than look. Seems to me ole Fur Coat is looking. She keeps looking while the dude moves down the aisle behind the counter, ducks down out of sight, reappears and comes back, dumping an armful of boxes on the counter.

"One box of Trojans and one box of Ramses," Ethel announces. "We want to do the comparison test."

"On the premises?" Lady G Fur says, planting a dignified hand on her collarbone.

"Egg-zack-lee."

"In your opinion, young man," Lady G Fur says, staying the arm of the brand tester, "which of the two is the best? Uhmm—the better of the two, that is. In your vast experience as lady-killer and cock hound, which passes the X test?" It's said kinda snotty. Me and Madeen exchange a look and dust around the cans of shoe polish.

"Well," the dude says, picking up a box in each hand, "in my opinion, Trojans have a snappier ring to em." He rattles the box against his ear, then lets Ethel listen. She nods approval. Fur Coat will not be swayed. "On the other hand, Ramses is a smoother smoke. Cooler on the throat. What do you say in your vast experience as—er—"

Ethel is banging down boxes of Kotex cracking up, screaming, "He gotcha. He gotcha that time. Old laundry bag got over on you, Helen."

Mrs. J comes out of the prescription booth and hustles her bulk to the counter. Me and Madeen clamp down hard on giggles and I damn near got to climb in with the neutral shoe polish to escape attention. Ethel and Fur Coat don't give a shit, they paying customers, so they just roar. Cept Fur Coat's roar is phony, like she really mad and gonna get even with the dude for not turning out to be a chump. Meanwhile, the dude is standing like a robot, arms out at exactly the same height, elbows crooked just so, boxes displayed between thumb and next finger, the gears in the wrist click, clicking, turning. And not even cracking a smile.

"What's the problem here?" Mrs. J trying not to sound breathless or angry and ain't doing too good a job. She got to say it twice to be heard.

"No problem, Mrs. Johnson," the dude says straight-face. "The customers are buying condoms, I am selling condoms. A sale is being conducted, as is customary in a store."

Mrs. J looks down at the jumble of boxes and covers her mouth. She don't know what to do. I duck down, cause when folks in authority caught in a trick, the first they look for is a scapegoat.

"Well, honey," Ethel says, giving a chummy shove to Mrs. J's shoulder, "what do you think? I've heard that Trojans are ultrasensitive. They use a baby lamb brain, I understand."

"Membrane, dear, membrane," Fur Coat says down her nose. "They remove the intestines of a four-week-old lamb and use the membrane. Tough, resilient, sheer."

"Gotcha," says Ethel. "On the other hand, it is said by folks who should know that Ramses has a better box score."

"Box score," echoes Mrs. J in a daze.

"Box score. You know, honey—no splits, breaks, leaks, seeps."

"Seepage, dear, seepage," says Fur Coat, all nasal.

"Gotcha."

"The solution," says the dude in an almost robot voice, "is to take one small box of each and do the comparison test as you say. A survey. A random sampling of your friends." He says this to Fur Coat, who is not enjoying it all nearly so much as Ethel, who is whooping and hollering.

Mrs. J backs off and trots to the prescription booth. Nazi Youth peeks over the glass and mumbles something soothing to Mrs. J. He waves me and Madeen away like he somebody we got to pay some mind.

"We will take one super-duper, jumbo family size of each."

"Family size?" Fur Coat is appalled. "And one more thing, young man," she orders. "Wrap up a petite size for a small-size smart-ass acquaintance of mine. Gift-wrapped, ribbons and all."

It occurs to me that Fur Coat's going to present this to the dude. Right then and there I decide I don't like her. She's not discriminating with her stuff. Up till then I was thinking how much I'd like to trade Aunt Harriet in for either of these two, hang out with them, sit up all night while they drink highballs and talk about men they've known and towns they've been in. I always did want to hang out with women like this and listen to their stories. But they beginning to reveal themselves as not nice people, just cause the dude is rough dry on Christmas Eve. My Uncle Henry all the time telling me they different kinds of folks in the community, but when you boil it right down there's just nice and not nice. Uncle Henry say they folks who'll throw they mamas to the wolves if the fish sandwich big enough. They folks who won't whatever the hot sauce. They folks that're scared, folks that are dumb; folks that have heart and some with heart to spare. That all boils down to nice and not nice if you ask me. It occurs to me that Fur Coat is not nice. Fun, dazzling, witty, but not nice.

"Do you accept Christmas gifts, young man?" Fur Coat asking in icy tones she ain't masking too well.

"No. But I do accept Kwanza presents at the feast."

"Quan . . . hmm . . ."

Fur Coat and Ethel go into a huddle with the stage whispers. "I bet he thinks we don't know beans about Quantas . . . Don't he know we are The Ebony Jet Set . . . We never travel to kangaroo land except by . . ."

Fur Coat straightens up and stares at the dude. "Will you accept a whatchamacallit gift from me even though we are not feasting, as it were?"

"If it is given with love and respect, my sister, of course." He was sounding so sincere, it kinda got to Fur Coat.

"In that case . . ." She scoops up her bundle and sweeps out the place. Ethel trotting behind hollering, "He gotcha, Helen. Give the boy credit. Maybe we should hire him and do a threesome act." She spun the turnstile round three times for she got into the spin and spun out the store.

"Characters," says Piper on tiptoe, as we all can hear him. He laughs and checks his watch. Madeen slinks over to Tobacco to be in asking distance in case he don't already have a date to the dance. Miz Della's patting some powder on. I'm staring at the door after Fur Coat and Ethel, coming to terms with the fact that my daddy ain't coming. It's gonna be just Uncle Henry and Aunt Harriet this year, with maybe Mama calling on the phone between sets to holler in my ear, asking have I been a good girl, it's been that long since she's taken a good look at me.

"You wanna go to the Kwanza celebrations with me sometime this week or next week, Candy?"

I turn and look at the dude. I can tell my face is falling and right now I don't feel up to doing anything about it. Holidays are depressing. Maybe there's something joyous about this celebration he's talking about. Cause Lord knows Christmas is a drag. The sister who taught me how to wrap a gele asked me was I coming to the celebration down at the Black Arts Center, but I didn't know nothing about it.

"Look here," I finally say, "would you please get a pencil and paper and write your name down for me. And write that other word down too so I can look it up."

He writes his name down and spins the paper around for me to read.

"Obatale."

"Right," he says, spinning it back. "But you can call me Ali Baba if you want to." He is leaning over too far writing out Kwanza for me to see if that was a smile on his face or a smirk. I figure a smile, cause Obatale nice people.

Yule Tides and Water Buffalo

JASON TAYLOR

Carl and Dennis had been pretending to sleep for over an hour. The only sound came from the ceiling fan, and the way it ticked as it moved around and around, pushing its cool air on the brothers' faces. On most nights, the boys would take turns making up noises or funny games, or singing the wrong lyrics to songs. While they'd spent a thousand nights chattering themselves to sleep in a matter of minutes, Christmas Eve had brought upon an incurable case of insomnia.

Carl lay on his back with his legs crossed at the ankles and his hands folded over his chest, staring at the object leaning against the bookshelf. It was a brand new garden rake with a thick red ribbon tied around the handle, a gift from Uncle Sanderson. *Thank you, Lord. Thank you for letting Dennis and me share it.* It was the only time the boys looked forward to splitting a present. After years of receiving handmade gloves, used hats, and nonperishable canned goods, the brothers had long given up hope of opening anything fun from Uncle Sandy. Acting on his eternal assumption that the boys were identical twins, their uncle would occasionally send a matching set of clothes, such as bumblebee-striped pullovers and pointy wool toboggans. Aside from their blond hair, the brothers looked nothing alike. And even though Dennis was a year younger than Carl, he was already two inches taller.

Beneath the bookshelf were several empty and battered shoeboxes. A pair of old drumsticks waited next to them. Carl wondered how Santa would fit the drums he had asked for down the chimney. He thought about how long it would take to learn to play them. He thought about drum solos and cool hair and picking up Teresa Parkman in a limousine on the way to school. He'd be a baseball player, too, and would play shows after the games were over. He wondered why anyone wanted to be a scientist.

Across the room, Dennis's foot rested up against the windowsill as his body lay sideways above the covers. One arm crooked between his pillow and the mattress, as the other one dangled over the edge of the bed. His blue-gray eyes pierced the window's thin sheet of wet glass, swiveling between the dripping trees and garland-covered mailboxes, dodging parked cars and cheerful homes. It had rained all day but stopped just after dinner.

Dennis remembered when, during lunch period a few months earlier, Rusty Hayes proudly declared Santa Claus a fake. But what did Rusty know? He had been toiling in the second grade for three straight years. And everyone had heard the stories he told before. The tires on his flying bicycle were always flat. The pet water buffalo wasn't allowed at school. And the box of gold coins he found and buried were impossible to get to because some fool built a house over them. Rusty's pitiful tale didn't stand a chance, not with Dennis and Carl. They had proof that Santa existed.

On the Christmas before last, the boys had welcomed Santa with the traditional milk and cookies and a handful of vitamins. They also left an inkpad, a blank sheet of paper, and a note asking for fingerprints. It was their greatest day ever, as Santa delivered a mountain of presents, ate their food, and booked himself before disappearing through the chimney. And on Christmas Day last year, Santa called their house. Carl talked to him, and had marveled at how well he knew his parents.

Dennis's arm began to tingle as he realized he hadn't moved since his mother kissed him goodnight. *Will Santa remember everything? I don't need any more clothes. What if . . .* His thought was abruptly divided by the distinct and convivial rattle of sleigh bells.

As if jolted by a sudden burst of electricity, he gripped the edge of the mattress, whipped his legs onto the floor, and threw his body toward the window, forcing his chest and nose up against the chilled glass. With his mouth half opened and half contorted, his eyes dashed from one rooftop to another, gliding with the pinpoint accuracy of a sniper. Moved by the same electric current, Carl sprang across the room like a frightened gazelle, sinking himself at the end of Dennis's bed.

Without saying a word, the boys carefully scanned every inch of earth within view. Dennis closed his eyes and tilted his head toward the floor, hoping his ears would conjure Santa's next stop. Several minutes passed without a sound or expression. The brothers didn't speak out of fear that any words of hope or wonderment might drown the soft jingle of sleigh bells.

"Where do you think he is?" Carl finally whispered.

"I don't know," answered Dennis quickly.

Carl studied the rooftops again. "Maybe he left and isn't coming back until we're asleep."

"Yeah, maybe . . . but I don't think so."

"Why not?"

"Because he's too busy for that. Why would he waste time flying in circles, waiting for us to go to bed?"

"He is fast, you know. Maybe he already—"

A furious rattle of bells suddenly rang down from above, joined by the thunderous sound of booted footsteps. Santa was on their roof. The brothers sat frozen, as their thoughts tangled with visions of St. Nick rummaging through his magic bag, pulling out drums and candy and electric toys, stroking the powerful necks of the reindeer as he prepared for his leap through the hailing chimney.

Carl leaned forward, raising his head toward the commotion. But his squinting eyes were met only by the rusted belly of the rain gutter. The voluminous footsteps continued to bang a scribbled path from the brothers' room all the way to the living room, then across the hallway and back to the brothers' room. The old man seemed lost.

The bells shook again. This time they were joined by a deep, cackling "Ho! Ho! Ho!" The visitor continued to streak across the roof as if he were trying to wake the house.

The voice came again, this time shouting "Ho! Ho! JESUS!" A booming thud pounded the ceiling as the sleigh bells could be heard rolling down the slippery roof. Sounds of exploding Christmas bulbs, echoing like miniature cannon reports, followed the tumbling mass of Christmas glory as he shook the room, his shrieks of "HOLY JESUS!" vibrating throughout the neighborhood.

The boys braced for the inevitable. They'd watch the poor man plunge into the waiting bushes. They'd watch as he broke his leg or tangled his drawers on the rusted porch railing. They'd listen to his blistered lips moan of slipshod roofs and early retirement. Or would he just disappear?

Santa's descent slowed as he hacked and clawed at the guilty shingles. He softly halted to a stop, popping off several more bulbs, as he lay flattened. His foot dangled over the edge of the roof. His puckered clothes clung like a damp blanket. Slowly, the old man collected himself and began his retreat.

The brothers stared at the giant boot as it disappeared into the clearing sky. They listened as the footsteps dragged a cautious path back to the roof's crest, and then vanished. The boys sat, without a word, wondering if what had happened was a dream or a nightmare or both.

Carl took to his bed and lay on his back. He felt his heart pounding through his skin. He tried to pray but he couldn't, so he pretended to sleep. Across the room, Dennis again lay facing the window, this time smiling and with his body tucked beneath the covers. He thought about Rusty Hayes and his water buffalo. He thought about Santa and the exploding Christmas lights. He thought about sleeping, but he couldn't. So he just pretended.

The Silent Stars Go By

PHILIP LEE WILLIAMS

CHAPTER FOURTEEN

Every December, two or three weeks before Christmas, Daddy, Mark, and I would set out on a frosty Saturday morning and head for the woods. This was unusual because Daddy rarely came to the forest, being too busy with adult life. That year, Laura Jane was with us, and Mother exulted in the care of her new daughter, though Daddy doted, too. Since I was nine years older than the baby, whom we would come to call Lolly, I was not jealous of that attention. Besides, she was funny. She had huge blue eyes, laughed all the time, and loved to be held.

This trip was the most special of the year, when we went to hunt for the perfect Christmas tree. In the South there was only one true kind of Christmas tree: the cedar. The woods behind our house held a surprising number of fine cedars, from seedlings to huge ones with limbs reaching from sky to ground. Not only were cedars fine for climbing, they were ideal for hiding. The dense foliage, the close-packed limbs made them a perfect sanctuary. Often, when I was alone in the woods, I'd find a cedar to scale and stay up there for hours, listening to birds, pretending that Indian attack was imminent. It took a great deal of boredom for me to move much in those days. I could sit happily in one place for hours.

On one memorable trip for a Christmas tree, I think a year or two earlier, we had reached Rocky Island, where three creeks merged. At the edge of one small creek, Daddy told us to move back because he was going to try something. He paced off a distance from a huge pine, balanced himself, raised the hatchet and threw it. It flew awkwardly, almost in slow motion, like a road sign tumbling in a storm. Then, with a resounding thwack, it struck, the blade digging into the punky bark. Mark and I stood amazed at the sight. Daddy's throwing arm was still extended toward the tree, and we were all frozen in shock and admiration for the beauty of the motion. (Years later, Mark and I would order some Wham-O! Malayan Throwing Knives from the back of an issue of *Boy's Life* and do considerable damage to trees in our back yard.)

This year was at least the fifth year in which we had gone scouting for a Christmas tree, and we were determined to find the best cedar in the forest.

The pine woods might have been my bones. I knew them by this time so well that I could have walked through them blindfolded without striking my head on a single trunk. There were hardwoods here and there, especially near Rocky Island, but mostly we played, camped, and lingered among the pines. I loved the pines, but I worshiped the cedars.

First was their aroma, one of the loveliest natural smells on earth. You could stand near one and simply inhale that delicious fragrance, almost sip it, feel it rich and pleasant on the tongue. I never passed a cedar tree without thrusting my face (carefully) into its branches and taking a good whiff. More often, I could find some small branch and break it off, bringing it slowly to my nose. I carried it with me for hours, bringing it up for a sniff from time to time.

Just as pleasing was their shape. Nothing else in the woods looked like a Christmas tree except the cedar, and that blue-green foliage held its shape against wind and rain. The limb structure was also perfect for a climbing boy.

Daddy walked slowly, keeping his eyes open. He would come up to a tree that might have a bad side or was too fat or thin.

"What do you think of this one, boys?" he might ask.

"I don't know," I'd say, disappointed that he was even considering it. *That* tree would look terrible in our front room near the piano.

"Well, with the lights on, it might look pretty good," he'd say, watching us from the corner of his eye.

"If the lights are working," Mark might blurt.

"And some icicles," Daddy said. "We could cover up the bad spots with icicles."

Mark and I walked around the sad tree, feeling a bit downcast until Daddy, inevitably, smiled and told us to come on, that we could surely find a better tree than this in a whole forest. Mark and I whooped and dashed forward, on the lookout for the right cedar.

Finally, every year, Daddy somehow lead us to a spot deep in the woods, maybe farther than we normally ranged, and he would stop and point. And there, miraculously, unbelievably, was our Christmas tree. In my imagination and delight, I saw the right tree ringed in light, as if awaiting us in its sheer perfection. Then we walked around it, praising it shape, its aroma.

"What do you think of this one, boys?" Daddy then asked.

"*Unh huh!*" we'd cry.

Our breaths feathered the air. Daddy in his coat would kneel before the tree and lightly hack away the ground-hugging branches, then begin to cut it down. I watched with a rising joy, never once thinking of the tree we were killing but only of the beauty it would bring to our house. Once the Christmas tree was up and decorated, there was no doubt that the holiday was near.

So it was that December 1959. Mark and I watched as he finished chopping down the six-foot cedar and dragging it clear of the stump. He stood it on end and shook it three times to knock out loose and dead needles, and a small shower of cedar-leavings sifted beneath it. Then we turned and headed back through the woods toward the field and, across it, home.

Once the tree was in its stand, Daddy put on the lights. Finally, after an evening of fiddling with the tangled strands, they would work nicely. Daddy would stand them around the tree from top to bottom. I vaguely remember— did it happen at all?—Laura Jane sitting in her high chair and watching as we decorated the tree, and music from Handel's *Messiah* flowing gently in the background. We put on all the bulbs and balls that my parents had been collecting since their wedding in 1945. We boys broke so many that I suppose most weren't that old. We did have some plastic icicles with hooks on the end that had survived for years. The last of that pleasant chore (was Mother in the kitchen popping popcorn to eat afterward?) was the hanging of the stranded icicles.

Everyone is familiar with these shining strips, but in those days the icicles were made of lead instead of plastic. You could take two or three and crumple them up in your hand and make a small silvery ball that, with repeated rubbings on a hard surface, would gleam. We had no idea that they were poisonous but I don't recall anyone eating any. Then, as the tree was finished and stood gleaming with promise in our front room, we celebrated with hot chocolate, and I felt a perfect joy. The details always seemed to be the same, but that year I was the least bit uncomfortable. We still had a state championship to win, and I had asked for a red football uniform.

The only problem, once the lovely cedar tree stood in our house, was the waiting.

A Christmas Gift for General Sherman

KENNETH ROBBINS

I beg to present you as a Christmas gift, the city of Savannah, with one hundred and fifty guns and plenty of ammunition, also about twenty-five thousand bales of cotton.

—William T. Sherman to Abraham Lincoln, December 20, 1864

Dinner is silent for the most part. The chicken is perfectly baked, the lima beans heavenly soft, the gravy thick with giblets, the potatoes rich in butter, the salad relatively crisp and mostly green, the stewed apples worthy of praise, and the chocolate mousse a surprise even for Celestine. She had planned a soufflé for dessert since sugar is so rare. Where Henrietta had found sufficient chocolate for the surprising dish is and will remain a mystery.

With only two for dinner, there is plenty, especially since Celestine eats so little, leaving the rest to the ravishing general who devours the food with relish and actually asks for thirds.

"Camp food be damned," he announces to the portrait of Jefferson Davis that graces the dining room's west wall. "I'll come here for my meals if you'll but invite me."

"A man of your importance needs no invitation," Celestine says, watching Uncle Billy scrape the bottom of the mousse dish that had been intended for her father.

"Hey, woman!" he calls toward the door that leads to the kitchen. Henrietta is obviously in the next room, ear to the wood paneling, longing to know how her repast has been received, since she is in the dining room in an instant, dishrag in hand, smile on her face. "You are some cook, madam," Uncle Billy declares. "How about following me back to the Green mansion and cooking me a manly breakfast in the morning?"

Henrietta is pleased; that is obvious from the broadness of her grin. She says with no real deferment for the man's rank or importance, "I spect I'll retire from cooking after this night, Mister Man. Getting this here meal's just about caused this old woman to play herself out. You folks want any more chocolate pudding?"

Uncle Billy pushes his chair away from the table. "I'm stuffed, thank you very much."

Celestine rises. "We'll take our port in the sitting room, Henrietta. And be sure to put some food aside for Mr. Bell. He'll be famished when he finally decides to return home."

"He will revise his politics, I'm certain, Miss Henrietta, soon as he discovers the delicacies he missed out on tonight." He offers his arm to Celestine. "Madam?"

She takes it. And they stroll like an old married couple back to the comforts of the room where one is supposed to sit.

"That was a meal well worth savoring, Miss Bell," he says as he plops on the sofa with feet on the coffee table and cigar emerging from the inner sanctum of his tunic.

She perches on the edge of the easy chair, leaning forward to give him an unobstructed view of her cleavage while edging an ashtray, a finely cut crystal bowl, toward his anticipated after-dinner smoke. "I do wish you would call me Celestine. Miss Bell is so formal."

"A rose by any other name, eh?" He chuckles and relaxes on the sofa, sprawling being the word to describe his physical attitude. He smiles at her cleavage but it is clear: he has seen better and will most likely see better before the night is finished and he is back in the gaudy confines of the Green mansion. Whether he finds her attractive or not is unknown: he stares at her anyway as Henrietta brings a tray with a decanter of port and two stemmed glasses from the kitchen. "Celestine," he says with a brief sadness crossing his face. "That was my daughter's name as well. Celestine. The celestial one."

"Please convey my Christmas greetings to her. Perhaps we might meet one of these days."

"Celestine did not survive the birthing process," he says with far less remorse than she would have preferred.

"I'm so sorry," is her reply.

"Don't be. I have plenty of healthy children. They are my joy, along with their mother, of course."

He enjoys his unlit cigar a bit more than is necessary, Celestine notes. In his hands it takes on the attitude of something lewd, almost pornographic. She can't be certain, but it appears that the cigar is for show, not for smoking since he has made no effort to light it. Because of its phallic nature and his obvious management of it as such, Celestine blurts out, "I'm not married."

Now where had that come from is his ponderment. He had not asked for such information. In fact, he didn't need it. He states without equivocation, "I surmised as much. A beau, perhaps?"

"No. I mean, yes. Actually no. Papa needs me."

"Of course, I'm sure he does. And your mother, too, I would presume."

"She is no longer . . . living here," she says, cutting her eyes away from the treacherous suggestions emerging from his visage.

He breaks the tension by asking, "Do you mind if I smoke? A meal is incomplete without a cigar."

She fluffs the ribbons gathered in her coifed hair. "Not at all. You'll find a box of matches on the table. There, near your left boot."

"Thank you." He extracts a long-stem match from the frivolous container. "An unusual keepsake." He turns it over and sees the inscription that makes the box of matches so precious to its owner. "Fanny Kemble? I caught a perform-ance of hers in New York before the war. A striking lady."

He lights his cigar. "Yes," she agrees, "most striking."

Uncle Billy's cigar emits heinous aromas throughout the room, but Celestine says nothing. She abhors the stench, but determines in spite of her inclination to say nothing. It is he who says, "You know her well? The famous Fanny Kemble?"

Celestine's mood is fluctuating and she regrets this. Cigar smoke will do that for a woman more readily than any other known male habit. She conceals her dilemma, however, at some risk. "I never met her, though I, too, saw her perform—here, in Savannah. I don't really care for her acting. Too dishonest."

"Dishonest? Since when have acting and honesty shared anything in common?"

"It's a matter of taste, I presume."

"Then I must presume that you prefer fantasy to be dishonest, since to be honest would be the result?"

She sighs. The conversation is impossible to control. But control it she must. "Whenever possible. You, for example."

"Me? For example of what? Fantasy?"

"No. Honesty." She leans to one side, giving him a sidelong glance. "Are you honest?"

Uncle Billy chuckles. "If I answered that with any semblance of truth, I'd be lying."

"You sound like a politician."

"Generals," he says with a smirk, "in their effort to obtain that rank, are by their very nature politicians. Scoundrels all."

"It's none of my business, really, whether you are honest or not. Not at the moment."

"I am sinfully relaxed at the moment, if that has anything to do with being honest!"

She is up and off. She has no destination. She simply must be on her feet, moving, in control if at all possible. So, she moves. He, the gentlemanliness of earlier in the evening obviously employed for show, remains "sinfully relaxed" on the sofa. "Let's talk of something else."

He chuckles, relishing his "sin." "I am at your disposal. So to speak."

She strikes an alluring pose near the piano as she asks, "Do you find Savannah an attractive city?"

He sits forward, ignoring the sexy attitude she has assumed. "Savannah, in the words of a man who is prone to romantic notions, my second in command, General O. O. Howard, whom you must meet one of these days, is a jewel in the southern crown. I've anticipated my return for some time. Upon departing Atlanta, I set my sights on this charming port village. I'm no stranger here. But I suppose you know that?"

"Of course." She tosses her coy game to the wind and returns to her perch on the easy chair. "When you were here before, you were merely a captain."

"Fresh from the academy with worlds to conquer."

"And hearts as well. You conquered mine. Don't you recall?"

"Did I really? How?" So this is why I have been wined and dined, he surmises. The truth will out.

"We bumped into each other one Sunday morning." She waves the smoke from her face, wishing he would get the hint. "I was coming from church, you from somewhere else, I can only imagine where. The bump was a hefty one. You knocked me headlong into a mud puddle."

He guffaws. "You're joking. You had me going there for a minute."

"No joke. My dress was ruined and my ego shattered. I was twelve. Most impressionable, you see."

He is sitting forward now, searching her face for any hint of his being cajoled. There is none. "This is distressing. All because of my clumsiness?"

She smiles for the first time since his arrival. "No need to apologize. I was as much to blame as you since I chose not to avoid your approach. Besides, I bought a new dress the very next day and my ego mended readily. Here—" and she takes the treasured handkerchief from her bodice— "here is the handkerchief you gave me that morning to wipe the mud from my face. You see? Your initials in the corner?"

He takes the offered token, scans it, and emits a grunt of recognition as he tosses it back to its owner. "Again, I'm terribly sorry. Contrite. How can I repay you?"

She has him. "By being my guest this evening. A most gracious guest, I might add."

He inhales a deep draught from the wretched cigar and allows the smoke to ease from his mouth as he says, "Such a long time ago. I strutted, didn't I."

"Maybe a little."

His memories of his youth are storming his strongholds. His brow is creasing and his eyes lost in a distant haze. "I was proud of my uniform in those days. I even wore it to bed until I learned I could not afford the cost of pressing my pants. Did you know that?"

"How could I?"

"You seem to know so much."

"Very little, actually."

He stands, struts a little, then assumes a military pose with his hand on the mantel, his elbow akimbo. "Have I changed since then?"

She feigns surveying him, another move for show since she has already studied him and come to her conclusions. "You've grayed a bit. Your wrinkles about the eyes have deepened. Your midsection is so-so. But generally, you're still the strutting same."

He laughs at her descriptions. "Not even the least bit grander?"

Such an opportunity. She is unable to avoid it. Her coyness back in place for a full frontal assault, she whispers, "You could hardly look more grand than you did that day with such an attractive woman on your arm and you dressed in your finest blue uniform."

He is taken aback. Apparently, he had disremembered the event. "There was a woman involved?"

"Yes, a most attractive brunette. Young. Swishy." She sees his mind working overtime to recall who the mystery woman might have been. This pleases her. It convinces her that she is indeed on the right path. "She smelled of orange blossoms. I recall visiting several shops in town in search of her fragrance in a bottle. I've often wondered if the lady were your wife. I naturally assumed she was."

"Yes," he says far too quickly for his own good. "Yes, my wife. So, Miss Bell, have you lived in Savannah long?"

She presses her advantage. "All my life. Are you certain she was your wife, General?"

He shrugs. What does it matter anyway? "I don't recall. Is that port?"

She is quick to pour him a glass of the syrupy liquid. "Forgive me. I am forgetting my manners." She serves him the glass and takes one for herself. "So, General, to business."

"Business? On Christmas night?"

"What better time than now? What better place than here? What better business associate than you?" She slides onto the sofa beside him and clinks glasses with him. "To Savannah."

"To Savannah."

"What are your intentions regarding Savannah after you leave?"

He sips his port. It is not his favorite after-dinner drink. He would prefer a beer. But he pretends to enjoy it. "Who says I'm leaving?"

She cannot sit beside him long. The rancid cigar forces her away. "Oh, come now," she says with a toss of her head. "What is to keep you in Savannah? You didn't march all this way just to become stodgy and an 'Alice-Sit-By-the-Fire.' You're much too ambitious for that. There are victories to be won, armies to defeat. Savannah can be nothing more to you than a convenient supply depot. So. What do you have planned for us?"

He lifts his glass in her direction, acknowledging her astute assessment of his position. "I haven't decided."

"When will you make your decision?"

"Probably the day I leave. To your health, dear lady." He is by her side, preparing to finagle his arm around her waist.

"And to your future battles."

"May they become fewer as the days progress." And they drink.

She moves away from him again. She must remain in control. "I have relatives in Atlanta. They have told me of their straits and the horrors of war. I've wondered how I would face the reality of leaving my home and returning to it as my cousins experienced, to find it in ashes. I think my heart would break if that were to happen."

"We must protect your heart, mustn't we."

She ignores him and persists: "My relative from Atlanta wrote of what I describe, returning to her home after your departure—I don't mean to accuse. You must be fully aware of the disaster that affected her life so profoundly. She couldn't distinguish her pile of rubble from her neighbors'. But she and her parents, my aunt and uncle, are rebuilding even as we speak."

He replenishes his glass from the wine decanter. "It pleases me to hear that."

"Does it truly?"

"My dear, burning Atlanta was a necessity of war, not the act of any personal enjoyment."

"Honestly?"

He shrugs again. "Just as torching Savannah will eventually be a similar necessity. I would be remiss in my duty if Savannah were left untouched to continue supplying the enemy. It is really quite simple."

"Nothing is ever simple, General."

"Nothing is ever terribly complicated, my dear Celestine. A thing is either this or that, seldom the other. The answer to most questions is usually yes or no, rarely maybe."

She takes a moment before she poses the most telling question to him: "Then you intend to burn Savannah?"

"Maybe."

She moves closer to him, struggling with the right attitude to hold her head, her chest, and her hands. "Is there any way I might dissuade you?"

His smile is demeaning, not worthy of a man of his position. "We could pursue the question, if you wish."

"If I told you I know a way. What then?"

"I would welcome any persuasive techniques you possess. Shouldn't we close the drapes?"

She takes his glass and places it on the table. She then takes his hand and pulls him toward the door. "Your cigar has gone out. Come with me."

"But my dear Miss Bell—"

"Come."

And she leads him gently toward the door, a promise in her eyes that he recognizes with only a momentary pause. What the hell? He laughs lightly as she gently leads him up the hallway stairs. Imagine that. Laughter. Friendship. Promise. All available this Christmas evening in the fair and beautiful city of Savannah.

Celestine leads the way up the back stairs. Uncle Billy pauses on the second floor, assuming the doors he sees hide the expected bedroom. His anticipation contains comfortable contact, perhaps some unknown balm to ease the pains in his lower back and legs, a full body massage would be nice, and perhaps a trick or two involving leather or at least hemp.

Instead, she continues up the stairs toward the third, attic level. "Don't dawdle," she says over her shoulder. "It's not far." And she disappears around a corner of the narrow stairwell.

This is most unusual, he nearly says aloud. Instead, he does as she commands and follows, his expectations for the conclusion of the evening growing with each tread on the stairwell.

At the top, he finds what he least desires: an attic devoid of any physical convenience. It is an attic like any other, stacked with discarded boxes all filled most likely with the disappointing Celestine Bell's discarded wardrobe. He finds her at the far end of the cluttered room, opening one of the wooden crates.

"Your cigar, sir?"

"I don't really care to smoke at a time like this."

"But that is why we have come all this way—to relight your horrid stogy." The match flares in her hand. "I want you to be comfortable as we continue discussing business."

"Again business," he says as he draws the flame into his revived cigar.

"Bargaining, actually. You see, General, Savannah is a city that I love more dearly than my own life. I intend to see to it that it remains secure, untouched."

"It's Christmas, dear lady," he says and turns back toward the stairwell. "I've had a delightful evening, but it is time—"

She overturns the crate that she has opened. Matches by the thousands spill onto the wooden floor of the attic. She announces, "For you, sir."

She is pleased that his mouth falls open, that he is having difficulty processing exactly what it is he sees.

"Incredible" is all he is able to manage as he kneels to the floor and fingers the stash of matchsticks.

"Take your pick, General, from any box. I have matches of all kinds, shapes, and sizes. Flints, phosphorus, you name it, it's here somewhere." She opens a second crate and spills its contents and a third and is in the process of spilling a fourth when he stops her.

"This is most unexpected."

"What makes it even more unexpected is the fact that each of these boxes contains new and unused matches. How many boxes are there? I'll let you count them, but I estimate at least three wagons full, maybe more."

"Do you have any idea how valuable these things are?"

She smiles. "I can only imagine."

He is momentarily delighted, even youthful as he scoops his hands into pile after pile of matches. "Incredible."

"I haven't counted them yet, but I estimate there to be at least five million matches here in my attic."

He snuffs his cigar out on the floor, a precaution against an unwanted spark. He admits without giving any thought to his words, "I've had a difficult time locating matches here in Savannah. It seems there are no matches to be found anywhere inside the city."

There is profound pride in her voice as she says, "I have them all."

He stands, squares his shoulders. "Yes, business. Now I understand. I could use every match you own. What's your price?"

She bows modestly in his general direction. "They are yours. Christmas present."

"Business is the word you used. You have obviously put a great deal of effort into this collection. How much?"

"May we get serious, General?"

"I am serious."

"Then these articles of war are my gift to you—in exchange for your Christmas gift to me."

"And just what might that be?"

"Savannah."

He is confused. His confusion is displayed across his face. "I don't understand."

"In exchange for my collection, you must agree to leave Savannah untouched." This is playing out exactly as she has rehearsed it in her head time and time again. "You are to avoid setting even a single fire upon your departure. You are to assign a military governor to oversee our safety and well-being—"

"Impossible."

"But, sir, think of what you are getting in return. All the matches you'll need for making South Carolina plea for pity. My price is really quite minimal considering just how desperate you are at the moment for matches."

"I'm desperate for nothing."

"Honestly? I could have sworn you just said—"

"I remarked that we are low. We're never desperate for any supplies. Besides, there are plenty more matches—"

"Which will take months to order and obtain. There are no matches available in Savannah. We have seen to that. If you burn Savannah, you won't have enough matches to do anything at all across the river. And you cannot afford to wait around for a shipment from outside. We both know that Lee can't last much longer in Virginia and that Wade Hampton hasn't a prayer of giving him the reinforcements he so desperately needs. If you do not head north soon, the war will be over and you will not have had any part in the final cessation of hostilities. Grant will be the national hero and you an afterthought. Is that your ultimate life goal, to be another hero's shadow?"

"Where do you get your information?"

"That's not really important, is it?"

He senses the nature of the trap she has set for him, but he is unsure of its power. Just how committed is this southern Bell who confronts him? He needs to know. "What assurance do I have that the people in Savannah won't continue supplying Lee and Hood?"

She shrugs her shoulders. "That is simple. Your retainer force will see to that. The military commander and his garrison can easily control the import and export of military goods. Ideally, Savannah could become your major supply base as the army moves into South Carolina."

"I haven't decided where we will go from here—south to Florida or by boat to Virginia—"

"Columbia is undoubtedly your best route."

"I know."

"You take Columbia and you've successfully broken South Carolina's back. It's the major railroad center remaining in the Confederacy—"

"I know, I know."

"Take Columbia and Charleston will wither. Take Columbia and you'll be front-page news around the world." He is silent. He does not move. She is patient for a moment or two before she asks, "Well?"

He gazes deep into her eyes. "I could confiscate these here and now. There is a patrol right outside your house—"

"I'd set fire to the whole shebang."

"You wouldn't."

"Oh, but I would."

"You'd be destroying your home."

"I know."

"I could arrest you."

"Yes, you could. Then my organization would destroy the matches as you transported them down the street."

"Organization?"

"You don't think I collected all my matches by myself, do you?"

"I don't know what to think anymore. I come here, in friendship, for a quiet Christmas dinner, and . . ."

She arranges writing materials on one of the crates—inkwell, pen, paper, and blotter. "Take my offer, General. It's easy, direct, and necessary. My matches for the city of Savannah."

He paces, no longer in control of the situation and he knows it. He must be in charge. He must regain the upper hand here. "Ah, the hell with it. I'll have you arrested—"

She strikes a match and holds it over the spilled crates.

He holds his hands up in a gesture of patience. "Now listen here, Miss Bell, you must be reasonable."

She strikes four more matches and watches them burn. "I understand your dilemma. You can't go into the field of battle without being fully armed. Without matches you may as well stay home in Ohio. It will be months before your supply from outside the city can get here. By then Grant will have defeated Lee and you're a footnote in history. Don't you see? Savannah's not that important when all is said and done."

"You drive a hard bargain. How do I know you have as many matches as you claim? These boxes could all be empty."

"Select one—any one, I don't care. Open it. See for yourself."

He does. Matches fill the box. He selects another crate from the bottom of a stack. It, too, is filled with matches. He shakes his head.

"Are you convinced?" she asks.

"Let me make sure I understand you. All that are here—in exchange for—"

"Savannah. Not a single fire to be set."

"I'll have to set at least three. Otherwise my men would revolt."

"Three then, on the outskirts of the city, on the South Carolina bank of the river."

"And you swear to me that none of these crates have been tampered with—watered down or anything like that."

"My word of honor. There has been no tampering. You are getting state-of-the-art matches, sir."

He surveys the attic one final time. He surveys his hostess one final time. He extends his right hand. "Done."

She takes his hand in both of hers. "You agree?"

"I agree. You have my word on it."

She steps away from the writing materials and wafts him to them. "In writing."

He guffaws. "You're joking."

"Is this a joking matter? I want it in writing that you will spare Savannah in exchange for the war machines which I consign to you. Signed, please."

He tries his most winning smile on her. "This is hardly necessary. My word is . . ."

Again she indicates the paper and pen.

"Oh, very well, if my word isn't good enough."

He scribbles a note on the paper, the pen making a rasping sound as it crosses the sheet. He steps aside. "There. Will that do?"

She reads his words. "Almost. Add: I also agree to leave a full garrison of trained soldiers in Savannah to maintain law and order for the duration of the war."

"The duration? That could be four more years. How much do you think these things are worth?"

"Far more than I'm asking."

He adds the phrase.

"Now, sign it."

He signs the note and hands it to her for her inspection. "Satisfied?"

She folds the paper and places it inside her trusted bodice. "Very good. Your hand, my good sir."

He ignores her offer, pushing past her and finding a match to relight his cigar. He rushes down the stairs as he calls, "That's a weight off me, let me tell you that. I didn't want to burn this city. It's too—what, too precious? Hardly. It's too damn cute to torch. Though it would have made a tidy little blaze." He gathers his things in the sitting room, she directly behind him. He turns to her and clicks his heels. "Thank you, Celestine, for a most entertaining evening. One I will remember for quite some time. I'll have my men come by in the morning."

She bows as she says, "It has been a pleasure doing business with you, Cump."

"Cump?" His eyes flash. "Well, what the hell. Give my regards to your father." He stops beneath the chandelier. "Isn't this mistletoe, dear lady?"

She goes to him. "I believe it is." She kisses him on the mouth, a kiss that she intended to be short and sweet but becomes extended as he readily responds.

He clears his throat as he pulls away and places his hat at a cocky angle. "Mrs. Sherman never kisses like that."

"And the woman who graced your arm that bright Sunday morning?"

"Yes." He marches to the door. "Good evening, Miss Bell. I hope to see you again. Some day."

"That won't be necessary. We're even now. You bumped me and I've bumped you back. Let's call it quits, shall we?"

"We'll see, my dear. We'll see." When he opens the door to the outside, the patrol snaps to attention. "Your servant, ma'am."

"May your journey through South Carolina be ablaze with glory, sir." And she slams the door closed.

Once a Thief

JANICE DAUGHARTY

This time The Count was moving us in a wheelbar, which made perfect sense to a drunk, because then Uncle King, at the corner filling station, would have to suffer seeing us suffer while load after load of our scrappy belongings got wheeled from the shack at Cornerville crossing, east along the sidewalk between the post office and the new courthouse—at sundown, in thirty-degree cold, on Christmas Eve. Uncle King's own runny-nosed nieces tracking behind the wheelbar, toting peed-on quilts and clothes and shoes, and finally the old lady in her purple housecoat trailing on the last load with her juiceharp and a flurry of fyce dogs.

I would like to of told The Count that even supposing Uncle King was watching us, he couldn't see us suffer no futher than maybe the Methodist Church, other side of the post office. And what big difference did that make if he couldn't see us when we turned off at the new schoolhouse and headed toward the shack in the colored quarters? I would like to of told The Count that we would still be at the mercy of Uncle King, whose house we was moving out of at the crossing just to move in another of his houses in the quarters, and who could care less if we froze, starved, or died of shame.

But The Count done knowed all of that. He was just drunk. And when he got drunk, he got spiteful, proud and sorry for hisself, and me nor Lovie nor Mama neither one didn't try to tell him nothing.

"There's Santy Claus," said Lovie, slipping her thumb from her puckered lips to point at the house across the road. A lectric Santy face with chapped cheeks beamed from the screen door of one of the white houses lined up from the courthouse to the schoolhouse. Warm smell of vanilla, cold smell of pine.

Sucking her thumb again, Lovie twirled one of her brown curls on her finger while we followed The Count with his wheelbar across the road to the turnoff leading to the quarters. Him and the wheelbar both wobbling like shoats. No cars coming and it was a good thing, since he didn't even look. I grabbed holt of Lovie's bony hand anyhow. We walked fast.

We could hear Mama behind us with the dogs, just their claws on the gravel—pck, pck, pck. Her juiceharp playing "Silent Night."

I'd be glad when Christmas was done with.

"There's the schoolhouse," said Lovie, this time not pointing, just resting her thumb on her bottom lip. Her swole brown eyes set shallow in puffy sockets. Worms, according to the county nurse, was how come Lovie stay about the same size since she was four. She was seven now, like a dog that stays puppy-size.

"I see it," I said. Truth was, I'd been seeing the schoolhouse up close, for a couple of months then. Slipping out at night and slinking in the shadows along each new wall smelling of brick dust and uncured cement. Just to show

Miss Annar the teacher and Berk Sirmons the principal, who wadn't even there, that Shirley Trevor could come back to school anytime she felt like it and didn't have to come if she didn't feel like it. I didn't mess with nothing.

Colored cutouts of snowflakes and Christmas trees was pasted on the door-sized windows now. Right after Christmas, I would make Lovie go back to school, but I wouldn't go. I'd made up my mind. Nobody couldn't make me. Me and Lovie had been turned out about a year ago, when Miss Annar the teacher and Berk Sirmons the principal got wind of the fact that Mama had colored blood. Wadn't long before they was begging us back—the fact wadn't a fact after all—to keep peace with The Count, and like they said, intergration was coming anyhow. Too late. I was going on thirteen and half-grown, and already taking over Mama's washerwoman job at Miss Lular's and looking out for another job paid money stead of hand-me-down clothes.

"Sister," Lovie said, sidling close, "you reckon Santy Claus'll find our new house?"

"Didn't never find the last one, as I know of."

Tarry green britches bagging to his knees, The Count was mumbling, swaying, weaving the wheelbar up the dirt road with a five-gallon can of kerosene and a hairy rug toward the first shack in the half-circle of shacks that wrapped around a fenced-in field, south end of the school grounds. Last place in the world I wanted to live— overlooking the school grounds. Not to mention living in the quarters.

"Mommer told him to look out for me," said The Count, blubbering and wiping his nose on his black coat sleeve. "Told him on her deathbed."

Up ahead, colored younguns and their dogs looped from the run-together yards to the footprinted road, squealing and tussling in the last smudge of daylight. Yard fires out-shining the puny orange sun now setting beyond the background of scrub oaks, black gums and pines; ever unseen dead limb and falling leaf seen in the backlight. Smoke shooting from the chimleys of shotgun shacks, where inside babies cried—too tired to go on, too miserable to quit. Drenty wash on clotheslines. Men idling about the crescent, smoking cigarettes, and women shouting from porches at deaf-acting younguns and dogs. Christmas lights etching out each doorway, doors standing wide. A song somewhere.

Behind us seemed to be waiting for Christmas; ahead seemed like Christmas could come or don't. The games would go on, the racket would go on. One more night of cold and burning boards off porches to warm by. One more day of grubbing for food. Babies crying. At a giant live oak dividing the road in two, about halfway between the schoolhouse and the shack we was moving into, The Count let the wheelbar down on its hind standards and began plundering for his whiskey bottle beneath the cotton batting he'd stole and stored at Uncle King's turpentine vat in the woods: the reason this time Uncle King had kicked him out of the house at the Cornerville crossing—"I ain't having nothing else to do with you till the hairs of my backend turn white." Uncle King was always saying that, always going back on his word.

I had lost track of the last reason Uncle King had threatened never to have nothing to do with The Count no more. But he did, and he never let us starve. Just almost.

Come dark, The Count had grieved and drunk hisself into a stupor, and lay sprawled on a mattress with his gray-whiskered chin jutted toward the ceiling where devils of firelight romped.

One thing you could count on The Count to do was build fires—big fires, bad fires. And not just to warm by. After me and Lovie got sent home from school cause of Mama's bad blood, The Count had built a fire. After Uncle King swindled The Count out of the timberland left by their daddy, The Count had built a fire. Schoolhouse and courthouse both burnt to the ground. And I expected before daybreak he'd burn down our old house at the Cornerville crossing too.

But for now, things was quiet. Except for the old lady rocking before the braiding fire, strumming "Silent Night" on her juiceharp, and the same sad-happy racket playing out in the quarters like a record somebody got for Christmas. Mama had been working on the same song for going on a month. Socked feet crossed, and her wrapped in her fuzzy purple housecoat, firelight mingled in her polleny stubbled hair. She held the juiceharp to her mouth with her left hand and plucked at the strings with her right hand. Green eyes blared and fire-bright. Not a care, looked like.

Me and Lovie was sleeping on another mattress with our feet to the fire, our heads cold from the air sucking along the vee-ceiled walls. Tomorrow we might open up the other rooms and sweep out the trash left by the last family, but till then we'd all have to sleep in this one room together. Mama's blowed-up, rocking shadow on the east wall made the room rock like a boat. I rolled over, facing Lovie's cheeky dark face and long lashes lapped over stained eye sockets; seemed like she was all that was sweet and new in that musty old house, maybe in the world. I felt as old and spent as The Count and Mama, who got bedraggled from his drinking and her sorry ways. I was getting just like them—settling into being hopeless and poor—except for that something inside me I couldn't name that made me want to get up and make something happen I couldn't name.

We had gone to bed hungry before—lots of befores— but this was Christmas Eve, and somehow going to bed hungry on Christmas Eve didn't seem fair. No Santy Claus for Lovie didn't seem fair. I listened to her suck her thumb, a slisking sound around the balking chords of "Silent Night" and dogs barking to be barking and the coloreds whooping to be whooping. And later I listened to the old lady sliding out of her rocker and punching up the fire and settling in on her mattress facing The Count's. No shortage of mattresses: The Count had snitched about a dozen of them from a old man had a mattress factory at his house near the Alapaha River bridge. What The Count done, according to Uncle King, was wait till the old man lay dead, then sneaked in his house and start toting out mattresses. "Low-principled, no-count thief," Uncle King said to The Count, adding, "Once a thief, always a thief." And for about the ten-thousandth time, Uncle King washed his hands of The Count.

He come by the name of "Count" honest—his dead mama had named him that—but when Uncle King and everbody else went to calling him "No-count," I started calling him "The Count" out of pride and spite.

With the juiceharp silent now, I could hear clear the laughing and whooping and crying next door, and next door, and next door. Linking racket. Lardy smell of fried mullet seeped through the chinks of the chimley where fire licked at the fat litard boards. When we'd got to the shack at sundown, Lovie had set in to begging Mama to let her go eat with the neighbors, but Mama said no, said me nor Lovie neither one better not be caught messing around with the coloreds. So Lovie had give up and gone to sleep hungry.

At least, when we used to go to school, we'd get one square meal a day. Free lunches for poor people. One reason I was bound and determined to make Lovie go back. You might get embarrassed to death at school, but you wouldn't starve to death at school. Miss Annar the teacher would say, "You free-lunchers line up last." That kind of thing.

I got up and laid another stick of wood on the fire, then tipped to the front door, opened it and stepped out on the airish porch. Smoky fires in all the yards on my right, people and their shadows like couples strolling. Gunfire like screen doors clapping from one of the houses on the far side of the field.

You could believe about half of what they taught you in school—specially the reading books with Dick and Jane and Mom and Dad—but if you didn't believe what they taught in Sunday school, you could wind up in hell. So, to be on the safe side, I tried to single out the star that led the wisemen to baby Jesus. So many, like nail pricks in tin, I just picked one. What mattered was that I believed, not what was true. Believe on the Lord Jesus Christ and thou shalt be saved. Thou shalt not kill, thou shalt not steal . . .

I was fixing to steal anyway.

I tiptoed inside and picked up The Count's black coat by his mattress and slipped it on, hearing in the right pocket a rattly box of matches. After I put on my shoes, I went back to the porch, stepping down where the doorsteps used to be before The Count burnt them for firewood, and started walking up the dirt road with my eyes on the flared oak shadow. Cold already. Cold soaking into the loose weave of The Count's black overcoat. Leaving behind the noise of the quarters on Christmas Eve, I thought I could hear The Count's dogs barking, blending in with the other dogs.

The Count was forever towing dogs home. Most got hit on the highway or died from worms.

In the pewter glow of starlight, I could see the twin hills of the high school roof that The Count had pounded a keg of nails a day into after burning down the other school. Two red brick buildings joined together—the high school and the grammar school—like a box with one side cut out. Just past the live oak, I angled across the playground on the south end of the high school with its same old whirl-a-way and swing sets—smutty metal reminding me of the fire and why the fire come to be in the first place. I'd been to the new school one Saturday and the smut smell wadn't half as strong during the day as at night. I stepped up on the sidewalk running along the grammar school wing—a row of doors set in the brick wall—to the lunchroom.

Knowing what I was fixing to do, I oughta been scared, but I wadn't, not this time. Right at first, when I'd walk about the new school at night, or on that Saturday, I'd be scared of Miss Annar the teacher and Berk Sirmons the principal, same way I was scared of Uncle King and Jesus. They made the rules we was belonged to live by, they was the keepers of the ten commandments and chalk and paddles and land and sky. Maybe I wadn't scared that night since I'd made up my mind not to live by their rules no more. Except for Jesus—when I could.

I stopped at the first jalousie window of the lunchroom, which I'd peeped through a bunch of times, and looked left at the dead-grass square, between the high school and the grammar buildings. Not even a shadow, just open space like a field of dried cornshucks. I hooked the fingers of my right hand under the rim of the window frame and prized up. It creaked and give about a inch, then snapped to on my froze fingers. But I found that if I kept working up on the metal frame of the panel, little by little, it was opening wider and wider. Wide enough for me to crawl through, but too high for me to climb up to. I remembered the garbage cans on a wood platform, other side of the lunch-room, and headed for the corner of the grammar wing where a breezeway hooked the two buildings together. A sucking blackness, sealed on each end with waxy gray light, and not a sound save for my shoe soles grating sand on cement. But the cold streaming through was like some-thing alive that would show itself any minute—Miss Annar the teacher or Berk Sirmons the principal or Uncle King or Jesus. I breathed in and kept walking, doing what I had to, going for one of the garbage cans to climb up on. All empty, all upside-down with lids on top that would clang to the ground if I bumped them.

Back through the breezeway with one of the cold garbage cans hugged close, again I checked for shadows along the walkway and the dead grass of the courtyard, then set the garbage can upside down under the sprung window and hiested myself up and squeezed through the bottom pane of the jalousie like a snake.

The garbage can plooped from where my knees had dented the metal, but still I wadn't scared. I kept telling myself I wadn't scared. Not half as scared as hungry, not half as scared as determined to do what I had in mind for Lovie's Christmas.

A rip in The Count's silky coat lining got snagged on one of the window cranks along the wall, and I had to rip it futher to free the crank. A loud sound in the froze dark static of the lunchroom. I kept walking, feeling my way between the rounded backs of metal chairs and the wall of windows that give off a watery glow like mud puddles at dusk.

I knowed that place, knowed it well, though I'd never stepped foot inside. My favorite part of this schoolhouse and the other schoolhouse. I knowed the kitchen section of the lunchroom was just ahead, dark as a closet—a clock ticking, a motor humming that had to be the icebox. I used to spend lunchtime watching the lunchroom ladies opening the door of the icebox for great blocks of butter and cheese and logs of balonny. My mouth went to watering. I had to be close. I could smell yeast dough and sour milk and fake lemon floor cleaner.

Feeling my way through the swinging half-door to the kitchen, I squinched my eyes trying to see what was ahead, but it was like walking blind. I reached out to locate the icebox humming on my right and banged my head on a hanging pot that set off a chiming along the line of other hanging pots. I steadied one and then the other till the chiming stopped. I struck my first match. The tiny orange flame showed the serving counters on the left instead of the right, the giant stove against the north wall, the—I struck another match—big icebox on my right, and beyond it shelfs of giant cans of mixed vegetables and peaches and beans and jars of peanut butter. Everthing scoured chrome and white and giant-size, like a blowed-up picture of a kitchen. The flame singed my finger and thumb and I shook the match out. Smell of sulphur, smell of smoke.

Still not scared. Still not scared enough. This was Christmas Eve, and who would be at the schoolhouse on Christmas Eve? Nobody but maybe The Count, who might be pilfering just like me if he wasn't passed out drunk at the house. I had to use both hands to pull up on the handle of the icebox to open it; and all at once, cold light and vapors gusted over me and clouded the room. And then I was scared. I started to close it, to head for the window on the wall now doused in blackness, but instead I lifted down one of the great galvanized pots behind me and set it on the floor before the gusting cold light and started filling it with blocks of butter and cheese and logs of balonny. Other stuff I didn't know what was. I hadn't meant to take so much, but there was so much to take. I was so hungry.

Hurrying now, though not scared anymore, just cold, so cold that my nose was leaking to the cement floor, I lugged the pot to the door on the west wall of windows, which I would use to go out if I could get it open. No problem, I flipped a latch and the door swung wide like somebody was opening it from outside. I closed it, leaning against it, sucking in and blowing out; then in a minute, I started back to the kitchen where the chute of light from the open icebox made the rest of the lunchroom darker but spotlighted two red Christmas stockings hanging from a dishrag line on the facing white wall. Mesh stockings full of candy and nuts and bubble-gum machine type toys.

All the time I was filling another tub-like pot with light bread and peanut butter and crackers from the row of shelfs on the other side of the icebox, I kept glancing at the Christmas stockings with my chest heating up and my kneecaps quivering, because I knowed I'd take one—just one. A real sin, real stealing, since I didn't need it but just wanted it.

While I lugged the second pot to the door, I could feel myself snatching down one of them stockings; I could feel it so strong that when I finally did snatch the stocking down, it felt like I'd done it already and I didn't feel half so bad about my first theft.

To make up for taking what I didn't need, I filled another tub with giant cans of mixed vegetables and beans, which I couldn't imagine no use for. So heavy I had to drag it across the cement floor—sounded like I was stealing the stove—out the door and across the frosty grass, leaving behind the choice food with the Christmas stocking till the last trip, as punishment. Back bent and tugging at the pot, I stayed along the shoulder in the cold-parched briars and dog fennels, the smooth dirt road alongside bucking as my eyes jerked around, behind and ahead. Nobody in sight, no tracks. Even the quarters snored with the same old racket of babies crying and grownups laughing at low pitch. Rectangles of red, yellow, blue, and green Christmas lights bright behind dull yard fires where dogs slept.

Leaving the first tub of food by the front porch of our shack, I took The Count's wheelbar to pick up the second load—froze cheese and butter and balonny. On the third load—the lightest but heaviest on my heart—I had to push the wheelbar a couple of feet and stop to rest, staying on the road this time, because I might as well. The mashed-down dog fennels and briars would tell what would be told anyhow.

On the porch, eating light bread from its cold plastic sack, I stood and watched daylight bloom in the east sky and located the star I believed had led the wisemen to baby Jesus.

Forgive me, Lord, for I have sinned.

Waking in the cold gelled light of Christmas morning to the fireplace sucking fire, I could hear younguns shouting and laughing and the quarters dogs barking, and on the front porch The Count cackling, talking to hisself like he was praying.

"I knowed he'd come around," The Count said. "Yessir, he's done overed hit."

Then he come strutting into the room with his bony chest bowed and his dingy white T-shirt shining at the neck of his green shirt and a open loaf of light bread in his left hand. He took out a slice and bit into it, gumming with his rind lips rolling to his hawk nose.

"Hey," he yelled, "old lady! Come see what King brung us. Enough vittles to last the rest of our natural lives."

She mumbled something, cleared her throat, swung around on the mattress and pulled her purple housecoat to in front. "What you talking bout?"

"Look ahere," he said and held out the loaf of light bread, green eyes lit in that wet-clay face.

She kneeled on the mound of quilts and stood up, tripping toward the fire. Took her snuff can down off the mantelshelf and doped her bottom lip.

It hit me then that I'd wore The Count's coat, that I'd took The Count's wheelbar, that The Count could be tracked to our house and might be blamed for robbing the lunchroom. Who else in Swanoochee County was known for a thief? Who else in Swanoochee County but The Count was known for stealing women's underdrawers off their clotheslines, and wash pots out of their yards, then giving what he stole to some other woman along the same road? Once he broke into the schoolhouse and stole a bunch of stage props from the auditorium closet, among the props a blue net evening gown The Count made a gift of to Uncle Kings daughter, who, unbeknowest to The Count, was the owner of the dress in the first place. Who else but The Count went to jail maybe once a month and got bailed out by his brother ever single time? Who else could care less where he was, setting in the jailhouse or setting at the house on Christmas Day? Lovie set up on the mattress, next to me, sucking her thumb, and watched The Count and the old lady through pus-stuck eyelashes. She crawled to the foot of the mattress and stood with a black plastic strap around her right ankle. She bent down and slid it over her tiny dark foot and stood up holding the red Christmas stocking with her face smiling though her lips was still working at her thumb. "Santy Claus!" she said around her thumb.

Peeping from beneath a quilt, I watched her and wondered if I'd done the right thing. Not just the stealing, which I'd about talked myself into believing was a need as much as a want. I wondered if I'd done the right thing by putting Santy Claus, who couldn't be trusted, on the same level with Jesus and Uncle King, who could.

Little Things Mean a Lot to Little Ones

LEWIS GRIZZARD

Jordan, experiencing her fourth Christmas, dove into the mound of packages under the tree with a terrible resolve.

All laws of space and time were suspended. The child was ripping through two and sometimes three packages at once.

Wrapping paper flew. Ribbons flew. She was Jordan Scissorhands. She was Jordan Chainsawhands.

"Slow down!" admonished her mother.

Do you tell the wind to slow down? Do you attempt to impede the progress of a raging river?

I saw a Ken doll emerge from an ever-growing tower of boxes and ripped-away paper and ribbons.

And there was a Cinderella doll.

And two stuffed bears from granny.

There was a set of fingerpaints. Jordan would do a lovely mural on the living-room wall later in the day.

I noticed a child's computer freed from a box. Not to mention a Little Mermaid exercise suit and a Little Mermaid battery-powered toothbrush.

There was a Beauty and the Beast home video and a game called Frog Soccer.

I did not give Jordan the Frog Soccer game because I don't even like soccer when it is played by participants who don't eat flies.

I did play a quick game of Frog Soccer with Jordan because she asked me to. She beat me 7–3, which is the most scoring in the history of any kind of soccer game.

I gave Jordan a doll house. I paid a guy $50 to put it together. There were parts that attached to other parts that could not be seen by the naked eye. Frank Lloyd Wright would have had a difficult time assembling the thing.

As I was unloading the doll house from my car, however, the top floor came apart. I spent a great deal of Christmas Eve trying to do what I'd paid the guy the $50 to do. But to no avail.

When Jordan saw the house, she was excited, but she wanted to know, "What happened to the top floor?"

"Termites," I said.

Somewhat confused, Jordan leapt at one last unwrapped gift. It was from Santa.

Once the paper was off, she opened the box. I couldn't believe what I saw.

It was a Slinky.

Surely you remember Slinkies. They've been around since I was a child.

A Slinky is nothing more than a series of circular divisions of a long wire that has an accordion effect to it.

Pull one of the circular divisions and the rest follow. You can make a Slinky jump from one of your hands to the other. A Slinky can even walk down steps.

Slinkies were big for Christmas when I was a kid back in ought-eight, or whenever it was, and now little Jordan's got one for Christmas 1992.

"Show me how this works," Jordan said to me.

I made the Slinky go from my right hand to my left. I played the Slinky like a yo-yo. I made it take two consecutive leaps along the carpet.

Jordan was beside herself with wonder and glee, and I'm thinking here are all these expensive complicated gifts—including a doll house with 14,806 parts, 4,739 of which are no longer attached—and it's this cheap, simple, good ol' standby Slinky that has her attention.

So maybe kids aren't that different today. Remember opening your toys in the morning and then spending the afternoon playing with the boxes?

Something else did finally take Jordan's attention away from the Slinky. It was the packing around the toys that had been mailed to her. It was a cellophane substance with bubble-like protrusions. When you stomped on those bubbles it made neat, popping sounds.

Jordan stomped out every bubble and never again mentioned the insect-ridden doll house I had given her.

The Education
of Edie Mac

JACK SLAY, JR.

The shriek of metal on metal, a train piling into the side of a not-quite-quick-enough semi. The mournful low of a cow twisted in calf. The squawk of a seagull wheeling in hurricane winds. Sounds: all of them, and a thousand cacophonous more, emitted from my trumpet in the sixth grade.

I was stockyard, I was big-city traffic jam, I was noise.

And band there in Stretch, that small Georgia hamlet, was Hell, Edie Mac my own personal Satan. It didn't help that I had zero talent, the trumpet in my hands just so much metal and air. I'd pucker and blow just like all the other sixth graders, but what came from me blasphemed the melody that came from them.

I joined the band to find Tie, but also to save my life. Rule was if you were in band, you had to drop gym. I picked up the trumpet after a marathon game of "murder ball," the logo of a ball I had not dodged still imprinted across my forehead. I was the smallest in gym, easy meat. Ship Tatum, my best friend, said I'd gone down like wet cement—but not before letting loose a scream Mrs. Husk, our ninety-year-old biology teacher, might have made. I remember nothing after the ball caromed off my head— except my Uncle Jeb coming to me and telling me to follow the music. I don't have an Uncle Jeb.

Ship picked up the trombone.

Band, at first, was not bad. We were a motley crew of earnest noise led by a Debbie Crews, a music major from the nearby college. Miss Crews smiled a lot and said things like "music is God's aural sunflower," and "keep trying and the melody will find you." I blew until my face pinked and my lungs withered and still produced nothing but the sounds of barnyard animals in varying degrees of pain. My fingers were thick and unbending as sausage on the valves, my lips fat as bicycle tires on the mouthpiece.

I practiced nearly every afternoon, thumping and blowing for exactly thirty minutes, my foot tapping epileptic time. Neighbors complained, my parents found errands to run, dogs howled. By Christmas I could blat out the first few bars of "Hawaii Five-O" and part of "Louie, Louie." But in early November, when Miss Crews had the rest of the band limping heroically through "When the Saints Go Marching In," I was still leading Mary's lamb to bloody slaughter.

Ship, of course, was a natural. The trombone in his hands like liquid brass, its slide an extension of his thoughts, its voice that of a rotund angel. He was sixth-grade melody, easily the best in our ragtag band. "I don't know how I do it," he told me. "I just blow and it comes out music."

I blew and it came out pain.

There were nearly fifty of us in band that year. Seven trombones and Ship never sat lower than second chair— and the only reason he wasn't first that week was that he came to tryouts with a fever of 102. "Be damned if Annie May Leer is going to take first chair from me," he said. She did that time, but never again.

Fifteen trumpets: I sat fourteenth. Which was fine by me: I was happy at the tail end of the trumpet line. There was little pressure down there and I wasn't being imprinted with murder balls. Two months into band I discovered that if I saved up for the whole hour, I could open my spit valve and create a puddle the size of a small lake. By then, Ship was playing something by Beethoven, maybe Pink Floyd, one of those old guys.

Two days before Thanksgiving break Miss Crews bounced into the music room, tapped her baton on the metal music stand, and said, "Guess what, guess what?" She didn't wait for us to respond: "I got us a spot in this year's Christmas parade!"

We gaped at her. The high school and junior high bands always marched in the parade—but never the sixth-grade starter band. We looked at each other and then broke into cheers, mostly because Miss Crews so obviously wanted us to. The parade happened every year, an endless meandering of tattered floats, Shriners on miniature vehicles, mobs of stomping kids. The next-to-the-last float was always First Baptist's nativity scene, a moonfaced Mary toting a rubber baby Jesus, mangy shepherds, a dog in sheep's clothing. Last came Santa, Mr. Logan who ran the pawnshop, huge and sweaty, tossing hard candy. Ship and I usually went together, claiming curbside in front of the Western Auto, catcalling to everyone we knew.

Miss Crews handed out sheet music for "Jingle Bells" and "We Wish You a Merry Christmas," told us to learn it over break, said we'd work on our marching first thing after Thanksgiving.

Her fever caught: we left abuzz with the idea of parade. Even I felt a tremble of excitement, had visions of me and my trumpet leading the band. I fingered my valves nervously and studied the sheet music, a flock of blackbirds starving in a blanket of snow.

Miss Crews never returned from Thanksgiving break; news of her disappearance swept through the school like an electric current: she'd run off with Mr. Taylor, the seventh-grade shop teacher. Rumor abounded. She was pregnant, she was lesbian, she had killed a man in Reno. Mr. Taylor had leukemia, he'd had an affair with one of his students, he was Amish.

We sat in the band hall, tittering with speculation, only a little worried about the parade. I studied my sheet music, paper I'd not held since last in this room. My trumpet was cold, the valves gluey. I couldn't find my mouthpiece.

The door to the classroom opened and she walked in. My heart froze, knowing before the rest of me. The band fell still.

Edie Mac.

We all knew her, of course, had heard tales of her since first picking up our instruments. Edie Mac was director of the junior high band, a woman who demanded perfection, who squashed anything less. We'd heard of screaming fits, of batons flung, of flutes bent double in rage. Ship told me later that he'd heard she'd once directed with a. 38 instead of a baton when the junior high couldn't get "You Are My Sunshine" right.

Edie Mac—Editha McNair her real name—strode to the director's stand and picked up the baton. She smiled broadly, her teeth yellow and all the same size. "Good morning, children," she said. "Let's make music."

Edie Mac's hair towered in a bouffant of shellac and sheen. Halfway down her nose perched a pair of thick cat-eyed glasses. She wore a flowery blouse and a bright green miniskirt. She tapped the music stand and a voice from the back said, "Oh my god, it's Nancy Sinatra."

The room erupted in laughter; me too, though I had no idea who Nancy Sinatra was. I could see Ship two rows in front of me chortling into his cupped hands.

Edie Mac's smile dropped from her face, ice slid into her eyes. "HEY!" The laughter dried up. "Give me a C *now*." We warbled into slow life. Her face twisted, looked like she'd just eaten something bad. "B-flat scale," she said, counting us off, and we began, the slow drone of notes rising. Halfway through, Edie Mac dropped her baton and glared at us with feral eyes. The band petered out, a series of squawks, a flock of geese murdered one by one. Not me, though—I still hadn't found my mouthpiece.

"That was the worst thing I ever heard. Let's start from ground zero, section at a time." She pointed and the section wailed its way through the A scale: the flutes ("horrendous"), the trombones ("not terrible"), the herd of clarinets ("you sound like an auto wreck"). Eventually, she found us. "Okay, trumpets, show them how it's done." We started well—then she spotted me, my horn hovering before my lips, unsounding. Halfway through the flutes I remembered I had used my mouthpiece as a duck call the day after Thanksgiving.

"Stop, stop, stop!" She pointed at me. "Son, what's your name?"

I told her.

"Why aren't you playing?"

"Forgot my mouthpiece at home." My voice trembled.

"Forgot your mouthpiece. At home. *Forgot* your mouthpiece. At *home*." She smacked her stand with the baton. It

snapped in two and a piece flipped off into the flute section. Hey, I thought, someone could lose an eye like that—
but I didn't say anything.

She said, her voice razor thin, "When you come in here
tomorrow, know the A scale, play it perfectly." She looked
at me. "And if it's not inconvenient, bring your mouthpiece
and join us." She flung the broken baton at the wall behind
her and stomped out.

Tie died when I was four. It happened in his upstairs bedroom, something terrible and unspoken. Seven years later I
still did not have all the pieces put together. I remember sheets
of thick red, my only glimpse through the closing door reveal-
ing the carpet sodden, the walls dripping. Mom cried a lot.
Dad grew silent, his mouth like a knife slash, still is. I often
heard them murmuring in the next room, their voices like the
chuckle of water, falling silent whenever I appeared.

Tie was twelve years older than me, a boy with bright eyes,
a mop of curly blond hair. I remember the coffin, the heavy
sadness that settled on the house like a fresh load of dirt.

What I remember most, though, is Tie's clarinet. He
played that thing like a motherfucker, his hands like spi-
ders up and down the keys. He made it talk, made it sing,
music drifting through the house like the warble of an
exotic bird, one that flew endlessly, invented songs. I
remember waking from four-year-old naps, the bed filled
with music like water, like sun. Tie's grinning face.

He's the real reason I picked up the trumpet, the clarinet
too sacred. I wanted to see if he left me the magic, if I could
find my brother.

We began to meet after school, marching for endless, monotonous hours, Edie Mac bellowing like a drill sergeant.

Marching wasn't so bad, the sun, the air, the possibility of escape.

During band, we practiced "Jingle Bells" and "Merry Christmas." I had found my mouthpiece, but not much had improved beyond that. The bridge at the end of "Jingle Bells" gave me fits, as did most of "Merry Christmas." By the first week of December I hated both songs. I also began to dream about Edie Mac, her wicked baton, her square, yellow teeth. Once she appeared naked, holding just her baton. I didn't eat for most of the next day.

Two weeks before the parade we sounded not bad. We'd do, she told us. During our last band hall run-through, we turned into the bit about dashing through the snow when I popped a note dead center of a two-beat rest, a noise as terse as a fart. Edie Mac turned red, the band stopped playing, I froze, my trumpet glued to my white lips, my eyes wide as drumheads. I hoped she'd suspect someone else—though there was little chance of that. It was hardly the first time I'd blatted drunkenly into rests. Edie Mac's cat-eyed scowl settled on me, everyone else looked elsewhere.

I whispered a prayer to Tie, hated my trumpet.

Wordlessly, Edie Mac dipped to the floor, came back up with fluid ease, her arm swinging in a quick clockwise motion. Something flew through the air, sailed just over the heads of the band. I watched in horror, unable to move, trumpet still held stupidly to my lips. It hit me square in the forehead, spreading both astonishment and pain through the reverberating plates of my skull. I went down, collapsing into my own spit puddle, but not before hearing someone say, "Jesus, he's been *shoed*!"

Next thing I knew I was in the nurse's station. She wrapped gauze around my forehead, tutting, "Not the first student I've had in here because of her. What she don't do for her band." She spoke with unmistakable admiration.

Walking home, Ship said, "I think Tie took the magic with him."

"Yeah, me too."

I took the bandage off before I got home. Edie Mac's pump had left a yellowing bruise, a small dent. I wondered if Tie had ever made such sacrifices. I refused to quit, certain that Tie hid in the music.

Ship was my sixth-grade Virgil, forever leading me down paths astray. In Tie's absence he had shown me how to fish for crawdads, how to roll a house and almost get away, how to balance a hurtling bicycle between my legs with no hands.

In fourth grade, he showed me my first naked woman.

Ship also had an older brother, Custer, a rangy tenth grader, face peppered with acne, hands always wet with sweat. He was little more than a shadow to us, always leaving the house on covert missions. He led a secret life, one we wordlessly envied.

Once when he left their shared room, a meeting suddenly remembered, Ship said, "Wanna see something cool?" Always up for coolness, I nodded, more interested in the bottle rocket we were modifying.

Ship shut the bedroom door, drew the curtains. He walked over to Custer's bed, plunged his hands between the mattresses, and withdrew a magazine. It glowed in his hands.

"*Playboy*," he whispered.

I'd heard of it, but had dismissed it as playground lore. He placed the magazine reverently on the floor and I bowed beside him. He let it fall open to the middle, pulled out the folded page. Another door in my hallwayed life kicked open.

The woman smiled, happy to see us. She was for some reason draped over a haybale in some nearly vacant loft, had inexplicably lost most of her clothes. She was as beautiful as any angel I'd ever imagined. I fell thunderously in love. Her name was Astra. I memorized her, relieved to discover that in other pictures she'd found some if not all of her clothing, mostly overalls with broken buckles, denim shirts with apparently no buttons, the occasional hat. From what I could figure, she worked on a farm, the pictures showing her in various degrees of disrobement, positioned awkwardly over one farming implement or another. I'd never seen anyone hoe naked, but, studying Astra, decided it seemed reasonable enough. I wondered about sunburn. I worried that the farmer would show up, fire her for lollygagging naked on the job. I delighted in her thigh-high farming boots, the way she handled a pitchfork, and her turn-ons, namely, spring rain and fresh corn.

I thought of Astra the rest of the year, dreaming of her in social studies and math, walking the hallways hunched over because of her.

"Astra, Astra," I would whisper into my pillow at night. "Astra," Ship would mutter to me in class and we would snicker until the teacher banished us to the hallway.

Day after my shoeing, two weeks before the parade, Edie Mac moved the band out to Jackson, a small street that wound its way around the school property. She gave everyone a handout printed with the Rules of March: shoulders back, horns perpendicular, right foot forward. It may as well have been written in Japanese. She lined us up, five abreast, ten rows, drums in the back, trumpets in front of them. Trombones led us, their slides like feelers probing the future.

Marching was yet another endeavor I had no talent for. I was forever throwing a left foot forward when the band was thrusting right. I lagged, giving our line a snakelike curl. Focusing on my feet, I let my horn droop. Four times that morning, Edie Mac stormed over to shout, "Horn up!" Her voice was like a jagged rock ricocheting around in my brain.

Things got worse when we started to play. It didn't help that I'd memorized only the first half of "Jingle Bells" and only jags of "Merry Christmas." The songs issued from my horn in mournful bleats. I sounded like a sleigh wreck, my jingled passengers pulped and bloody.

By Thursday, Edie Mac spent most of her time marching alongside me, smacking her hands together, occasionally popping the back of my head, shouting in my ear, "ONE TWO THREE *FOUR* ONE TWO THREE *FOUR!*" I prayed for Edie Mac to spontaneously combust, for Tie to fill my soul with music, for the parade to be cancelled, for a meteor to smash through Edie Mac's skull. I needed relief.

After practice Ship would walk back with me to the band hall, everyone else having decided I had something akin to leprosy.

"Why don't you quit?" he asked.

"Can't."

"Why not? Parents making you stay?"

"No," I said, putting away my horn. "My folks could care less." I looked at Ship. "I think Tie's here. I won't quit till I find him."

"Hang in there," he said, nodding.

"Trying."

On Friday Edie Mac, stomping beside me, seething at every misstep and bad note, shouted for a halt. The band wound down, a single flute playing for several beats.

"It's no hope," she shouted at the band. "What do I do?" She walked circles around me, gesticulated wildly. "What do I do?" She glared at me.

"He's hopeless, I can't do any more than what I've already done. Can't."

Her circle widened, she flailed between the flutes, stomped through the clarinets. No one said a word, everyone looking straight ahead. I stood ramrod straight, trumpet tucked under my arm. I'd not greased my valves in over a month; they were sluggish as Monday morning.

Edie Mac crashed back through the ranks, stopped before me. Her eyes were like tennis balls, magnified by her glasses. She grimaced, her hundred teeth flashing in the sun.

"Don't play," she said. "Just march. Don't play."

She turned to leave and I said. "Um. For today?"

She wheeled around and said, "For *ever*. Don't play. Maybe if you focus on one thing and one thing only you can pull it off. You're not going to ruin my parade."

So I marched without playing, trumpet angled before me, silent, useless. I fingered the valves, warmed the brass with my breath, even faked a spit take every once in a while. But it was all for nothing: everyone knew. I saw their cupped grins, heard their whispered laughs. I tried to ignore them, held my horn high.

For the first couple of days Edie Mac marched right beside me, told me once, "Better." Then she dashed off to yell at a flute for not having her instrument at the correct angle.

My marching was better, a little. I popped the right foot forward and mostly kept up with the line. Halfway through Tuesday, Edie Mac jumped on Charlie Turner, reamed him good. He'd been showing out, sliding so far that his horn came apart in his hands. "You do that in the parade," Edie Mac shrieked, jots of spittle peppering Charlie's face, "and I'll wrap that slide around your scrawny neck." She faced the band: "No one's going to ruin my parade."

We marched again, Edie Mac stomping Godzilla-like between Charlie and Ship. While she was preoccupied, I cut a quick jag in "Jingle Bells," just the bit about bobtails brightening spirits. I didn't really care about playing; it was just the fact that I couldn't. Edie Mac was on me instantly, a fly on roadkill.

"You crazy?" she screamed, her face red, a tiny vein in her forehead throbbing; it looked like a worm trying to burrow its way out. "You gonna ruin my parade? One more time—*one more time*—and you are banned for life. You understand?"

I nodded, staring straight ahead. I thought about not playing for the rest of my life and found myself not horrified by the idea. I thought about quitting, dropping my horn and walking off the street. Mom and Dad would probably never notice. Tie, though, would be disappointed. So I'd stick it out a little longer. For Tie.

Thursday, the day before the parade, Ship said he had something for me.

"Another *Playboy*?"

"No, better. You've had a tough couple of weeks, this'll smooth things out."

"I've had a tough damn life."

"Good for what ails you," Ship said and answered no more questions.

That afternoon I followed him back to his room. He shut the door and burrowed for several minutes in his closet. Custer was gone, a new after-school job. "Something down at the Western Auto," Ship said, his head and shoulders buried in the detritus of his closet. "He's counting screws and lining up hammers. Not too hard on the brain. *Ah-ha*!"

Ship emerged, holding a small baggie filled with lawn clippings.

"Grass?"

"You could say that." He opened the bag and held it under my face. Close up it looked like something my mom tossed into spaghetti sauce.

"Oregano? This is good for what ails me?"

Ship cackled. "It's pot, you idiot. Marijuana."

I backed away, horrified. "The pot," I said, shaking my head. "I'm too young to be hooked, I wouldn't know where to find the connection." I had listened well to all the dope lectures at school. "I can't be a sixth-grade monkey on my back! I don't wanna be a crack whore!"

"Hey! Calm down! Jesus, it's just a little grass. Won't hurt you, just mellow you out. But if you don't want to, no problem." He folded the baggie back up.

I eyed him sulkily. "What's it do?"

"I've only done it once, Custer showed me. Told him I'd tell Mom and Dad if he didn't. Makes you feel loopy and silly for a couple of hours and then nothing."

I sat on Ship's bed and wondered what Astra would do, what Tie would say. "I dunno," I said. "Seems kind of dangerous."

"Think of it this way," Ship said, sitting beside me, my leering Virgil, putting his arm around me. "It's the best way to deal with Edie Mac. When she starts to scream at you,

you just flash back to this afternoon, remember the mellow. And everything'll be all right."

I eyed the baggie and said, "Maybe just a little."

Ship held the baggie open and I took a small pinch, put it in my mouth. It was crunchy, tasted like sticks and dead grass might.

"Jesus Q. Christ, where the hell were you born? You don't eat it, you *smoke* it." He reached in the baggie and pulled out a small hand-rolled cigarette. He tucked it behind his ear and reburied the pot in the closet. He opened the window and set up two chairs beneath it.

"What about your parents?"

"Not home till after six, Custer too." He put the cigarette in his mouth and lit it with a Bic lighter. He inhaled, his chest puffing up like a rooster. He coughed immediately, spitting smoke. He grinned, offered me the cigarette, and said, "Smooth."

I took a small puff and coughed it out. I took another and trapped it inside me. It burned my mouth, my throat, filled my lungs with fire. I was sure my uvula was aflame.

"Hold it inside."

I coughed, spewing smoke.

"Fucking dragon," Ship said and took another drag. I took another small one. We fanned the smoke outside and I worried about stoned sparrows, could see them crashing into walls, falling from trees.

"Nothing's happening."

"Give it a minute."

I thought about Edie Mac, wondered whether I should bother showing up tomorrow night. Probably what she wanted. I wondered if she was as mean to her own children and if I was addicted to marijuana yet. All I needed to accompany my band woes was a sixth-grade habit. I took

102

another drag, this time the smoke smoother, a warm liquid easing down my throat, filling me from the inside out.

Ship nudged me and I dragged again. My lungs felt as big and fine as Astra's. I realized I'd never seen quite the blue of Ship's pillowcase, was fascinated by its blueness, wanted to ask Ship where he'd found it, wanted one just like it. I was in love with Annie May Leer, her eyes the color of Ship's pillowcase. Life was a river. I knew if I put my hand in the bell of my trumpet, I could *feel* the notes, squirmy and slippery as tadpoles.

The room moved in a slow train around me. My head floated, filled with smoke, light as sunbeams. The room shifted, meandered in the opposite direction. I understood the Pythagorean theorem, remembered where I'd hidden my skate key in the second grade.

Ship stared at his shoe, pulled at a loose piece of rubber. He looked up at me and said, his voice smoky, "Shoe."

I giggled, said, "Shoe." It was the funniest word I'd ever heard. I laughed, stomach-doubling, head-hollowing bursts of laughter. I collapsed on the floor and Ship fell on top of me. "Shoe," he gasped, guffawing. "Shoe!"

We laughed for another four or five hours, time, I realized, also like a river. Later, little burps of laughter still coming up, stomach and head aching pleasantly, I reached for my trumpet, fingered the valves. I blew and from my horn came a sound as beautiful as I'd ever heard, a sonorous note smooth as sunshine. The trumpet warmed in my hands, became almost too hot to hold. It began to squirm, seemed on the verge of melting.

Then, my note filling the room, a mist wafted from the bell, a wispy fog that twined with the music, that was somehow the tone corporalized. I stared, mesmerized, and on I blew.

The mist swirled and twirled, became denser. The note still pouring from me like liquid sound, the fog took shape, became, before my disbelieving eyes, the figure of a boy sitting at the edge of Ship's bed.

My magical note evaporated and I put the trumpet aside.

"Tie," I said.

He smiled. He had his clarinet tucked under his arm.

"You okay, little brother?"

He looked older than I remembered, his face tanned and sharp, his hair still a tangled mess. I stared at him, my head looping, my eyes swimming.

"Hear you got troubles with Edie Mac."

I nodded, tongue too thick to say anything.

"Me, too. She hated me, wouldn't let me play in the Christmas parade one year, said I was banned for life."

I reached out to touch him, my eyes filled with tears, and my hand passed through him, Tie as ephemeral as smoke.

"You really here?"

"You bet, little brother. I've *always* been here."

Then he climbed off the bed, hunkered down in front of me. "Here's what you do." His eyes were an icy blue, swimming pools in summer. He smelled of wildflowers.

"You happy, Tie?"

"More than ever." He told me what to do and then was gone. I tried to feel the blue of Ship's pillowcase, wondered whether I was too young for Astra, what brand of toothpaste Annie May Leer used. I was glad I'd seen Tie, glad I'd finally found my brother again.

Next day my head was clear, bright, and I wanted to think Tie was just a pot dream, a figment of my polluted mind. But he'd seemed far too real, his presence as vivid as that magical note. I dreamed Tie, felt him at long last in my world, him and his plan lodged firmly in my heart.

The band ran through a last practice, Edie Mac shouting all the way. On the way back to the band hall, she stopped me, tugged at my shirtsleeve. "We don't play, remember?" she said. "We don't ruin the parade, right?"

The day dragged by, each class slower than the one before. "Tie, Tie," I whispered. "You sure this is the way?" No one answered.

Home, I polished my horn, oiled the valves, warmed the mouthpiece, all empty tasks. At least I'll look good, I thought.

Soon enough, butterflies as big as sparrows, I arrived at the First Baptist parking lot at the end of Main Street, found Ship, and lined up with the band and a half dozen other groups: the junior and senior high school bands, a gaggle of Girl and Boy Scouts, a renegade nativity scene.

Edie Mac marched over, led us through an A and C scale and then a pretty sorry chromatic. I didn't play, my horn sparking in the moonlight. Edie Mac looked disgusted, like she wanted to spit, to hurl a shoe. "Don't make me look bad," she breathed through clenched teeth.

Then she straightened, smiled for the cameras, said, "You'll do fine. Remember: I'll be with the junior high, fifteen slots behind you. You'll be on your own. But I know you can do it. We've practiced hard. You'll do fine."

She turned to go, looked back over her shoulder. "If not," she said, "I'll see you on Monday."

Parade started, the Shriners leading the way, farting along Main in their miniature convoy. A couple floats followed, a herd of Scouts, the town wrecker adorned in holly, lights flashing, horn blaring. I shifted from foot to foot, polished the bell of my trumpet with my shirtsleeve, prayed to Tie. "You sure, you sure?" I whispered. The high school disembarked, another Scout trooplet, more floats, then us. We moved smoothly into the street, our stride as unisoned as chorus girls.

Stepping off the curb and onto Main I saw Edie Mac. She grimaced, shot me the evil eye, mouthed, "Don't."

I grinned, waved, and said through my teeth, "Eat shit, Edie Mac." She took a step forward and I was sure she'd heard me—then I was swept into Main and the Christmas parade, and Edie Mac fell behind.

I focused on marching: right, left, right, left. Held my horn just right, blew warm air through the silent mouth-piece, fingered my valves. The band lurched into "Jingle Bells," wavered, smoothed, sounded fine. We followed quickly with "We Wish You a Merry Christmas," sounded even better. Edie Mac told us we'd get in six or seven repetitions. Tie had suggested the third playing; by then we'd be middle of Main.

A float jammed a block ahead of us and the band marked time. Halfway through "Merry Christmas" a wafting of leftover pot drifted through my brain and I floated, happy, light-headed. We marched on.

Just short of halfway, we launched into "Merry Christmas," a reversal planned by Edie Mac. Toward the end, I realized I was not going to follow Tie, not then, probably not ever. My brother's plan unraveled, fell like damp linen around my feet. *Coward*, I muttered to myself, *you big fat sissy coward*. The band warbled through its third "Jingle Bells" and I remained quiet, stupidly fingering noiseless valves.

Still muttering, anger like a black eye riding through my head, I marched in perfect step. Passing Western Auto, I saw him.

Saw Tie.

He stood, a dark figure behind the crowd, his head and shoulders visible between a fat man and big-haired woman. Shadows dappled his face, but there was no doubt it was Tie, that mop of hair, that certain slouch. He waved with his clarinet, tipped it to his head, seemed to say *It's okay, man, don't worry about it.* Seemed to say *I'm here.*

I tilted my horn to him and it all came crashing together, like celestial cymbals, my head caught between: Ship and Astra, the pot, Tie and his beautiful clarinet, his music like water filling my youth.

I grinned at him and blew air through my ax, got ready.

The band hit "Jingle Bells" hard, confident, the end of Main in sight. I waited, butterflies gone, a pleasant loopiness still floating round my brain. I waited, breathing evenly, filling my lungs. The band arrived at the rest, the two-, three-beat pause at the end of "Jingle Bells," the bit where you usually shouted "Hey!"

In the near silence of that crystal night, I pursed my lips and blew. The air circled my trumpet, the valves full open, and blasted from my bell in a ringing blat, the sound of a mad elephant, a rhinoceros explosively farting.

The band stumbled, missed their steps, horns faltered, wavered, a couple managed a few sickly bleats into "Dashing through the snow." But by then I was blatting again, tremendous blasts of air exploding from my horn; your drunken uncle bellowing over Christmas dinner, tornadoes touching down in your front yard, air raid sirens.

Some of the band tried to find "Merry Christmas," but it was too late. I roared over them, a mile-high wall of sound. I marched on, stepping lively, horn held high, and the rest of the band hurried to keep pace. I could see Ship shaking with laughter, head high, horn at rest. Someone said, "You're gonna get it." Another said, "Stop, please stop." I blared on, lost in my own Christmas world, angels stoned.

I counted in my head, just as Tie had suggested. Saw in my mind Edie Mac charging toward us, leaving her precious junior high band, passing Brownies, knocking over an oily-haired Mary, bulling her way through a somnambular troop of Masons.

On I marched, on I blatted.

Then waited until I heard her scream my name, waited until I felt the band behind me part as she hurtled through. I ran, bolting through the ranks, just ahead of her outstretched arms. I could feel her breath, could feel anger coming off her like radiation.

But just as I bolted, I made the mistake of looking back. Edie Mac's face was twisted, not in rage but in hurt. I'd ruined it for her, taken her greatest joy and stomped amok over it. In that single second I actually felt sorry for her, could almost feel her pain. I knew immediately, though, what hell there would be to pay on Monday. I realized, too, that life hereafter would be a little less sympathetic, a little harder.

I dropped my trumpet, heard it hit the macadam, heard the crash of a bass drum going over, heard Edie Mac shriek. I dodged into the crowd and found Ship running beside me, breathing hard, laughing, trombone in his hands.

I passed Tie in the crowd, clarinet under his arm. He stepped back, let me through, a grin as big as summer plastered across his ghostly face.

My man, I heard him say, *my brother*, as I ran to beat the devil, ran headlong into the world.

The Brown- and Blue-Eyed Santa Claus

LAURA DABUNDO

(Found crumpled in a wastebasket on December 26.)

Dear Little Girl,

I am sorry that I don't know what your name is (or even, really, that you are a little girl since you didn't sign the letter you slid under my door, but I don't think a little boy would write a letter like yours)—but, then again, without your name, I can't mail this letter so I don't even know why I am writing you, but, hey, it's late, it's Christmas Eve, I'm feeling sorry for myself and who knows.

Anyway, I am just writing to tell you that I can't bring back the brown- and blue-eyed Santa Claus. And, really, Little Girl, I can't see why anyone would want to. A more slovenly, lazy, no-good, son of—but of course, I have to maintain the pretense that I am writing to a little girl and try to watch my potatoes here.

How did you know he was sent packing anyhow? It was late last night, right before closing. I know we weren't in my office, but the lights had been dimmed to discourage the late shoppers, and pretty much all of them—really, *all of them*, I am sure of it—had been sent scurrying for the exits. Our voices got pretty loud, but I am sure we would have heard if anyone else was around.

No, Little Girl, I guess I need to be honest to you. My voice got pretty loud. Naturally, the sniveling, whining, self-pitying sorry excuse for a Santa Claus never opened his mouth. How well I know that he never opened his mouth. This is what made dealing with him so frustrating. He never got mad. He never defended himself. He just took it. I mean, I don't want sass; I don't want employees talking back to me, which includes these Santa Clauses—forgive me, Little Girl, I guess you know that the Spirit of Santa Claus hovers over department stores and malls and can descend into a multitude of Santa Clauses at any one time, so that there can seem to be a lot of them when there really is just one up at the North Pole, in his workshop with the elves, blah, blah, blah: if I could mail this letter I would clean it up for your innocent ears. Nah, why would I? It is never too early to learn, right? Face the music, Little Girl. There are loads of Santa Clauses. And they are all fakes. You too can be a Santa Claus. I can be a Santa Claus. We all can be a Santa Claus. Hurrah for Christmas. We all have to be Santa Claus. Well, that's right in a way. Santa Claus is all of our responsibilities. We all have to do it.

And that's why I had to fire him, Little Girl, send him packing into the cold, cruel world, right before Christmas. Because he was letting down all the little children every time he let us down. Every time that sniveling, sneaky, slimy, sly, weasely old man—or young man, I wasn't really ever sure—anyway, "sneaky" is right. You'd turn around and there he was, where he wasn't supposed to be, talking to children in the Women's Shoe Department (the Women's Shoe Department, for heaven's sake) when he was supposed to be posing for pictures with children on his lap in the

Christmas Shoppe! And once we even found him in Housewares! And in Lingerie! And in the Men's Department! I could go on. He was a sneak! Just like how he had eyes of different colors; he wasn't one or the other; he wasn't where he should have been. In the god-, that is, the gosh-darned Christmas Shoppe! Where lines of screaming kids and screaming parents who had paid good, hard-earned *cash, cash,* what keeps us all going here, for a picture with their sniveling, screaming, whining babies on his lap, one after another after another after another after another. That is where we paid him to be.

No, Little Girl, he was in the freaking Women's Shoe Department. I know, I know. He had children on his lap there. But their parents hadn't paid for the privilege of having him hold children there. And there were no pictures! No pictures! There is no photographer in the Women's Shoe Department. And were those people about to tie up their business in the Women's Shoe Department, go to the Christmas Shoppe and stand in a long line and *pay* to have their pictures taken with Santa Claus, when they had already had their precious experience of him for *free,* in the freaking Women's Shoe Department? No siree bob! And Santa Claus wouldn't be there; anyway, he'd be off in Pots and Pans, by then, or Electronics or Luggage. That's where he needed to be, all right, in Luggage. Getting ready to pack up and leave.

Well, I am sorry, Little Girl, I am sorry you feel sorry. Because I am not sorry. No siree, I am not sorry!

I am sorry I hired him in the first place. But there we were, shorthanded, our best Santa Claus, I mean the best Santa Claus ever, did what he was told, stayed where he was supposed to be, didn't complain when the little brats, hot and tired and overwhelmed, threw up in his beard or went to the toilet in his lap—yes, Little Girl, that is what being Santa Claus is really like, our best Santa Claus, Charlie Conrad, *quit! Quit!* Just up and quit! How do you like that? Said he had a better offer at Macy's! I like that! Like it isn't all the same, everywhere. Anyway, there we were, mothers screaming, the line getting longer, and all of a sudden I get a phone call from Women's Shoes (Hmm, Women's Shoes, must be something about shoes that he liked), saying there was a random Santa Claus down there, getting underfoot (ha, that's good, underfoot in the Shoe Department!), getting in the way, and would we come and get him. So I did! I knew it wasn't one of ours, but hell (oh, hell, I'll clean this up later), I charged down there and I said, "Hey, you, Santa Claus! " He looked at me with those two-color eyes, and I swear it was the weirdest thing, you know. I guess you know about his eyes, since you mentioned them in your letter. Anyway, it was as if, suddenly, all the sounds in the store went quiet. All the yelling, all the screaming. Everything went still. And I said, "I need a Santa Claus right now, upstairs. Right now." Then I lowered my voice, as I added, "Fifteen bucks an hour plus overtime; we'll do the paperwork later. Go! " And he went, but he never stayed. He kept wandering off. I would get calls from all over the store, and I would have to go chasing off after him, but I learned never to look in his eyes when I told him to get back to where he was supposed to be. No siree. Made me nervous, those eyes. Like they looked right into my soul and didn't like what they saw. Well, why should they? My wife didn't like what she saw when she looked in there. Nor my kids. That's why I am here, on Christmas Eve, after closing, with the typewriter and my Santa Claus, this good little ol' brown bottle of bourbon. Yes, sir, that's my Santa Claus. As I said, all the other ones are fake; they all let you down. Everyone wanders off; everyone leaves. What stays is what you buy yourself. For yourself. That's it; that's all. That's all there ever is.

As I said, we all have to be Santa Claus. There is no Santa Claus in the North Pole, Little Girl. Now, don't cry, I am doing you a favor here. What there is instead is all of us, doing our jobs, doing the right thing, being where we are supposed to be when we are supposed to be there. And then there will be Santa Clauses where they are supposed to be. Sitting on a velvet throne in a woolen suit under hot lights in the Christmas Shoppe. There aren't supposed to be Santa Clauses in Women's Shoes or in Lingerie or in Luggage or in the Men's Department.

Well, thank God, I am shed of him now. Just the way he shed his suit. It's right there in the corner of my office. But even in leaving he made work for me.

Right before closing, my phone rings, and it's the manager in Women's Shoes. He said he just found a Santa Claus suit there. So once again I had to trot down there to tend to business concerning that different-eyed Santa Claus. But this time it was just an empty suit, so I brought it up here and threw it in the corner. And there it can remain until kingdom come and good riddance to no-good Santa Clauses. Merry Christmas. Cheers.

Hey, this is weird. I just went over and kicked the suit, and a little index card fell out. I picked it up and saw an address typed on it. Of all things, it's my ex's address.

I haven't lived there in years. Why would that address be there? That's funny. Her address. Their address. The kids' address. That's where they live. With her. Without me. Without their dad. Without their daddy. At Christmas. Or ever. But especially at Christmas. Their address. In a Santa Claus suit. In a discarded Santa Claus suit. But with no

Santa Claus in the Santa Claus suit. Just an empty suit. Just an empty—

Let's see, what time is it?

Hmm, it's not that late yet. The kids would still be up.

What if I just ran past the toy department, picked up some things, left some money, put on that stupid suit, and went over to the house?

Nah. I can't do that. That's not what I am supposed to do.

Still, it is Christmas Eve. I am not doing anything here except feeling sorry for myself.

She doesn't have to know it's me. It won't be me. I wouldn't do something like that. Because I am not supposed to be there. That isn't where I am supposed to be.

But I could just pretend. I could just pretend to be the brown- and blue-eyed Santa Claus. He's never where he's supposed to be. Not hard to do. I can just take out a blue contact lens. They don't need to know who it is. And no one will know, just me and you, Little Girl.

But I'll tell you this, Little Girl, I'll be your brown- and blue-eyed Santa Claus. You can count on me. If you come back here next year, I promise you, we'll have a brown- and blue-eyed Santa Claus.

Hell, we'll fill the store with them. Everywhere you look, there'll be one. Everywhere, Electronics, Housewares, Luggage, Women's Shoes, everywhere. Just you wait! We'll all be Santa Claus. Because if we aren't, there won't be any, ever, anywhere. Just empty suits.

Merry Christmas, Little Girl! And Merry Christmas to all! Hurrah for Christmas!

A Conscript's Christmas

JOEL CHANDLER HARRIS

On a Sunday afternoon in December, 1863, two horsemen were making their way across Big Corn Valley in the direction of Sugar Mountain. They had started from the little town of Jasper early in the morning, and it was apparent at a glance that they had not enjoyed the journey. They sat listlessly in their saddles, with their carbines across their laps, and whatever conversation they carried on was desultory.

To tell the truth, the journey from Jasper to the top of Sugar Mountain was not a pleasant one even in the best of weather, and now, with the wind pushing before it a bitterly cold mist, its disagreeableness was irritating. And it was not by any means a short journey. Big Corn Valley was fifteen miles across as the crow flies, and the meanderings of the road added five more. Then there was the barrier of the foothills, and finally Sugar Mountain itself, which when the weather was clear lifted itself above all the other mountains in that region.

Nor was this all. Occasionally, when the wind blew aside the oilskin overcoats of the riders, the gray uniform of the Confederacy showed beneath, and they wore cavalry boots, and there were tell-tale trimmings on their felt hats. With these accoutrements to advertise them, they were not in a friendly region. There were bushwhackers in the mountains, and, for aught the horsemen knew, the fodder stacks in the valley, that rose like huge and ominous ghosts out of the mist on every side, might conceal dozens of guerrillas. They had that day ridden past the house of the only member of the Georgia State convention who had refused to affix his signature to the ordinance of secession, and the woods, to use the provincial phrase, were full of Union men.

Suddenly, and with a fierce and ripping oath, one of the horsemen drew rein. "I wish I may die," he exclaimed, his voice trembling with long pent up irritation, "if I ain't a great mind to turn around in my tracks an' go back. Where does this cussed road lead to anyhow?"

"To the mountain—straight to the mountain," grimly remarked the other, who had stopped to see what was the matter with his companion.

"Great Jerusalem! Straight? Do you see that fodder stack yonder with the hawk on the top of the pole? Well, we've passed it four times, and we ain't no further away from it now than we was at fust."

"Well, we've no time to stand here. In an hour we'll be at the foot of the mountain, and a quarter of a mile further we'll find shelter. We must attend to business and talk it over afterwards."

"An' it's a mighty nice business, too," said the man who had first spoken. He was slender in build, and his thin and straggling mustache failed to relieve his effeminate appearance. He had evidently never seen hard service. "I never have believed in this conscriptin' business," he went on in a complaining tone. "It won't pan out. It has turned more men agin the Confederacy than it has turned fer it, or else my daddy's name ain't Bill Chadwich, nor mine neither."

"Well," said the other curtly, "it's the law, Bill Chadwick, and it must be carried out. We've got our orders."

"Oh, yes! You are the commander, Cap'n Moseley, an' I'm the army. Ain't I the gayest army you ever had under you? I'll tell you what, Cap'n Moseley (I'd call you Dick, like I useter, if we was n't in the ranks), when I j'ined the army I thought I was goin' to fight the Yankees, but they slapped me in the camp of instruction over there at Adairsville, an' now here we are fightin' our own folks. If we ain't fightin' 'em, we are pursuin' after 'em, an' runnin' 'em into the woods an' up the mountains. Now what kind of soldier will one of these conscripts make? You need n't tell me, Cap'n! The law won't pan out."

"But it's the law," said Captain Moseley. The captain had been wounded in Virginia, and was entitled to a discharge, but he accepted the position of conscript officer. He had the grit and discipline of a veteran, and a persistence in carrying out his purposes that gave him the name of "Hardhead" in the army. He was tall and muscular, but his drooping left shoulder showed where a Federal bullet had found lodgment. His closely cropped beard was slightly streaked with gray, and his face would have been handsome had not determination left its rude handwriting there.

The two rode on together in silence a little space, the cold mists, driven by the wind, tingling in their faces. Presently Private Chadwick, who had evidently been ruminating over the matter, resumed the thread of his complaints.

"They tell me," he said, "that it's a heap easier to make a bad law than it is to make a good one. It takes a lot of smart men a long time to make a good one, but a passel of blunderbusses can patch a bad one up in a little or no time. That's the way I look at it.

"What's the name of this chap we are after? Israel Spurlock? I'd like to know, by George, what's the matter with him! What makes him so plague-taked important that two men have to be sent on a wild-goose chase after him? They yerked him into army, an' he yerked himself out, an' now the word is that the war can't go on unless Israel Spurlock is on hand to fling down his gun an' run when he hears a bung-shell playin' a tune in the air."

Captain Moseley coughed to hide a smile.

"It's jest like I tell you, Cap'n. The news is that we had a terrible victory at Chattanooga, but I notice in the Atlanta papers that the Yankees ain't no further north than they was before the fight; an' what makes it wuss, they are warmin' themselves in Chattanooga, whilst we are shiverin' outside. I reckon if Israel Spurlock had been on hand at the right time an' in the right place, we'd a drove the Yanks plumb back to Nashville. Lord! I hope we'll have him on the skirmish line the next time we surround the enemy an' drive him into a town as big as Chattanooga."

Private Chadwick kept up his complaints for some time, but they failed to disturb the serenity of the captain, who urged his horse forward through the mist, closely followed by his companion. They finally left the valley, passed over the foothills, and began the ascent of Sugar Mountain. Here their journey became less disagreeable. The road, winding and twisting around the mountain, had been cut through a dense growth of trees, and these proved to be something of a shelter. Moreover, the road sometimes brought the mountain between the travelers and the wind, and these were such comfortable intervals that Mr. Chadwick ceased his complaints and rode along good-humoredly.

The two horsemen had gone about a mile, measuring the mountain road, though they were not more than a quarter of a mile from the foot, when they came suddenly on an old man sitting in a sheltered place by the side of the road. They came on the stranger so suddenly that their horses betrayed alarm, and it was all they could do to keep the animals from slipping and rolling into the gorge at their left. The old man was dressed in a suit of gray jeans, and wore a wool hat, which, although it showed the signs of constant use, had somehow managed to retain its original shape. His head was large and covered with a profusion of iron-gray hair, which was neatly combed. His face was round, but the lines of character obliterated all suggestions of chubbiness. The full beard that he wore failed to hide evidences of firmness and determination; but around his mouth a serene smile lingered, and humor sparkled in his small brown eyes.

"Howdy, boys, howdy!" he exclaimed. "Tired as they look to be, you er straddlin' right peart creeturs. A flirt or two more an' they'd 'a' flung you down the hill, an' 'a' follered along atter you, headstall an' stirrup. They done like they were n't expectin' company in an' around here."

The sonorous voice and deliberate utterance of the old man bespoke his calling. He was evidently a minister of the gospel. This gave a clew to Captain Moseley's memory.

"This must be Uncle Billy Powers," said the captain. "I have heard you preach many a time when I was a boy."

"That's my name," said Uncle Billy; "an' in my feeble way I've been a-preachin' the Word as it was given to me forty year, lackin' one. Ef I ever saw you, the circumstance has slipped from me."

"My name is Moseley," said the captain.

"I useter know Jeremiah Moseley in my younger days," said Uncle Billy, gazing reflectively at the piece of pine bark he was whittling. "Yes, yes! I knowed Brother Moseley well. He was a God-fearin' man."

"He was my father," said the captain.

"Well, well, well!" exclaimed Uncle Billy, in a tone that seemed to combine reflection with astonishment. "Jerry Moseley's son; I disremember the day when Brother Moseley came into my mind, an' yit, now that I hear his name bandied about up here on the hill, it carries me back to ole times. He weren't much of a preacher on his own hook, but let 'im foller along for to clench the sermon, an' his match could n't be foun' in them days. Yit, Jerry was a man of peace, an' here's his son a-gwine about with guns an' pistols, an' what not, a-tryin' to give peaceable folks a smell of war."

"Oh, no!" said Captain Moseley, laughing; "we are just hunting up some old acquaintances,—some friends of ours that we'd like to see."

"Well," said Uncle Billy, sinking his knife deep into the soft pine bark, "it's bad weather for a frolic, an' it ain't much better for a straight-out, eve'y-day call. Speshually up here on the hill, where the ground is so wet and slipperyfied. It looks like you've come a mighty long ways for to pay a friendly call. An' yit," the old man continued, looking up at the captain with a smile that well became his patriarchal face, "thar ain't a cabin on the hill whar you won't be more than welcome. Yes, sir; wheresomever you find a h'a'thstone, thar you'll find a place to rest."

"So I have heard," said the captain. "But maybe you can cut our journey short. We have a message for Israel Spurlock."

Immediately Captain Moseley knew that the placid and kindly face of Uncle Billy Powers had led him into making a mistake. He knew that he had mentioned Israel Spurlock's name to the wrong man at the wrong time. There was a scarcely perceptible frown on Uncle Billy's face as he raised it from his piece of pine bark, which was now assuming the shape of a horseman's pistol, and he looked at the captain through half-closed eyelids.

"Come, now," he exclaimed, "ain't Israel Spurlock in the war? Did n't a posse ketch 'im down yander in Jasper an' take an' cornscrip' 'im into the army? Run it over in your mind now! Ain't Israel Spurlock crippled some'r's, an' ain't your message for his poor ole mammy?"

"No, no," said the captain, laughing, and trying to hide his inward irritation.

"Not so?" exclaimed Uncle Billy. "Well, sir, you must be shore an' set me right when I go wrong; but I'll tell you right pine blank, I've had Israel Spurlock in my min' off an' on' ev'ry since they run him down an' kotch him an' drug 'im off to war. He was weakly like from the time he was a boy, an' when I heard you call forth his name, I allowed to myself, says I, 'Israel Spurlock is sick, an' they 've come atter his ole mammy to go an' nuss him.' That's the idee that riz up in my min'."

A man more shrewd than Captain Moseley would have been deceived by the bland simplicity of Uncle Billy's tone.

"No," said he; "Spurlock is not sick. He is a sounder man than I am. He was conscripted in Jasper and carried to Adairsville, and after he got used to the camp he concluded that he would come home and tell his folks good-bye."

"Now that's jes like Israel," said Uncle Billy, closing his eyes and compressing his lips—"jes like him for the world. He knowed that he was drug off right spang at the time he wanted to be getherin' in his craps, an' savin' his ruffage, an' one thing an' another bekaze his ole mammy did n't have a soul to help her but 'im. I reckon he's been a-housin' his corn an' sich like. The ole 'oman tuck on might'ly when Israel was snatched into the army."

"How far is it to shelter?" inquired Captain Moseley.

"Not so mighty fur," responded Uncle Billy, whittling the pine bark more cautiously. "Jes keep in the middle of the road an' you'll soon come to it. Ef I ain't thar before you, jes holler for Aunt Crissy an' tell her that you saw Uncle Billy some'r's in the woods an' he told you to wait for 'im."

With that, Captain Moseley and Private Chadwick spurred their horses up the mountain road, leaving Uncle Billy whittling.

"Well, dang my buttons!" exclaimed Chadwick, when they were out of hearing.

"What now?" asked the captain, turning in his saddle. Private Chadwick had stopped his horse and was looking back down the mountain as if he expected to be pursued.

"I wish I may die," he went on, giving his horse the rein, "if we ain't walked right square into it with our eyes wide open."

"Into what?" asked the captain, curtly.

"Into trouble," said Chadwick. "Oh," he exclaimed, looking at his companion seriously, "you may grin behind your beard, but you just wait till the fun begins—all the grins you can muster will be mighty dry grins. Why, Cap., I could read that old chap as if he was a newspaper. Whilst he was a-watchin' you I was a-watchin' him, an' if he ain't got a war map printed on his face I ain't never saw none in the 'Charleston Mercury.' "

"The old man is a preacher," said Captain Moseley in a tone that seemed to dispose of the matter.

"Well, the Lord help us!" exclaimed Chadwick. "In about the wuss whippin' I ever got was from a young feller that was preachin' an' courtin' in my neighborhood. I sorter sassed him about a gal he was flyin' around, an' he upped an' frailed me out, an' got the gal to boot. Don't tell me about no preachers. Why, that chap flew at me like a Stonefence rooster, an' he fluttered twice to my once."

"And have you been running from preachers ever since?" dryly inquired the captain.

"Not as you may say, constantly a-runnin'," replied Chadwick; "yit I ain't been a-flingin' no sass at 'em; an' my reason tells me for to give 'em the whole wedth of the big road when I meet 'em."

"Well," said the captain, "what will you do about this preacher?"

"A man in a corner," responded Chadwick, "is obleeged to do the best he kin. I'll jest keep my eye on him, an' the fust motion he makes, I'll"—

"Run?" suggested the captain.

"Well, now," said Chadwick, "a man in a corner can't most ingener'lly run. Git me hemmed in, an' I'll scratch an' bite an' scuffle the best way I know how. It's human natur', an' I'm mighty glad it is; for if that old man's eyes did n't tell no lies we'll have to scratch an' scuffle before we git away from this mountain."

Captain Moseley bit his mustache and smiled grimly as the tired horses toiled up the road. A vague idea of possible danger had crossed his mind while talking to Uncle Billy Powers, but he dismissed it at once as a matter of little importance to a soldier bent on carrying out his orders at all hazards.

It was not long before the two travelers found themselves on a plateau formed by a shoulder of the mountain. On this plateau were abundant signs of life. Cattle were grazing about among the trees, chickens were crowing, and in the distance could be heard the sound of a woman's voice singing. As they pressed forward along the level road they came in sight of a cabin, and the blue smoke curling from its short chimney was suggestive of hospitality. It was a comfortable-looking cabin, too, flanked by several out-houses. The buildings, in contrast with the majestic bulk of the mountain, that still rose precipitously skyward, were curiously small, but there was an air of more than ordinary neatness and coziness about them. And there were touches of feminine hands here and there that made an impres-sion—rows of well-kept boxwood winding like a green serpent through the yard, and a privet hedge that gave promise of rare sweetness in the spring.

As the soldiers approached, a dog barked, and then the singing ceased, and the figure of a young girl appeared in the doorway, only to disappear like a flash. This vision, vanishing with incredible swiftness, was succeeded by a more substantial one in the shape of a motherly looking woman, who stood gazing over her spectacles at the horse-men, apparently undecided whether to frown or to smile. The smile would have undoubtedly forced its way to the pleasant face in any event, for the years had fashioned many a pathway for it, but just then Uncle Billy Powers himself pushed the woman aside and made his appearance, laughing.

" 'Light, boys, 'light!" he exclaimed, walking nimbly to the gate. " 'Light whilst I off wi' your creeturs' gear. Ah!" he went on, as he busied himself unsaddling the horses, "you thought that while your Uncle Billy was a-moonin' aroun' down the hill yander you'd steal a march on your Aunt Crissy, an' maybe come a-conscriptin' of her into the army. But not—not so! Your Uncle Billy has been here long enough to get his hands an' his face rested."

"You must have been in a tremendous hurry," said Captain Moseley, remembering the weary length of moun-tain road he had climbed.

"Why, I could 'a' tuck a nap an' 'a' beat you," said the old man.

"Two miles of tough road, I should say," responded Moseley.

"Go straight through my hoss lot and let yourself down by a saplin' or two," answered Uncle Billy, "an' it ain't more'n a good quarter." Whereupon the old man laughed heartily.

"Jes leave the creeturs here," he went on. "John Jeems an' Fillmore will ten' to 'em whilst we go in an' see what your Aunt Crissy is gwine to give us for supper. You won't find the grub so mighty various, but there is plenty enough of what they is."

There was just enough of deference in Aunt Crissy's greeting to be pleasing, and her unfeigned manifestations of hospitality soon caused the guests to forget that they might possibly be regarded as intruders in that peaceful region. Then there were the two boys, John Jeems and Fillmore, both large enough, and old enough, as Captain Moseley quietly observed to himself, to do military service, and both shy and awkward to a degree. And then there was Polly, a young woman grown, whose smiles all ran to blushes and dimples. Though she was grown, she had the ways of a girl—the vivacity of health and good humor, and the innocent shyness of a child of nature. Impulsive and demure by turns, her moods were whimsical and elusive and altogether delightful. Her beauty, which illumined the old cabin, was heightened by a certain quality that may be described as individuality. Her face and hands were browned by the sun, but in her cheeks the roses of youth and health played constantly. There is nothing more charming to the eye of man than the effects produced when modesty parts company with mere formality and conventionality. Polly, who was as shy as a ground squirrel and as graceful, never pestered herself about formalities. Innocence is not infrequently a very delightful form of boldness. It was so in the case of Polly Powers, at any rate.

The two rough soldiers, unused to the society of women, were far more awkward and constrained than the young woman, but they enjoyed the big fire and the comfortable supper none the less on that account. When, to employ Mrs. Powers's vernacular, "the things were put away," they brought forth their pipes; and they felt so contented that Captain Moseley reproved himself by suggesting that it might be well for them to proceed on their journey up the mountain. But their hosts refused to listen to such a proposal.

"Not so," exclaimed Uncle Billy; "by no means. Why, if you knowed this hill like we all, you'd hoot at the bar' idee of gwine further after nightfall. Besides," the old man went on, looking keenly at his daughter, "ten to one you won't find Spurlock."

Polly had been playing with her hair, which was caught in a single plait and tied with a bit of scarlet ribbon. When Spurlock's name was mentioned she used the plait as a whip, and struck herself impatiently in the hand with the glossy black thong, and then threw it behind her, where it hung dangling nearly to the floor.

"Now I tell you what, boys," said Uncle Billy, after a little pause; "I'd jes like to know who is at the bottom of this Spurlock business. You all may have took a notion that he's a no-count sorter chap—an' he is kinder puny; but what does the army want with a puny man?"

"It's the law," said Captain Moseley, simply, perceiving that his mission was clearly understood. "He is old enough and strong enough to serve in the army. The law calls for him, and he'll have to go. The law wants him now worse than ever."

"Yes," said Private Chadwick, gazing into the glowing embers—"lots worse'n ever."

"What's the matter along of him now?" inquired Mrs. Powers, knocking the ashes from her pipe against the chimney jamb.

"He's a deserter," said Chadwick.

"Tooby shore!" exclaimed Mrs. Powers. "An' what do they do wi' 'em, then?"

For answer Private Chadwick passed his right hand rapidly around his neck, caught hold of an imaginary rope, and looked upwards at the rafters, rolling his eyes and distorting his features as though he were strangling. It was a very effective pantomime. Uncle Billy shook his head and groaned, Aunt Crissy lifted her hands in horror, and then both looked at Polly. That young lady had risen from her chair and made a step toward Chadwick. Her eyes were blazing.

"You'll be hung long before Israel Spurlock!" she cried, her voice thick with anger. Before another word had been said she swept from the room, leaving Chadwick sitting there with his mouth wide open.

"Don't let Polly pester you," said Uncle Billy, smiling a little at Chadwick's discomfiture. "She thinks the world an' all of Sister Spurlock, an' she's been a-knowin' Israel a mighty long time."

"Yes," said Aunt Crissy, with a sigh; "the poor child is hot-headed an' high-tempered. I reckon we've sp'ilt 'er. 'T ain't hard to spile a gal when you hain't got but one."

Before Chadwick could make reply a shrill, querulous voice was heard coming from the room into which Polly had gone. The girl had evidently aroused some one who was more than anxious to engage in a war of words.

"Lord A'mighty massy! whar's any peace?" the shrill voice exclaimed. "What chance on the top side of the yeth is a poor sick creetur got? Oh, what makes you come a-tromplin' on the floor like a drove of wild hosses, an' a-shakin' the clabberds on the roof? I know! I know!"—the voice here almost rose to a shriek,—"it's 'cause I'm sick an' weak, an' can't he'p myself. Lord! Ef I but had strength!"

At this point Polly's voice broke in, but what she said could only be guessed by the noise in the next room.

"Well, what ef the house an' yard was full of 'em? Who's afeard? After Spurlock? Who keers? Hain't Spurlock got no friends on Sugar Mountain? Ef they are after Spurlock, ain't Spurlock got as good a right for to be after them? Oh, go 'way! Gals hain't got no sense. Go 'way! Go tell your pappy to come here an' he'p me in my cheer. Oh, go on!"

Polly had no need to go, however. Uncle Billy rose promptly and went into the next room.

"Hit's daddy," said Aunt Crissy, by way of explanation. "Lord! Daddy used to be a mighty man in his young days, but he's that wasted wi' the palsy that he hain't more'n a shadder of what he was. He's jes like a baby, an' he's mighty quar'lsome when the win' sets in from the east."

According to all symptoms the wind was at that moment setting terribly from the east. There was a sound of shuffling in the next room, and then Uncle Billy Powers came into the room, bearing in his stalwart arms a big rocking-chair containing a little old man whose body and limbs were shriveled and shrunken. Only his head, which seemed to be abnormally large, had escaped the ravages of whatever disease had seized him. His eyes were bright as a bird's and his forehead was noble in its proportions.

"Gentlemen," said Uncle Billy, "this here is Colonel Dick Watson. He used to be a big politicianer in his day an' time. He's my father-in-law."

Uncle Billy seemed to be wonderfully proud of his connection with Colonel Watson. As for the Colonel, he eyed the strangers closely, apparently forgetting to respond to their salutation.

"I reckon you think it's mighty fine, thish 'ere business er gwine ter war whar they hain't nobody but peaceable folks," exclaimed the colonel, his shrill, metallic voice being in curious contrast to his emaciated figure.

"Daddy!" said Mrs. Powers in a warning tone.

"Lord A'mighty! Don't pester me, Crissy Jane. Hain't I done seed war before? When I was in the legislatur' did n't the boys rig up an' march away to Mexico? But you know yourself," the colonel went on, turning to Uncle Billy's guests, "that this hain't Mexico, an' that they hain't no war gwine on on this 'ere hill. You know that mighty well."

"But there's a tolerable big one going on over yonder," said Captain Moseley, with a sweep of his hand to the westward.

"Now, you don't say!" exclaimed Colonel Watson, sarcastically. "A big war going on an' you all quiled up here before the fire, out'n sight an' out'n hearin'! Well, well, well!"

"We are here on business," said Captain Moseley, gently.

"Tooby shore!" said the Colonel, with a sinister screech that was intended to simulate laughter. "You took the words out'n my mouth. I was in-about ready to say it when you upped an' said it yourself. War gwine on over yander an' you all up here on business. Crissy Jane," remarked the colonel in a different tone, "come here an' wipe my face an' see ef I'm a-sweatin'. Ef I'm a-sweatin', hit's the fust time since Sadday before last."

Mrs. Powers mopped her father's face, and assured him that she felt symptoms of perspiration.

"Oh, yes!" continued the colonel. "Business here an' war yander. I hear tell that you er after Israel Spurlock. Lord A'mighty above us! What er you after Israel for? He hain't got no niggers for to fight for. All the fightin' he can do is to fight for his ole mammy."

Captain Moseley endeavored to explain to Colonel Watson why his duty made it imperatively necessary to carry Spurlock back to the conscript camp, but in the midst of it all the old man cried out:—

"Oh, I know who sent you!"

"Who?" the captain said.

"Nobody but Wesley Lovejoy!"

Captain Moseley made no response, but gazed into the fire. Chadwick, on the other hand, when Lovejoy's name was mentioned, slapped himself on the leg, and straightened himself up with the air of a man who has made an interesting discovery.

"Come, now," Colonel Watson insisted, "hain't it so? Did n't Wesley Lovejoy send you?"

"Well," said Moseley, "a man named Lovejoy is on Colonel Waring's staff and he gave me my orders."

At this the old man fairly shrieked with laughter, and so sinister was its emphasis that the two soldiers felt the cold chills creeping up their backs.

"What is the matter with Lovejoy?" It was Chadwick who spoke.

"Oh, wait!" cried Colonel Watson; "thes wait. You may n't want to wait, but you'll have to. I may look like I'm mighty puny, an' I 'spec' I am, but I hain't dead yit. Lord A'mighty, no! Not by a long shot!"

There was a pause here, during which Aunt Crissy remarked, in a helpless sort of way:—

"I wonder wher' Polly is, an' what she's a-doin'?"

"Don't pester 'long of Polly," snapped the paralytic. "She knows what she's a'doin'."

"About this Wesley Lovejoy," said Captain Moseley, turning to the old man: "you seem to know him very well."

"You hear that, William!" exclaimed Colonel Watson. "He asts me ef I know Wes. Lovejoy! Do I know him? Why, the triflin' houn'! I've knowed him ev'ry sence he was big enough to rob a hen-roos'."

Uncle Billy Powers, in his genial way, tried to change the current of the conversation, and he finally succeeded, but it was evident that Adjutant Lovejoy had one enemy, if not several, in that humble household. Such was the feeling for Spurlock and contempt for Wesley Lovejoy that Captain Moseley and Private Chadwick felt themselves to be inter-lopers, and they once more suggested the necessity of pur-suing their journey. This suggestion seemed to amuse the paralytic, who laughed loudly.

"Lord A'mighty!" he exclaimed, "I know how you feel, an' I don't blame you for feelin' so; but don't you go up the mountain this night. Thes stay right whar you is, beca'se ef you don't you'll make all your friends feel bad for you. Don't ast me how, don't ast me why. Thes you stay. Come an' put me to bed, William, an' don't let these folks go out'n the house this night."

Uncle Billy carried the old man into the next room, tucked him away in his bed, and then came back. Conversation lagged to such an extent that Aunt Crissy once more felt moved to inquire about Polly. Uncle Billy responded with a sweeping gesture of his right hand, which might mean much or little. To the two Confederates it meant nothing, but to Aunt Crissy it said that Polly had gone up the moun-tain in the rain and cold. Involuntarily the woman shuddered and drew nearer the fire.

It was in fact a venturesome journey that Polly had undertaken. Hardened as she was to the weather, familiar as she was with the footpaths that led up and around the face of the mountain, her heart rose in her mouth when she found herself fairly on the way to Israel Spurlock's house. The darkness was almost overwhelming in its intensity. As Uncle Billy Powers remarked while showing the two Confederates to their beds in the "shed-room," there "was a solid chunk of it from one end of creation to t'other." The rain, falling steadily but not heavily, was bitterly cold, and it was made more uncomfortable by the wind, which rose and fell with a muffled roar, like the sigh of some Titanic spirit flying hither and yonder in the wild recesses of the sky. Bold as she was, the girl was appalled by the invisible contention that seemed to be going on in the elements above her, and more than once she paused, ready to flee, as best she could, back to the light and warmth she had left behind; but the gesture of Chadwick, with its cruel significance, would recur to her, and then, clenching her teeth, she would press blindly on. She was carrying a message of life and freedom to Israel Spurlock.

With the rain dripping from her hair and her skirts, her face and hands benumbed with cold, but with every nerve strung to the highest tension and every faculty alert to meet whatever danger might present itself, Polly struggled up the mountain path, feeling her way as best she could, and pulling herself along by the aid of the friendly saplings and the overhanging trees.

After a while—and it seemed a long while to Polly, contending with the fierce forces of the night and beset by a thousand doubts and fears—she could hear Spurlock's dogs barking. What if the two soldiers, suspecting her mission, had mounted their horses and outstripped her? She had no time to remember the difficulties of the mountain road, nor did she know that she had been on her journey not more than half an hour. She was too excited either to reason or to calculate. Gathering her skirts in her hands as she rose to the level of the clearing, Polly rushed across it towards the little cabin, tore open the frail little gate, and flung herself against the door with a force that shook the house.

Old Mrs. Spurlock was spinning, while Israel carded the rolls for her. The noise that Polly made against the door startled them both. The thread broke in Mrs. Spurlock's hand, and one part of it curled itself on the end of the broach with a buzz that whirled it into a fantastically tangled mass. The cards dropped from Israel's hands with a clatter that added to his mother's excitement.

"Did anybody ever hear the beat of that?" she exclaimed. "Run, Iserl, an' see what it is that's a-tryin' to tear the roof off'n the house."

Israel did not need to be told, nor did Mrs. Spurlock wait for him to go. They reached the door together, and when Israel threw it open they saw Polly Powers standing there, pale, trembling, and dripping.

"Polly!" cried Israel, taking her by the arm. He could say no more.

"In the name er the Lord!" exclaimed Mrs. Spurlock, "wher' 'd you drop from? You look more like a drownded ghost than you does like folks. Come right in here an' dry yourse'f. What in the name of mercy brung you out in sech weather? Who's dead or a-dyin'? Why, look at the gal!" Mrs. Spurlock went on in a louder tone, seeing that Polly stood staring at them with wide-open eyes, her face as pale as death.

"Have they come?" gasped Polly.

"Listen at 'er, Iserl! I b'lieve in my soul she's done gone an' run ravin' deestracted. Shake 'er, Iserl; shake 'er."

For answer Polly dropped forward into Mrs. Spurlock's arms, all wet as she was, and there fell to crying in a way that was quite alarming to Israel, who was not familiar with feminine peculiarities. Mrs. Spurlock soothed Polly as she would have soothed a baby, and half carried, half led her to the fireplace. Israel, who was standing around embarrassed and perplexed, was driven out of the room, and soon Polly was decked out in dry clothes. These "duds," as Mrs. Spurlock called them, were ill-fitting and ungraceful, but in Israel's eyes the girl was just as beautiful as ever. She was even more beautiful when, fully recovered from her excitement, she told with sparkling eyes and heightened color the story she had to tell.

Mrs. Spurlock listened with the keenest interest, and with many an exclamation of indignation, while Israel heard it with undisguised admiration for the girl. He seemed to enjoy the whole proceeding, and when Polly in the ardor and excitement of her narration betrayed an almost passionate interest in his probable fate, he rubbed his hands slowly together and laughed softly to himself.

"An' jest to think," exclaimed Polly, when she had finished her story, "that that there good-for-nothin' Wesley Lovejoy had the imperdence to ast me to have him no longer'n last year, an' he's been a-flyin' round me constant."

"I seed him a-droppin' his wing," said Israel, laughing. "I reckon that's the reason he's after me so hot. But never you mind, mammy; you thes look after the gal that's gwine to be your daughter-in-law, an' I'll look after your son."

"Go off, you goose!" cried Polly, blushing and smiling. "Ef they hang you, whose daughter-in-law will I be then?"

"The Lord knows!" exclaimed Israel, with mock seriousness. "They tell me that Lovejoy is an orphan!"

"You must be crazy," cried Polly, indignantly. "I hope you don't think I'd marry that creetur. I wouldn't look at him if he was the last man. You better be thinkin' about your goozle."

"It's ketchin' befo' hangin'," said Israel.

"They've mighty nigh got you now," said Polly. Just then a hickory nut dropped on the roof of the house, and the noise caused the girl to start up with an exclamation of terror.

"You thought they had me then," said Israel, as he rose and stood before the fire, rubbing his hands together, and seeming to enjoy most keenly the warm interest the girl manifested in his welfare.

"Oh, I wisht you'd cut an' run," pleaded Polly, covering her face with her hands; "they'll be here therreckly."

Israel was not a bad-looking fellow as he stood before the fire laughing. He was a very agreeable variation of the mountain type. He was angular, but neither stoop-shouldered nor cadaverous. He was awkward in his manners, but very gracefully fashioned. In point of fact, as Mrs. Powers often remarked, Israel was "not to be sneezed at."

After a while he became thoughtful. "I jest tell you what," he said, kicking the chunks vigorously, and sending little sparks of fire skipping and cracking about the room. "This business puzzles me—I jest tell you it does. That Wes. Lovejoy done like he was the best friend I had. He was constantly huntin' me up in camp, an' when I told him I would like to come home an' get mammy's crap in, he jest laughed an' said he did n't reckon I'd be missed much, an' now he's a-houndin' me down. What has the man got agin me?"

Polly knew, but she didn't say. Mrs. Spurlock suspected, but she made no effort to enlighten Israel. Polly knew that

Lovejoy was animated by blind jealousy, and her instinct taught her that a jealous man is usually a dangerous one. Taking advantage of one of the privileges of her sex, she had at one time carried on a tremendous flirtation with Lovejoy. She had intended to amuse herself simply, but she had kindled fires she was powerless to quench. Lovejoy had taken her seriously, and she knew well enough that he regarded Israel Spurlock as a rival. She had reason to suspect, too, that Lovejoy had pointed out Israel to the conscript officers, and that the same influence was controlling and directing the pursuit now going on.

Under the circumstances, her concern—her alarm, indeed—was natural. She and Israel had been sweethearts for years,—real sure-enough sweethearts, as she expressed it to her grandfather,—and they were to be married in a short while; just as soon, in fact, as the necessary preliminaries of clothes-making and cake-baking could be disposed of. She thought nothing of her feat of climbing the mountain in the bitter cold and the overwhelming rain. She would have taken much larger risks than that; she would have faced any danger her mind could conceive of. And Israel appreciated it all; nay, he fairly gloated over it. He stood before the fire fairly hugging the fact to his bosom. His face glowed, and his whole attitude was one of exultation; and with it, shaping every gesture and movement, was a manifestation of fearless-ness which was all the more impressive because it was unconscious.

This had a tendency to fret Polly, whose alarm for Israel's safety was genuine.

"Oh, I do wisht you'd go on," she cried; "them men'll shorely ketch you ef you keep on a-stayin' here a-winkin' an' a-gwine on makin' monkey motions."

"Shoo!" exclaimed Israel. "Ef the house was surrounded by forty thousan' of 'em, I'd git by 'em, an', ef need be, take you wi' me."

While they were talking the dogs began to bark. At the first sound Polly rose from her chair with her arms outstretched, but fell back pale and trembling. Israel had disappeared as if by magic, and Mrs. Spurlock was calmly lighting her pipe by filling it with hot embers. It was evidently a false alarm, for, after a while, Israel backed through the doorway and closed the door again with comical alacrity.

"Sh-sh-sh!" he whispered, with a warning gesture, seeing that Polly was about to protest. "Don't make no fuss. The dogs has been a-barkin' at sperits an' things. Jest keep right still."

He went noiselessly about the room, picking up first one thing and then another. Over one shoulder he flung a canteen, and over the other a hunting-horn. Into his coat-pocket he thrust an old-fashioned powder-flask. Meanwhile his mother was busy gathering together such articles as Israel might need. His rifle she placed by the door, and then she filled a large homespun satchel with a supply of victuals— a baked fowl, a piece of smoked beef, and a big piece of light bread. These preparations were swiftly and silently made. When everything seemed to be ready for his departure Israel presented the appearance of a peddler.

"I'm goin' up to the Rock," he said, by way of explanation, "an' light the fire. Maybe the boys'll see it, an' maybe they won't. Leastways they're mighty apt to smell the smoke."

Then, without further farewell, he closed the door and stepped out into the darkness, leaving the two women sitting by the hearth. They sat there for hours, gazing into the fire and scarcely speaking to each other. The curious reticence that seems to be developed and assiduously cultivated by the dwellers on the mountains took possession of them. The confidences and sympathies they had in common were those of observation and experience, rather than the result of an interchange of views and opinions.

Towards morning the drizzling rain ceased, and the wind, changing its direction, sent the clouds flying to the east, whence they had come. About dawn, Private Chadwick, who had slept most soundly, was aroused by the barking of the dogs, and got up to look after the horses. As he slipped quietly out of the house he saw a muffled figure crossing the yard.

"Halt!" he cried, giving the challenge of a sentinel. "Who goes there?"

"Nobody ner nothin' that'll bite you, I reckon," was the somewhat snappish response. It was the voice of Polly. She was looking up and across the mountains to where a bright red glare was reflected on the scurrying clouds. The density of the atmosphere was such that the movements of flames were photographed on the clouds, rising and falling, flaring and fading, as though the dread spirits of the storm were waving their terrible red banners from the mountain.

"What can that be?" asked Chadwick, after he had watched the singular spectacle a moment.

Polly laughed aloud, almost joyously. She knew it was Israel's beacon. She knew that these red reflections, waving over the farther spur of the mountain and over the valley that nestled so peacefully below, would summon half a hundred men and boys—the entire congregation of Antioch Church, where her father was in the habit of holding forth on the first Sunday of each month. She knew that Israel was safe, and the knowledge restored her good humor.

"What did you say it was?" Chadwick inquired again, his curiosity insisting on an explanation.

"It's jest a fire, I reckon," Polly calmly replied. "Ef it's a house burnin' down, it can't be holp. Water could n't save it now."

Whereupon she pulled the shawl from over her head, tripped into the house, and went about preparing breakfast, singing merrily. Chadwick watched her as she passed and repassed from the rickety kitchen to the house, and when the light grew clearer he thought he saw on her face a look that he did not understand. It was indeed an inscrutable expression, and it would have puzzled a wiser man than Chadwick. He chopped some wood, brought some water, and made himself generally useful; but he received no thanks from Polly. She ignored him as completely as if he had never existed.

All this set the private to thinking. Now a man who reflects much usually thinks out a theory to fit everything that he fails to understand. Chadwick thought out his theory while the girl was getting breakfast ready.

It was not long before the two soldiers were on their way up the mountain, nor was it long before Chadwick began to unfold his theory, and in doing so he managed to straighten it by putting together various little facts that occurred to him as he talked.

"I tell you what, Captain," he said, as soon as they were out of hearing; "that gal's a slick 'un. It's my belief that we are gwine on a fool's errand. 'Stead of gwine towards Spurlock, we're gwine straight away from 'im. When that gal made her disappearance last night she went an' found Spurlock, an' ef he ain't a natchul born fool he tuck to the woods. Why, the shawl the gal had on her head this mornin' was soakin' wet. It were n't rainin', an' hadn't been for a right smart while. How come the shawl wet? They were n't but one way. It got wet by rubbin' again the bushes an' the limbs er the trees."

This theory was plausible enough to impress itself on Captain Moseley. "What is to be done, then?" he asked.

"Well, the Lord knows what ought to be done," said Chadwick; "but I reckon the best plan is to sorter scatter out an' skirmish aroun' a little bit. We'd better divide our army. You go up the mountain an' git Spurlock, if he's up thar, an' let me take my stan' on the ridge yander an' keep my eye on Uncle Billy's back yard an' hoss lot. If Spurlock is r'ally tuck to the woods, he'll be mighty apt to be slinkin' 'roun' whar the gal is."

Captain Moseley assented to this plan, and proceeded to put it in execution as soon as he and Chadwick were a safe distance from Uncle Billy Powers's house. Chadwick, dismounting, led his horse along a cow-path that ran at right angles to the main road, and was soon lost to sight, while the captain rode forward on his mission.

Of the two, as it turned out, the captain had much the more comfortable experience. He reached the Spurlock house in the course of three-quarters of an hour.

In response to his halloo Mrs. Spurlock came to the door.

"I was a-spinnin' away for dear life," she remarked, brushing her gray hair from her face, "when all of a sudden I hearn a fuss, an' I 'lows ter myself, says I, 'I'll be boun' that's some one a-hailin',' says I; an' then I dropped ever'thin' an' run ter the door an' shore enough it was. Won't you 'light an' come in?" she inquired with ready hospitality. Her tone was polite, almost obsequious.

"Is Mr. Israel Spurlock at home?" the captain asked.

"Not, as you might say, adzackly at home, but I reckon in reason it won't be long before he draps in. He hain't had his breakfas' yit, though hit's been a-waitin' for him tell hit's stone col'. The cows broke out last night, an' he went off a-huntin' of 'em time it was light good. Iserl is thes ez rank after his milk ez some folks is after the'r dram. I says, says I, 'Shorely you kin do 'thout your milk one mornin' in the year;' but he would n't nigh hear ter that. He thes up an' bolted off."

"I'll ride on," said the captain. "Maybe I'll meet him coming back. Good-by."

It was an uneventful ride, but Captain Moseley noted one curious fact. He had not proceeded far when he met two men riding down the mountain. Each carried a rifle flung across his saddle in front of him. They responded gravely to the captain's salutation.

"Have you seen Israel Spurlock this morning," he asked.

"No, sir, I hain't saw him," answered one. The other shook his head. Then they rode on down the mountain.

A little farther on Captain Moseley met four men. These were walking, but each was armed—three with rifles, and one with a shot-gun. They had not seen Spurlock. At intervals he met more than a dozen—some riding and some walking, but all armed. At last he met two that presented something of a contrast to the others. They were armed, it is true; but they were laughing and singing as they went along the road, and while they had not seen Spurlock with their own eyes, as they said, they knew he must be farther up the mountain, for they had heard of him as they came along.

Riding and winding around upward, Captain Moseley presently saw a queer-looking little chap coming towards him. The little man had a gray beard, and as he walked he had a movement like a camel. Like a camel, too, he had a great hump on his back. His legs were as long as any man's but his whole body seemed to be contracted in his hump. He was very spry, too, moving along as active as a boy, and there was an elfish expression on his face such as one sees in old picture-books—a cunning, leering expression, which yet had for its basis the element of humor. The little man carried a rifle longer than himself, which he flourished about with surprising ease and dexterity—practicing apparently some new and peculiar manual.

"Have you seen Israel Spurlock?" inquired Captain Moseley, reining in his horse.

"Yes! Oh, Yes! Goodness gracious, yes!" replied the little man, grinning good-naturedly.

"Where is he now?" asked the captain.

"All about. Yes! All around! Gracious, yes!" responded the little man, with a sweeping gesture that took in the whole mountain. Then he seemed to be searching eagerly in the road for something. Suddenly pausing, he exclaimed: "Here's his track right now! Oh yes! Right fresh, too! Goodness, yes!"

"Where are you going?" Moseley asked, smiling at the antics of the little man, their nimbleness being out of all proportion to his deformity.

For answer the little man whirled his rifle over his hump and under his arm, and caught it as it went flying into the air. Then he held it at a "ready," imitating the noise of the lock with his mouth, took aim and made believe to fire, all with indescribable swiftness and precision. Captain Moseley rode on his way laughing; but, laugh as he would, he could not put out of his mind the queer impression the little man had made on him, nor could he rid himself of a feeling of uneasiness. Taking little notice of the landmarks that ordinarily attract the notice of the traveler in a strange country, he suddenly found himself riding along a level stretch of tableland. The transformation was complete. The country roads seemed to cross and recross here, coming and going in every direction. He rode by a little house that stood alone in the level wood, and he rightly judged it to be a church. He drew rein and looked around him. Everything was unfamiliar. In the direction from which he supposed he had come, a precipice rose sheer from the tableland more than three hundred feet. At that moment he heard a shout, and looking up he beheld the hunchback flourishing his long rifle and cutting his queer capers.

The situation was so puzzling that Captain Moseley passed his hand over his eyes, as if to brush away a scene that confused his mind and obstructed his vision. He turned his horse and rode back the way he had come, but it seemed to be so unfamiliar that he chose another road, and in the course of a quarter of an hour he was compelled to acknowledge that he was lost. Everything appeared to be turned around, even the little church.

Meanwhile Private Chadwick was having an experience of his own. In parting from Captain Moseley he led his horse through the bushes, following for some distance a cow-path. This semblance of a trail terminated in a "blind path," and this Chadwick followed as best he could, picking his way cautiously and choosing ground over which his horse could follow. He had to be very careful. There were no leaves on the trees, and the undergrowth was hardly thick enough to conceal him from the keen eyes of the mountaineers. Finally he tied his horse in a thicket of black-jacks, where he had the whole of Uncle Billy Powers's little farm under his eye. His position was not an uncomfortable one. Sheltered from the wind, he had nothing to do but sit on a huge chestnut log and ruminate, and make a note of the comings and goings of Uncle Billy's premises.

Sitting thus, Chadwick fell to thinking; thinking, he fell into a doze. He caught himself nodding more than once, and upbraided himself bitterly. Still he nodded—he, a soldier on duty at his post. How long he slept he could not tell, but he suddenly awoke to find himself dragged backward from the log by strong hands. He would have made some resistance, for he was a fearless man at heart and a tough one to handle in a knock-down and drag-out tussle; but resistance was useless. He had been taken at a disadvantage, and before he could make a serious effort in his own behalf, he was lying flat on his back, with his hands tied, and as helpless as an infant. He looked up and discovered that his captor was Israel Spurlock.

"Well, blame my scaly hide!" exclaimed Chadwick, making an involuntary effort to free his hands. "You're the identical man I'm a-huntin'."

"An' now you're sorry you went an' foun' me, I reckon," said Israel.

"Well, I ain't as glad as I 'lowed I'd be," said Chadwick. "Yit nuther am I so mighty sorry. One way or 'nother I knowed in reason I'd run up on you."

"You're mighty right," responded Israel, smiling not ill-naturedly. "You fell in my arms same as a gal in a honeymoon. Lemme lift you up, as the mule said when he kicked the nigger over the fence. Maybe you'll look purtier when you swap een's." Thereupon Israel helped Chadwick to his feet.

"You ketched me that time, certain and shore," said the latter, looking at Spurlock and laughing; "they ain't no two ways about that. I was a settin' on the log thar, a-noddin' an' a-dreamin' 'bout Christmas. 'Tain't many days off, I reckon."

"Oh, yes!" exclaimed Spurlock, sarcastically; "a mighty purty dream, I bet a hoss. You was fixin' up for to cram me in Lovejoy's stockin'. A mighty nice present I'd 'a' been, tooby shore. Stidder hangin' up his stockin', Lovejoy was a-aimin' for to hang me up. Oh, yes! Christmas dreams is so mighty nice an' fine, I'm a great min' to set right down here an' have one er my own—one of them kin' er dreams what's got forked tail an' fireworks mixed up on it."

"Well," said Chadwick, with some seriousness, "whose stockin' is you a-gwine to cram me in?"

"In whose else's but Danny Lemmons's? An' won't he holler an' take on? 'N' why, I wouldn't miss seein' Danny Lemmons take on for a hat full er shinplasters. Dang my buttons ef I would!"

Chadwick looked at his captor with some curiosity. There was not a trace of ill-feeling or bad humor in Spurlock's tone, nor in his attitude. The situation was so queer that it was comical, and Chadwick laughed aloud as he thought about it. In this Spurlock heartily joined him, and the situation would have seemed doubly queer to a passer-by chancing along and observing captor and prisoner laughing and chatting so amiably together.

"Who, in the name of goodness, is Danny Lemmons?"

"Lord!" exclaimed Spurlock, lifting both hands, "don't ast me about Danny Lemmons. He's—he's—well, I tell you what, he's the bull er the woods, Danny Lemmons is; nuther more ner less. He hain't bigger'n my two fists, an' he's 'flicted, an' he's all crippled up in his back, whar he had it broke when he was a baby, an' yet he's in-about the peartest man on the mountain, an' he's the toughest an' the sooplest. An' more'n that, he's got them things up here," Spurlock went on, tapping his head significantly. Chadwick understood this to mean that Lemmons, whatever might be his afflictions, had brains enough and to spare.

There was a pause in the conversation, and then Chadwick, looking at his bound wrists, which were beginning to chafe and swell, spoke up.

"What's your will wi' me?" he asked.

"Well," said Spurlock, rising to his feet, "I'm a-gwine to empty your gun, an' tote your pistol for you, an' invite you down to Uncle Billy's. Oh, you needn't worry," he went on, observing Chadwick's disturbed expression, "they're expectin' of you. Polly's tol' 'em you'd likely come back."

"How did Polly know?" Chadwick inquired.

"Danny Lemmons tol' 'er."

"By George!" exclaimed Chadwick, "the woods is full of Danny Lemmons."

"Why, bless your heart," said Spurlock, "he thes swarms roun' here."

After Spurlock had taken the precaution to possess himself of Chadwick's arms and ammunition, he cut the cords that bound his prisoner's hands, and the two went down the mountain, chatting as pleasantly and as sociably as two boon companions. Chadwick found no lack of hospitality at Uncle Billy Powers's house. His return was taken as a matter of course, and he was made welcome. Nevertheless, his entertainers betrayed a spirit of levity that might have irritated a person less self-contained.

"I see he ketched you, Iserl," remarked Uncle Billy, with a twinkle in his eye. "He 'lowed las' night as how he'd fetch you back wi' him."

"Yes," said Israel, "he thes crope up on me. It's mighty hard for to fool these army fellers."

Then and afterward the whole family pretended to regard Spurlock as Chadwick's prisoner. This was not a joke for the latter to relish, but it was evidently not intended to be offensive, and he could do no less than humor it. He accepted the situation philosophically. He even prepared himself to relish Captain Moseley's astonishment when he returned and discovered the true state of affairs. As the day wore away it occurred to Chadwick that the captain was in no hurry to return. Even Uncle Billy Powers grew uneasy.

"Now, I do hope an' trust he ain't gone an' lost his temper up thar in the woods," remarked Uncle Billy. "I hope it from the bottom of my heart. These here wars an' rumors of wars makes the folks mighty restless. They'll take resks now what they would n't dassent to of tuck before this here rippit begun, an' it's done got so now human life ai'nt wuth shucks. The boys up here ain't no better'n the rest. They fly to pieces quicker'n they ever did."

No trouble, however, had come to Captain Moseley. Though he was confused in his bearings, he was as serene and as unruffled as when training a company of raw conscripts in the art of war. After an unsuccessful attempt to find the road he gave his horse the rein, and that sensible animal, his instinct sharpened by remembrance of Uncle Billy Powers's corn-crib and fodder, moved about at random until he found that he was really at liberty to go where he pleased, and then he turned short about, struck a little canter, and was soon going down the road by which he had come. The captain was as proud of this feat as if it were due to his own intelligence, and he patted the horse's neck in an approving way.

As Captain Moseley rode down the mountain, reflecting, it occurred to him that his expedition was taking a comical shape. He had gone marching up the hill, and now he came marching down again, and Israel Spurlock, so far as the captain knew, was as far from being a captive as ever—perhaps farther. Thinking it all over in a somewhat irritated frame of mind, Moseley remembered Lovejoy's eagerness to recapture Spurlock. He remembered, also, what he had heard the night before, and it was in no pleasant mood that he thought it all over. It was such an insignificant, such a despicable affair, two men carrying out the jealous whim of a little militia politician.

"It is enough, by George!" exclaimed Captain Moseley aloud, "to make a sensible man sick."

"Lord, yes!" cried out a voice behind him. Looking around, he saw the hunchback following him. "That's what I tell 'em; goodness, yes!"

"Now, look here!" said Captain Moseley, reining in his horse, and speaking somewhat sharply. "Are you following me, or am I following you? I don't want to be dogged after in the bushes, much less in the big road."

"Ner me nurther," said the hunchback, in the cheerfulest manner. "An' then thar's Spurlock—Lord, yes; I hain't axt him about it, but I bet a hoss he don't like to be dogged atter nuther."

"My friend," said Captain Moseley, "you seem to have a quick tongue. What is your name?"

"Danny Lemmons," said the other. "Now don't say I look like I ought to be squoze. Ever'body inginer'lly says that," he went on with a grimace, "but I've squoze lots more than what's ever squoze me. Lord, yes! Yes, siree! Men an' gals tergether. You ax 'em, an' they'll tell you."

"Lemmons," said the captain, repeating the name slowly. "Well, you look it!"

"Boo!" cried Danny Lemmons, making a horrible grimace; "you don't know what you're a-talkin' about. The gals all 'low I'm mighty sweet. You ought to see me when I'm rigged out in my Sunday-go-to-meetin' duds. Polly Powers she 'lows I look snatchin'. Lord, yes! Yes, siree! I'm gwin down to Polly's house now."

Whereat he broke out singing, paraphrasing an old negro ditty, and capering about in the woods like mad.

"Oh, I went down to Polly's house,
An' she was not at home;
I set myself in the big arm-cheer
An' beat on the ol' jaw-bone.
Oh, rise up, Polly! Slap 'im on the jaw,
An hit 'im in the eyeball—bim!"

The song finished, Danny Lemmons walked on down the road ahead of the horse in the most unconcerned manner. It was part of Captain Moseley's plan to stop at Mrs. Spurlock's and inquire for Israel. This seemed to be a part of Danny's plan also, for he turned out of the main road and went ahead, followed by the captain. There were quite a number of men at Mrs. Spurlock's when Moseley rode up, and he noticed that all were armed. Some were standing listlessly about, leaning against the trees, some were sitting in various postures, and others were squatting around whittling: but all had their guns within easy reach. Mrs. Spurlock was walking about among them smoking her pipe. But the strained and awkward manner of the men as they returned his salutation, or by some subtle instinct he could not explain, Captain Moseley knew that these men were waiting for him, and that he was their prisoner. The very atmosphere seemed to proclaim the fact. Under his very eyes Danny Lemmons changed from a grinning buffoon into a quiet, self-contained man trained to the habit of command. Recognizing the situation, the old soldier made the most of it by retaining his good humor.

"Well, boys," he said, flinging a leg over the pommel of his saddle, "I hope you are not tired waiting for me." The men exchanged glances in a curious, shame-faced sort of way.

"No," said one; "we was thes a-settin' here tallkin' 'bout ol' times. We 'lowed maybe you'd sorter git tangled up on the hill thar, and so Danny Lemmons, he harked back for to keep a' eye on you."

There was no disposition on the part of this quiet group of men to be clamorous or boastful. There was a certain shyness in their attitude, as of men willing to apologize for what might seem to be unnecessary rudeness.

"I'll tell you what," said Danny Lemmons, "They ain't a man on the mounting that's got a blessed thing agin you, ner again the tother feller, an' they ain't a man anywheres aroun' here that's a-gwine to pester you. We never brung you whar you is; but now that you're here we're a-gwine to whirl in an' ast you to stay over an' take Christmas wi' us, sech ez we'll have. Lord, yes! A nice time we'll have, ef I ain't forgot how to finger the fiddle-strings. We're sorter in a quandary," Danny Lemmons continued, observing Captain Moseley toying nervously with the handle of his pistol. "We don't know whether you're a-gwine to be worried enough to start a row, or whether you're a-gwine to work up trouble."

Meanwhile Danny had brought his long rifle into a position where it could be used promptly and effectually. For answer Moseley dismounted from his horse, unbuckled his belt and flung it across his saddle, and prepared to light his pipe.

"Now, then," said Danny Lemmons, "thes make yourself at home."

Nothing could have been friendlier than the attitude of the mountain men, nor freer than their talk. Captain Moseley learned that Danny Lemmons was acting under the orders of Colonel Dick Watson, the virile paralytic; that he and Chadwick were to be held prisoners in the hope that Adjutant Lovejoy would come in search of them—in which event there would be developments of a most interesting character.

So Danny Lemmons said, and so it turned out; for one day while Moseley and Chadwick were sitting on the sunny side of Uncle Billy's house, listening to the shrill, snarling tones of Colonel Watson, they heard a shout from the roadside, and behold, there was Danny Lemmons with his little band escorting Lovejoy and a small squad of forlorn-looking militia. Lovejoy was securely bound to his horse, and it may well be supposed that he did not cut an imposing figure. Yet he was undaunted. He was captured, but not conquered. His eyes never lost their boldness, nor his tongue its bitterness. He was almost a match for Colonel Watson, who raved at all things through the tremulous and vindictive lips of disease. The colonel's temper was fitful, but Lovejoy's seemed to burn steadily. Moved by contempt rather than caution, he was economical of his words, listening to the shrill invective of the colonel patiently, but with a curious flicker of his thin lips that caused Danny Lemmons to study him intently. It was Danny who discovered that Lovejoy's eyes never wandered in Polly's direction, nor settled on her, nor seemed to perceive that she was in existence, though she was flitting about constantly on the aimless little errands that keep a conscientious housekeeper busy.

Lovejoy was captured one morning and Christmas fell the next, and it was a memorable Christmas to all concerned. After breakfast Uncle Billy Powers produced his Bible and preached a little sermon—a sermon that was not the less meaty and sincere, not the less wise and powerful, because the English was ungrammatical and the rhetoric uncouth. After it was over the old man cleared his throat and remarked:—

"Brethern, we're gathered here for to praise the Lord an' do his will. The quare times that's come on us has brung us face to face with much that is unseemly in life, an' likely to fret the sperit an' vex the understandin'. Yit the Almighty is with us, an' of us, an' among us; an', in accordance wi' the commands delivered in this Book, we're here to fortify two souls in the'r choice, an' to b'ar testimony to the Word that makes lawful marriage a sacrament."

With that, Uncle Billy, fumbling in his coat pockets, produced a marriage license, called Israel Spurlock and his daughter before him, and in simple fashion pronounced the words that made them man and wife.

The dinner that followed hard on the wedding was to the soldiers, who had been subsisting on the tough rations furnished by the Confederate commissaries, by all odds the chief event of the day. To them the resources of the Powers household were wonderful indeed. The shed-room, running the whole length of the house and kitchen, was utilized, and the dinner table, which was much too small to accommodate the guests, invited and uninvited, was supplemented by the inventive genius of Private William Chadwick, who, in the most unassuming manner, had taken control of the whole affair. He proved himself to be an invaluable aid, and his good humor gave a lightness and a zest to the occasion that would otherwise have been sadly lacking.

Under his direction the tables were arranged and the dinner set, and when the politely impatient company were summoned they found awaiting them a meal substantial enough to remind them of the old days of peace and prosperity. It was a genuine Christmas dinner. In the centre of the table there was a large bowl of egg-nog, and this was flanked and surrounded by a huge dish full of apple dumplings, a tremendous chicken pie, barbecued shote, barbecued mutton, a fat turkey, and all the various accompaniments of a country feast.

When Uncle Billy Powers had said an earnest and simple grace he gave his place at the head of the table to Colonel Watson, who had been brought in on his chair. Aunt Crissy gave Chadwick the seat of honor at the foot, and then the two old people announced that they were ready to wait on the company, with Mr. Chadwick to do the carving. If the private betrayed any embarrassment at all, he soon recovered from it.

"It ain't any use," he said, glancing down the table, "to call the roll. We're all here an' accounted for. The only man or woman that can't answer to their name is Danny Lemmons's little brown fiddle, an' I'll bet a sev'm-punce it'd skreak a little ef he tuck it out'n the bag. But before we whirl in an' make a charge three deep, le's begin right. This is Christmas, and that bowl yander, with the egg-nog in it, looks tired. Good as the dinner is, it's got to have a file leader. We'll start in with what looks the nighest like Christmas."

"Well," said Aunt Crissy, "I've been in sech a swivet all day I don't reelly reckon the nog is wuth your while, but you'll ha' ter take it thes like you fin' it. Hit's sweetened wi' long sweet'nin', an' it'll ha' ter be dipped up wi' a gourd an' drunk out'n cups."

"Lord bless you, ma'm," exclaimed Chadwick, "they won't be no questions axed ef it's got Christmas enough in it, an' I reckon it is, kaze I poured it myself, an' I can hol' up a jug as long as the nex' man."

Though it was sweetened with syrup, the egg-nog was a success, for its strength could not be denied.

"Ef I had n't 'a' been a prisoner of war, as you may say," remarked Chadwick, when the guests had fairly begun to discuss the dinner, "I'd 'a' got me a hunk of barbecue an' a dumplin' or two, an' a slice of that chicken pie there—I'd 'a' grabbed 'em up an' 'a' made off down the mountain. Why, I'll tell you what's the truth—I got a whiff of that barbecue by daylight, an' gentulmen, it fairly made me dribble at the mouth. Nex' to Uncle Billy there, I was the fust man at the pit."

"Yes, yes," said Uncle Billy, laughing, "that's so. An' you holp me a right smart. I'll say that."

"An' Spurlock, he got a whiff of it. Did n't you all notice, about the time he was gittin' married, how his mouth puckered up? Along towards the fust I thought he was a fixin' to dip down an' give the bride a smack. But, bless you, he had barbecue on his min', an' the bride missed the buss."

"He did n't dare to buss me," exclaimed Polly, who was ministering to her grandfather. "Leastways not right out there before you all."

"Please, ma'am, don't you be skeered of Iserl," said Chadwick. "I kin take a quarter of that shote an' tole him plumb back to camp."

"Now I don't like the looks er this," exclaimed Uncle Billy Powers, who had suddenly discovered that Lovejoy, sitting by the side of Danny Lemmons, was bound so that it was impossible for him to eat in any comfort. "Come, boys, this won't do. I don't want to remember the time when any livin' human bein' sot at my table on Christmas day with his han's tied. Come, now!"

"Why, tooby shore!" exclaimed Aunt Crissy. "Turn the poor creetur loose."

"Try it!" cried Colonel Watson, in his shrill voice. "Jest try it!"

"Lord, no," said Danny Lemmons. "Look at his eyes! Look at 'em."

Lovejoy sat pale and unabashed, his eyes glittering like those of a snake. He had refused all offers of food, and seemed to be giving all his attention to Israel Spurlock.

"What does Moseley say?" asked Colonel Watson.

"Ah, he is your prisoner," said Moseley. "He never struck me as a dangerous man."

"Well," said Chadwick, "ef there's any doubt, jest take 'im out in the yard an' give 'im han'-roomance. Don't let 'im turn this table over, 'cause it'll be a long time before some of this company'll see the likes of it ag'in."

It was clear that Lovejoy had no friends, even among his comrades. It was clear, too, that this fact gave him no concern. He undoubtedly had more courage than his position seemed to demand. He sat glaring at Spurlock, and said never a word. Uncle Billy Powers looked at him, and gave him a sigh that ended in a groan.

"Well, boys," said the old man, "this is my house, an' he's at my table. I reckon we better ontie 'im, an' let 'im git a mou'ful ter eat. 'Tain't nothin' but Christian-like."

"Don't you reckon he'd better eat at the second table?" inquired Chadwick. This naïve suggestion provoked laughter and restored good humor, and Colonel Watson consented that Lovejoy should be released. Danny Lemmons undertook this gracious task. He had released Lovejoy's right arm, and was releasing the left, having to use his teeth on one of the knots, when the prisoner seized a fork—a large horn-handle affair, with prongs an inch long—and as quick as a flash of lightning brought it down on Danny Lemmons's back. To those who happened to be looking it seemed that the fork had been plunged into the very vitals of the hunchback.

The latter went down, dragging Lovejoy with him. There was a short, sharp struggle, a heavy thump or two, and then, before the company realized what had happened, Danny Lemmons rose to his feet laughing, leaving Lovejoy lying on the floor, more securely bound than ever.

"I reckon this fork'll have to be washed," said Danny, lifting the formidable-looking weapon from the floor.

There was more excitement after the struggle was over than there had been or could have been while it was going on. Chadwick insisted on examining Danny Lemmons's back.

"I've saw folks cut an' slashed an' stobbed before now," he exclaimed, "an' they did n't know they was hurt tell they had done cooled off. They ain't no holes here an' they ain't no blood, but I could 'most take a right pine-blank oath that I seed 'im job that fork in your back."

"Tut, tut!" said Colonel Watson. "Do you s'pose I raised Danny Lemmons for the like of that?"

"Well," said Chadwick, resuming his seat and his dinner with unruffled nerves, temper, and appetite, "it beats the known worl'. It's the fust time I ever seed a man git down on the floor for to give the in-turn an' the under-cut, an' cut the pigeon-wing an' the double-shuffle, all before a cat could bat her eye. It looks to me that as peart a man as Lemmons there ought to be in the war."

"Ain't he in the war?" cried Colonel Watson, excitedly. "Ain't he forever and eternally in the war? Ain't he my bully bushwacker?"

"On what side?" inquired Chadwick.

"The Union, the Union!" exclaimed the colonel, his voice rising into a scream.

"Well," said Chadwick, "ef you think you kin take the taste out'n this barbecue with talk like that, you are mighty much mistaken."

After the wedding feast was over, Danny Lemmons seized on his fiddle and made music fine enough and lively enough to set the nimble feet of the mountaineers to dancing. So that, take it all in all, the Christmas of the conscript was as jolly as he could have expected it to be.

When the festivities were concluded there was a consultation between Colonel Watson and Danny Lemmons, and then Captain Moseley and his men were told that they were free to go.

"What about Lovejoy?" asked Moseley.

"Oh, bless you! he goes over the mountain," exclaimed Danny, with a grin. "Lord, yes! Right over the mountain."

"Now, I say no," said Polly, blushing. "Turn the man loose an' let him go."

There were protests from some of the mountaineers, but Polly finally had her way. Lovejoy was unbound and permitted to go with the others, who were escorted a piece of the way down the mountain by Spurlock and some of the others. When the mountaineers started back, and before they had got out of sight, Lovejoy seized a musket from one of his men and turned and ran a little way back. What he would have done will never be known, for before he could raise his gun a streak of fire shot forth into his face, and he fell and rolled to the side of the road. An instant later Danny Lemmons leaped from the bushes, flourishing his smoking rifle.

"You see 'im now!" he cried. "You see what he was atter! He'd better have gone over the mountain. Lord, yes! Lots better."

Moseley looked at Chadwick.

"Damn him!" said the latter; "he's got what he's been a-huntin' for."

By this time the little squad of militia-men, demoralized by the incident, had fled down the mountain, and Moseley and his companion hurried after them.

Christmas Gift!

FERROL SAMS

I remember the year of '29, foundation for the mindset of an entire generation about material security. The year was lean and mean. There was no extra gift of clothing or toys under my stocking in '29 and only one Roman candle kept the sky rocket company. With a shrug of acceptance I sat down and forced a leisurely exploration of the stocking. If that was all there was to North Pole joy that morning, it behooved me to prolong it. I examined each piece of candy, speculating on which colored designs went all the way through and which would come off with the first two sucks. I sorted the nuts into neat little piles. I set the firecrackers aside. When I extracted the raisins I pulled two off and ate them, ignoring the clinging lint from the stocking and being careful of the seeds. I knew that if you swallowed a watermelon seed it would sprout and grow inside you. My grandfather had told me that was what had happened to Cuddin John McLean, and although it was absorbing to watch Cuddin John's watch fob jiggle in space while he led the singing on Sunday mornings, I had no desire to wake up some day with clusters of raisins hanging from my nose. There were perils in childhood greater than stepping on cracks.

At the very toe of my stocking was a foreign and unexpected object. On feeling it I imagined a dried biscuit. On delivery to vision it was a watch. A big, fat pocket watch. Like Pa Jim's, Comp's, Uncle Ed's. Like Daddy's. Mine was a shiny silver color, not white or yellow gold, but mine was thicker than any of theirs. Mine had Westclox on the face instead of Waltham or Hamilton, but mine ticked the loudest. Any forlornness vanished in an instant. I was a boy child. Some day I would be a man. Oh, Christmas gift!

Another Christmas morning of which I remember some vivid details was in a more affluent year. It was one of the times that LaLou brought with her from the opulence of Atlanta a gallon of fresh oysters for Auntie to put in the turkey dressing.

"A whole gallon? The menfolks can have some of them to eat with pepper sauce and we'll save some out for a stew. You shouldn't have spent that much, Addie Lou, but we can use them. They sure make the dressing richer. I don't mean to sound like I'm bragging, but the boarders at Woolsey always said my oyster dressing was the best they ever put in their mouths."

That was the Christmas that Santa Claus brought Ellen Jane and me bicycles, and that was the Christmas she and I quit believing in him. We were forced into it.

The protocol of belief was fairly well-defined. For several years a child had conviction. Then came the doubts. Often they were planted by an older child, often a schoolmate, one whose assumptions could be disregarded because for some reason he was usually not doing well in spelling or geography and lived in the academic danger of social promotion. The only thing he was good in was arithmetic. What did he know?

This was about the time that specific questions to parents about the mysteries and abilities of Saint Nicholas underwent drastic reduction in number. No child was obtuse enough to probe so deeply into the matter that all his doubts about the reality of Santa Claus lay bare before mother or father. When knowledge about Santa Claus became too definite to deny, we stood naked in truth. The custom was to gather then around our persons the magic protection of the Emperor's Clothes so that we might remain believers, at least in our parents' eyes. The illusion of innocence was preferable to no innocence at all. Through ages four, five, and six our parents were able to fool us. Through ages eight, nine and even ten, we were able in turn to fool them. I think. Christmas gift!

Of all the cousins, Ellen Jane and I were probably the closest. Certainly we were in age. I played with her and competed with her, but I never pushed too far. She was two weeks younger than I but a good head taller. When goaded too far, she could thrash me. I adored her; affection so often germinates from respect.

She and I shared more than Christmas. In our infancy, home deliveries and breast feedings were the highest and best standards of medical care. No child got a bottle unless he was weasly or had a mother who was delicate. Mothers stayed home out of necessity to be there when babies became hungry, for they were equipped with what my elders called "the dinner jug." The act of nursing was a modest act, one conducted in privacy, certainly out of sight of any menfolk, sometimes beneath a sheltering scarf or napkin. Aunt Ara was Ellen Jane's mama. She was the one who introduced brown eyes into our gene pool and her children consequently differed from the rest of us in appearance.

161

When Ellen Jane and I were babies, Little Daddy and Aunt Ara lived right across the field from us. That was when he still thought he could make a living farming and before he went to work for a road contractor. Our mothers, I was told in lowered voice, both had lots of milk. Certainly both ladies were full of energy and loved to be on the go. They were ideal baby-sitters for each other and their two babies were fed simultaneously, abundantly, and indiscriminately while the freed mother of the moment enjoyed carefree shopping or missionary meetings. The Common Cup. Mother's Day Out.

"You and Ellen Jane mustn't fuss with each other. In some ways she's closer than your sisters."

Auntie's elucidation was explicit but ladylike, although tinged with what I later identified as nulliparous wistfulness. Ambrosia, amalgamation cake and oyster dressing were a matter of perspective. When I became enough of an adult to realize that accomplishments are relative, I loved Auntie unconditionally. At the time I was outraged. My mother would never have shared my pottage which was also my birthright with another child, and that one a girl to boot.

Maybe Auntie was making it up to tease me. I consulted the Oracle of Delphi down at the woodpile. Mr. Jim cut a chew of tobacco so thin that it curled on itself and popped it into his mouth. "Sure, boy, that's the way it was. Y'all were what we call 'titty twins.' It was convenience, not necessity like some folks. Use to in old days, if a mama's milk was thin and the baby weasly, we'd get a colored woman who had lately freshened, one we knew was clean, to help out. Nothing unusual about that. Have to do it with calves now and then to this day, but you have to hold the cow. She'll kick and butt."

I was repelled. As an innocent, unsuspecting baby I had been periodically deserted to feed from an alien breast, to pull at a foreign pap, to fend off starvation the best I could with brown-eyed milk. Worse than that, my inherited bounty had been casually shared with another. Ellen Jane was probably bigger than I was because by some quirk of fate she had always managed to get the richer breast, wherever she happened to be suckling. I accosted my mother with diffidence and a little distrust. She assured me that this had been a happy time, a wonderful arrangement, that it was like having real twins, that there had been plenty to go around. The bond that I forged with Ellen Jane, nevertheless, was always tinged with just the faintest guilt of a secret that, if it was no longer dark, in my judgment should have been. I ate my peas, I gorged on cornbread, but I never caught her in growth. She had too good a head start.

The Christmas that I remember my titty twin most poignantly was the year we were confronted with harsh reality about Santa Claus, that year of the bicycles. Hers was blue and mine was red, and they glistened in the parlor beside our stockings with as much reflecting shine as the ornaments on the tree, so spanking new I felt they would squeak if I touched them. After daylight came and we were out in the yard trying to master them, we fell to assuring each other that Santa Claus did not have to do things exactly the way our ordinary perceptions dictated. My postulate was that a being who was capable of getting down a two-story chimney that had a coal-burning grate at the bottom of it surely had sense enough to unhook the front door and roll a couple of bicycles in, especially if he had just eaten that terrible tasting fruitcake and was full of buttermilk. Ellen Jane mused that perhaps he had brought them unassembled down the chimney in his pack and then put them together in the parlor while we slept. "In a twinkling," she said.

Pete overheard us. He was a year and a half older and at least a decade wiser. He lived in Atlanta.

"You two ninnies quit making up fairy tales and come with me."

He led us behind the barn where he had been potting at Mr. Jim's pigeons with his new air rifle and pointed. Secreted inside a shed, awaiting disposal, stood two cardboard cartons from Sears Roebuck, a picture of a girl's bike on one, of a boy's bike on the other. The papers diagramming their assembly were crumpled and stuffed loosely in the cartons.

"There! Now I guess you'll believe me. I've been knowing for three years but my mama said she'd snatch me bald-headed if I told you two. Besides, my daddy said driving down here he knew he'd be late getting to bed because he'd have to help Comp put y'all's bikes together. Said neither one of your daddies would get it right."

That statement about the daddies smacked of truth even more irrefutably than the empty cartons.

Ellen Jane burst into tears and fled toward the house. I followed her, ineffectual but loyal. We encountered Auntie on the back doorsteps.

"Girl, what are you crying about this time? You've got to quit being so tender-hearted. I declare you traipse around here sometimes like your bladder was behind your eyeballs."

We veered abruptly at a right angle and leaned in the sheltering corner of the east chimney. Ellen Jane hushed.

I borrowed from the wisdom of my grandfather in his assessment of one of our neighbors. "Don't pay any attention to Pete. He'd climb a tree to tell a lie when he could stand on the ground and tell the truth." Ellen Jane hic-cupped, but her soft shining eyes were non-acquiescent.

"Besides," I added staunchly, clinging to the myth for her benefit, "who's to say Sears Roebuck doesn't have a branch store at the North Pole?"

Ellen Jane burst into tears again and I lapsed into silence. Truth is truly naked when it appears explosively, and it can be painful when one is not even afforded the temporary dignity of the Emperor's Clothes.

We Are Looking at You, Agnes

ERSKINE CALDWELL

There must be a way to get it over with. If somebody would only say something about it, instead of looking at me all the time as they do, when I am in the room, there wouldn't be any more days like this one. But no one ever says a word about it. They sit and look at me all the time—like that—but not even Papa says anything.

Why don't they go ahead and say it—why don't they do something—They know it; everyone knows it now. Everybody looks at me like that, but nobody ever says a word about it.

Papa knows perfectly well that I never went to business college with the money he sent me. Why doesn't he say so—He put me on the train and said, Be a good little girl, Agnes. Just before the train left he gave me fifty dollars, and promised me to send me the same amount monthly through October. When I reached Birmingham, I went to a beauty-culture school and learned how to be a manicurist with the money he sent me. Everybody at home thought I was studying shorthand at the business college. They thought I was a stenographer in Birmingham, but I was a manicurist

166

in a three-chair barbershop. It was not long until in some way everybody at home found out what I was doing. Why didn't they tell me then that they knew what I was doing— Why didn't they say something about it—

Ask me, Papa, why I became a manicurist instead of learning to be a stenographer. After you ask me that, I'll tell you why I'm not even a manicurist in a three-chair barbershop any longer. But say something about it. Say you know it; say you know what I do; say anything. Please, for God's sake, don't sit there all day long and look at me like that without saying something about it. Tell me that you have always known it; tell me anything, Papa.

How can you know what I am by sitting there and looking at me—How do you know I'm not a stenographer— How am I different from everybody else in town—

How did you know I went to Nashville—ask me why I went there, then. Say it; please, Papa, say it. Say anything, but don't sit there and look at me like that. I can't stand it another minute. Ask me, and I'll tell you the truth about everything.

I found a job in a barbershop in Nashville. It was even a cheaper place than the one in Birmingham, where the men came in and put their hands down the neck of my dress and squeezed me; it was the cheapest place I had ever heard about. After that I went to Memphis; and worked in a barbershop there awhile. I was never a stenographer. I can't read a single line of shorthand. But I know all about manicuring, if I haven't forgotten it by this time.

After that I went to New Orleans. I wished to work in a fine place like the St. Charles. But they looked at me just like you are doing, and said they didn't need anyone else in the barbershop. They looked at me, just like Mamma is looking at me now, but they didn't say anything about it.

Nobody ever says anything about it, but everybody looks at me like that.

I had to take a job in a cheap barbershop in New Orleans. It was a cheaper place than the one in Memphis, or the one in Nashville. It was near Canal Street, and the men who came in did the same things the men in Birmingham and Nashville and Memphis had done. The men came in and put their hands down in the neck of my dress and squeezed me, and then they sat down and talked to me about things I had never heard of until I went to Birmingham to be a stenographer. The barbers talked to me, too, but nobody ever said anything about it. They knew it; but no one ever said it. I was soon making more money on the outside after hours than I was at the table. That's why I left and went to live in a cheap hotel. The room clerk looked at me like that, too, but he didn't say anything about it. Nobody ever does. Everyone looks at me like that, but there is never a word said about it.

The whole family knows everything I have done since I left home nearly five years ago to attend business college in Birmingham. They sit and look at me, talking about everything else they can think of, but they never ask me what I'm doing for a living. They never ask me what company I work for in Birmingham, and they never ask me how I like stenography. They never mention it. Why don't you ask me about my boss—But you know I don't work for a company. You know everything about me, so why don't you say something to me about it—

If somebody would only say it, I could leave now and never have to come back again once a year at Christmas. I've been back once a year for four years now. You've known all about it for four years, so why don't you say something—Say it, and it then will be all over with.

Please ask me how I like my job in Birmingham, Mamma. Mamma, say, Are your hours too long, Agnes—have you a comfortable apartment—is your salary enough for you—Mamma, say something to me. Ask me something; I'll not tell you a lie. I wish you would ask me something so I could tell you the truth. I've got to tell somebody, anybody. Don't sit there and look at me once a year at Christmas like that. Everyone knows I live in a cheap hotel in New Orleans, and that I'm not a stenographer. I'm not even a manicurist any longer. Ask me what I do for a living, Mamma. Don't sit there and look at me once a year at Christmas like that and not say it.

Why is everyone afraid to say it—I'll not be angry; I'll not even cry. I'll be so glad to get it over with that I'll laugh. Please don't be afraid to say it; please stop looking at me like that once a year at Christmas and go ahead and say it.

Elsie sits all day looking at me without ever asking me if she may come to visit me in Birmingham. Why don't you ask me, Elsie—I'll tell you why you can't. Go ahead and ask if you may visit me in Birmingham. I'll tell you why. Because if you went back with me you'd go to New Orleans and the men would come in and put their hands down the collar of your frock. That's why you can't go back to Birmingham with me. But you do believe I live in Birmingham, don't you, Elsie—Ask me about the city, then. Ask me what street I live on. Ask me if my window in Birmingham faces the east or west, north or south. Say something, Elsie; isn't anyone ever going to ask me something, or say something—

I'm not afraid; I'm a grown woman now. Talk to me as you would to anyone else my age. Just say one little something, and I'll have the chance to tell you. After that I'll leave and never come back again once a year at Christmas.

An hour ago Lewis came home and sat down in the parlor, but he didn't ask me a single question about myself. He didn't say anything. How does he know—Lewis, can you tell just by looking at me, too—Is that how everyone knows—Please tell me what it is about me that everyone knows. And if everyone knows, why doesn't someone say something about it—If you would only say it, Lewis, it would be all over with. I'd never have to come home again once a year at Christmas and be made to sit here and have everyone look at me like that but never saying anything about it.

Lewis sits there on the piano stool looking at me but not saying anything to me. How did you find it out, Lewis— Did someone tell you, or do you just know—I wish you would say something, Lewis. If you will only do that, it will be all over with. I'd never have to come back home once a year at Christmas and sit here like this.

Mamma won't even ask me what my address is. She acts as though I went upstairs and slept a year, coming down once a year at Christmas. Mamma, I've been away from home a whole year. Don't you care to ask me what I've been doing all that time—Go ahead and ask me, Mamma. I'll tell you the truth. I'll tell you the perfect truth about myself.

Doesn't she care about writing to me—doesn't she care about my writing to her—Mamma, don't you want my address so you can write to me and tell me how everyone is—Every time I leave they all stand around and look at me and never ask when I'm coming back again. Why don't they say it—If Mamma would only say it, instead of looking at me like that, it would be better for all of us. I'd never have to come back home again, and they'd never have to sit all day and look at me like that. Why don't you say something to me, Mamma—For God's sake, Mamma, don't sit there all day long and not say a word to me.

Mamma hasn't even asked me if I am thinking of marrying. I heard her ask Elsie that this morning while I was in the bathroom. Elsie is six years younger than me, and Mamma asks Elsie that but she has never asked me since I went to Birmingham five years ago to study shorthand. They don't even tell me about the people I used to know in town. They don't even say good-by when I leave.

If Papa will only say something about it, instead of looking at me like that all the time, I'll get out and stay out forever. I'll never come home again as long as I live, if he will only say it. Why doesn't he ask me if I can find a job for Lewis in Birmingham—Ask me to take him back to Birmingham and look after him to see that he gets along all right from the start, Papa. Ask me that, Papa. Please, Papa, ask me that; ask me something else then, and give me a chance to tell you. Please ask me that and stop sitting there looking at me like that. Don't you care if Lewis has a job—You don't want him to stay here and do nothing, do you—You don't want him to go downtown every night after supper and shoot craps until midnight, do you, Papa—Ask me if I can help Lewis find a job in Birmingham; ask me that, Papa.

I've got to tell somebody about myself. You know already, but I've got to tell you just the same. I've got to tell you so I can leave home and never have to come back once a year at Christmas. I went to Birmingham and took the money to study manicuring. Then I found a job in a barbershop and sat all day long at a little table behind a screen in the rear. A man came in and put his hand down the neck of my dress and squeezed me until I screamed. I went to Nashville, to Memphis, to New Orleans. Every time I sat down at the manicurist's table in the rear of the barber-shop, men came in and put their hands down my dress.

If they would only say something it would be all over with. But they sit and look, and talk about something else all day long. That's the way it's been once a year at Christmas for four or five years. It's been that way ever since I took the money Papa gave me and went to Birmingham to study stenography at the business college. Papa knows I was a manicurist in a barbershop all the time I was there. Papa knows, but Papa won't say it. Say something, Papa. Please say something, so I can tell you what I do for a living. You know it already, and all the others, too; but I can't tell you until you say something about it. Mamma, say something; Lewis, say something. Somebody, anybody, say something.

For God's sake, say something about it this time so I won't have to come back again next year at Christmas and sit here all day in the parlor while you look at me. Everybody looks at me like that, but nobody ever says it. Mamma makes Elsie stay out of the room while I'm dress-ing, and Papa sends Lewis downtown every hour or two. If they would only say something, it would be all over with. But they sit all day long in the parlor, and look at me with-out saying it.

After every meal Mamma takes the dishes I have used and scalds them at the sink. Why don't they say it, so I'll never have to come back—

Papa takes a cloth soaked in alcohol and wipes the chair I've been sitting in every time I get up and leave the room. Why don't they go ahead and say it—

Everyone sits in the parlor and looks at me all day long. Elsie and Lewis, Mamma and Papa, they sit on the other side of the room and look at me all day long. Don't they know I'll tell them the truth if they would only ask me—Ask me,

Papa; I'll tell you the truth, and never come back again. You can throw away your cloth soaked in alcohol after I've gone. So ask me. For God's sake, say something to me about it.

Once a year at Christmas they sit and look at me, but none of them ever says anything about it. They all sit in the parlor saying to themselves, We are looking at you, Agnes.

Healing the Sick

KAREN SCHWIND

The day Earl Thompson got run over by the Rototiller, Jody decided to go to college. He had been pestering her for years to go to Athens to the university so that she could get a degree and maybe teach school, but Jody always snorted at the thought. Instead, she worked days at Rose's Department Store.

Then one day, Earl was in the garden plowing and the tragedy occurred. We aren't sure what happened, but apparently he bent over to snatch a root out of the ground, and he slipped and let go of the Rototiller. Fortunately, Jody, his granddaughter and only living relative, didn't find him. Mr. Barnett did when he came to ask if Earl was going to the Moose Lodge meeting that night.

Tall and big boned the way some tall girls are, Jody had a grace to her that made her look like a willow tree when she walked. Her hair, soft and shiny, seemed to sort of blow back when she moved so that the gold strands glinted in the sun like corn silks, and her clear, white skin and simple cotton dresses told anybody what a farm girl she was.

She sleepwalked through the funeral. I think the doctor must have given her some of that Valium because she looked like a zombie from *Invasion of the Body Snatchers*.

After the funeral, Miss Mays, the postmistress, went to see if there was anything Jody needed. She knocked on the front door, but no one answered, so she went round to the back porch and rattled the screen.

"I come to see if you need any help," she said when Jody came to the screen door.

"No, ma'am. Actually, I am kind of busy," Jody replied.

Miss Mays said it was like a glass of ice water thrown in her face when Jody said she was busy.

When she asked if Jody needed help, Jody said no, that she had packed all she had. That's what we knew until Tom Sanders told Mr. Barnett that he and his family had moved into the Richards place and begun to farm it for Jody.

Turns out she was already in Athens by that time. We hardly saw a thing of her for four years, but what we did see about killed us. The next summer she came back, to check on things, Tom said, and she was wearing black from head to toe. Looked like she lived at a funeral parlor.

The next summer she had her head shaved, and she was still wearing black. Mrs. Patterson said she believed that Jody wore the same thing every day, but I don't know how you could tell.

Later we heard she went to New York and became an artist. My brother-in-law, Jack Baker, said he thought he saw her one day when he was up there on business. (Jack thinks he's Donald Trump because he had to go to New York on business once.) When he said she had her hair dyed purple, we wondered if we would ever see Jody again.

We did, though.

Tom and his family had long since built a house of their own and even bought a few acres, although they still farmed Jody's, too. Jody came back in the winter when the ground was iced over and the rain fell in torrents after heavy gray clouds finally let go. We didn't know for days that she was back. Then late one December day, while Tom cleared stumps out of the pasture, he noticed smoke coming from the chimney.

He said later that he thought a vagabond must have taken up in the house. Tom wasn't going to chase him off, mind you, but he did feel the need to make sure that everything was all right. He did feel some responsibility toward the place.

Stepping quietly through the front door, he craned his neck to see as far down the hall as he could, he said. When he went to step into the house, a large woman in an old gray jacket and overalls came through the kitchen door on the left and glared at him. He would have thought she was a man, but her hair, gray and shaggy, was long enough to hang down her back, so he supposed she was a woman. Still, he never would have recognized her if she hadn't called him by name.

"Tom? Tom?" she said. "How are you, Tom?"

He stayed for a few minutes, long enough to get a list of necessities that she needed, and went back to his tractor. Later he went home and got his truck so he could drive over to Zack's Big Buy.

The rest of us heard about the incident on Sunday. Tom's wife, Vivian, told us. If it had been up to Tom, we still wouldn't know she was over there. Some of the women thought a couple of us from the church should go over and invite her to Christmas pot luck, but the rest of us thought maybe we should wait until she called on us.

In the end, we all decided to wait.

After a respectable time, though, I thought I owed it to Earl and his family, whom I had known for four decades before his death, to go over there and see how Jody was.

I had to park almost down at the road because the spring rains the year before had washed what was left of the old driveway out: deep ruts pitted into red clay packed hard and full of rocks jutting out like the backs of whales. I felt like I walked on water, trying to keep my balance as I stepped between the gullies. The grass on either side of the drive had been allowed to grow high in the summer, and although it was now brown, it stood three feet tall or so. I thought once of trying to walk through it, but since I had on white tennis shoes, I stayed on the drive.

Intimidated by the unfriendly house with its black window-eyes shuttered and door riddled with cracked paint, I thought Jody might not let me in after all these years; but as it turns out, I had not made it to the steps when the door swung open and a shadow zigzagged across the threshold.

"Mrs. Baker?" Even after years in New York, Jody's voice, languid and soft, spoke of the South. I was glad. My heart felt lighter as I hurried a bit so the cold wouldn't take over the house on my account.

I tried not to stare when I walked into the room, bare and scattered with canvas easels. I was grateful that Vivian had warned us.

She was tall, but what once had been a supple, lithe body had become big and chunky, like a man's. She wore overalls and boots that looked like some kind of workman's footwear. Her skin was a sallow white, the once high, shiny cheeks now sagging in folds so that her eyes turned downward at the corners as if they were being pulled by tiny, unseen hands. Around her eyes were fine lines that crossed and recrossed and branched out, mapping the journeys she must have taken after she left McDonough.

I moved into the room to get a better look at the canvases. Large and covered with wide streaks of black and gray and dark blue, they seemed to be metaphorical.

After a brief glance, though, I had to turn around and look at Jody, who stood behind me, waiting. I could feel her waiting.

"Well," I said, feeling like one of those caged birds that chirps too loudly. "What brings you back to these parts? We heard you were an artist in New York City. That must have been so exciting. What brings you back to McDonough?"

"Would you like a cup of tea?" Jody looked at me as if I had become a three-headed Hydra, but her tone remained as polite as ever.

"Yes, please," I croaked, then stood in the middle of the room and waited while she went to the kitchen.

"Oh, sorry." Her voice reached me before I actually saw her. "Sit down anywhere. I don't have real chairs, but I have some stools scattered around. You'll have to sit on one of those."

"Why, thank you, Jody."

"I'll have to see about getting some chairs."

"Well, maybe I could help you with that. I know that John and I have some things up in the attic. When Ben and Caroline went off to college, they robbed us of almost everything they could get their hands on—John got up at five one morning to tie down the dining room table, just in case. But when they graduated and got jobs, they brought some of it back. I'll look to see what's up there tomorrow morning."

"Thank you, Mrs. Baker."

I sat awkwardly on a stool that had one broken leg taped and wobbled every time I tried to take a sip of tea. Staring at the painting nearest me, I tried to think of something to say, but I was fresh out of conversational ideas.

"What brings you back this way, Jody?" I finally managed to ask. I expected her to do what any southern woman would have done—offer some polite pleasantry and leave the truth hanging midair.

Instead she said, "I've come home to be healed."

I nearly fell off the wobbling stool. I had to grab the wall to keep from spilling tea all over myself.

Then I heard myself croak, "Well, that's wonderful, Jody."

She stood still as a lizard, eyes unblinking.

"But what exactly do you mean?" I finally had to ask.

"Three years ago, I found out that I had a lump in my breast. I had it taken out and it turned out to be malignant. I went through all that chemo, Mrs. Baker, and tried herbs and stopped eating dairy products altogether. I had quit eating meat years before, of course."

"Of course," I murmured.

"I thought it was gone," she continued mechanically, as if she had told this same story before, "but early November, I went for my checkup and found that it had returned."

"Oh, dear."

I thought Jody was going to laugh, but she smiled a quick, polite smile and went on: "The cancer had spread rapidly throughout my body. The doctor wanted to give me more chemo, but he said it wouldn't work. I've thought about this for the past several weeks, and I've decided that I want to be cured by faith."

She sat and looked at me as if she expected me to jump up and lay hands on her right then. When I failed to speak, sat there with my mouth open, she shifted on her box and started again, speaking slowly as if to a dull child.

"I want to be healed by faith, Mrs. Baker. People in New York have so little faith, you know. I've thought and thought and finally the answer came to me like writing on the wall: home, the First Baptist Church of McDonough."

"Wh-what can we do, Jody?" I stammered.

"Laying on of hands, Mrs. Baker. I want the women in First Baptist to lay their hands on me." The whole time she talked, she looked me straight in the eye and sort of leaned forward as if she could see better what was on my mind.

I heard myself gasp for breath. Why, she was talking about those people who threw snakes around. We never did that at First Baptist. Even Jerry Duncan never got beyond raising his hands and wriggling his fingers a little. Without real words, I finally told her I could call my prayer group and discuss it. "I'll get back to you," I promised.

I practically ran down that driveway, white shoes or no.

I rang the ladies, had them over to the house where we could have coffee and pound cake. I told them the whole story, including the deer I saw on my drive over. When I finished, they sat and stared at me.

"Do you think she's crazy?" Mary Jane asked at last.

"You know, I heard that some artist went crazy once from smelling paint all day. I bet that's what's happening here," nodded Miss Betty sagely. She was seventy-six and had not been sick a day in her life.

"Are we allowed to do this sort of thing?" I asked. "Isn't it against the rules of the Southern Baptist Convention?" I really wanted to know. That sort of rule could really get us off the hook.

By the time we had eaten and finished our second pot of coffee, we had decided that, rule or no rule, this request would take us dangerously close to acting like Holiness. I was told to decline the offer.

The next day I walked back up that drive, heart pounding, and knocked on the door. Standing in the bright sun,

Jody looked so pallid that she could have been mistaken for a ghost. She leaned on the door to keep from falling. I knew then that she was worse than I first thought.

"Come in," she mumbled, shuffling off to the back bedroom before I could speak. I followed her slowly, holding out my hand so that I might catch her if she fell.

When she was finally in bed, after I lifted her feet onto the old mattress and covered her with a torn blanket, I began to explain how hesitant we ladies were.

Jody lay in her bed, her hair streaming out in all directions from her face, and looked at me with accusing eyes, her breath jerking her body.

"Now, I'm not saying no, mind you, Jody. I didn't say that we weren't going to do it. Of course we will," I lied. "I just wanted to discuss the matter with you first."

"There's nothing to discuss," Jody whimpered. "You have to come and pray for me, Mrs. Baker. Nothing else will do."

I thought the ladies would die when I told them what I had done. None of us was younger than sixty-five. There we sat, five white and grey heads bobbing around like apples as we tried to figure out how one does such a thing.

"I am taking no part in this," Alice Hawkins declared. "Why, this is a sin. I know it is."

"What should we wear?" Miss Betty wanted to know.

"Well," said Mary Jane, ignoring Alice, "I guess it will be a little like goin' to church, so we should wear a nice dress and maybe a hat."

"What if we have to sit on the floor?"

"Her house is none too clean," I interjected, raising my eyebrows so that they would fully understand. "In fact, I think that we should take some sheets and blankets and towels before we actually try anything."

"I think we should take her a little Christmas tree, too," Miss Betty added.

"I think we should wear slacks if we are determined to do this thing," Alice spoke up again. "I think we should wear nice slacks, not jeans."

"I agree," said Mary Jane.

When I told Jody that we were going to do it, she smiled and said, "Thank you, Mrs. Baker. I know that with all the faith you ladies have, I'll be walking around in no time." Then she drifted back off to sleep while I cleaned the house, as much as I could, and put wood in the furnace.

We decided to do it on a Monday night when we had planned to do our last-minute Christmas shopping. That way no one would be suspicious of our being gone so long. We did tell our husbands that we were going to visit Jody first, and we borrowed Walter Hawkins's old four-wheel Chevrolet so we could get up the driveway.

As Alice drove slowly over the drive's ruts, Miss Betty suddenly took in all the air in the cab. "What if we have to go to the bathroom?" she whispered.

"We'll all go before we start," Alice said firmly.

"How long do you think this will take?" Mary Jane asked. "I told my daughter I'd call her tonight if I had time."

"Not long," Alice snorted.

She stopped the truck right in front of the door and got out. We followed behind her like lost sheep, not even knocking when we got to the door. Alice pushed it open and we scurried into the front room.

"Jody?" she shouted.

"Back here."

"Come on," Alice whispered through gritted teeth. "Let's get this over with."

We walked into the room, all of us wearing Belk's slacks with elastic around the waist, our tennis shoes scraping the floor as we shuffled around the bed and looked at Jody lying there, smiling. I noticed she had hung gold garlands across the windows.

"I have to go to the bathroom," whined Miss Betty, a little petulantly.

We trooped to the bathroom, one by one, then returned to stand around the bed.

Finally, Jody said, "Ready when you are," and smiled again. She looked relaxed and happy; we looked like a bunch of old turkeys, our necks stretched out before us.

I had no idea what to do, but then Ellen Watson, the fifth member of our group and the quietest, went to the front room and began to carry stools and boxes to the bedroom. When we each had one, we sat down and held hands.

"No, I think you should put your hands on me," Jody instructed, somewhat impatiently. I think she was disappointed. She had apparently been laboring under the misconception that we did this sort of thing on a regular basis.

We reached out our hands tentatively and placed them on the blanket resting on Jody.

"I think we should take off the blanket," Ellen whispered.

We took off the blanket and laid it carefully on the floor. We put our hands on Jody, all ten of them fluttering like butterflies that wanted to take off.

"Why don't we begin by praying silently?" Alice said as she gave each of us a stern glance.

We bowed our heads and began to pray. Once I opened an eye and glanced around, and I could see the other ladies moving their lips and sort of squinching their eyes shut.

I prayed the Lord's Prayer over and over. After a while, maybe thirty minutes, I began to feel kind of light and I felt myself sway on the stool. I wanted to open my eyes, but I couldn't. I started saying "Jesus, Jesus," over and over, not knowing what else to pray. I could feel Ellen sway against me every few minutes. After what seemed like a long time, I could feel—I don't know how else to explain it—I could feel Ellen rocking back and forth on the cardboard box she sat on.

Then I noticed that the ladies were praying out loud, whispering the name of Jesus over and over. I don't know what they were praying because I was praying too, only I don't know what I was praying either.

Jody lay silently on the bed.

The night moved on and the fire in the stove began to die down. The room grew cold, but no one seemed to mind and I could not open my eyes. I could hear the wind pushing against the windows, rattling one of the panes. I could hardly breathe; I kept hearing the name of Jesus so that it filled me up and seemed to spill over into the room and I felt that he was standing beside me.

When I turned to look, to see if he was there, Jody sat bolt upright in bed and said slowly and distinctly, not screaming, "Forgive me, Lord, for I am a sinner." She lay back down. I felt all of this rather than saw it, for I could not open my eyes.

Then, just as I thought that we would all explode into song, Ellen said, "She's healed."

Everyone stopped praying. We sat, breathing hard. I heard Miss Betty sniffle, then rustle in her pocket for a tissue.

I wanted to open my eyes, but I could not. I sat for what seemed like hours, trying to open my eyes. Finally, I opened them a tiny slit and saw that we had forgotten to turn on any light except the one in the hall. The room was almost dark, moonlight coming in the window and casting a pale glow over us. I could see the other ladies' faces illuminated and thought of the picture of Mary, the mother of Christ, we had put up on the bulletin board for Christmas.

Slowly, we got up and walked around like people who had been sleeping all our lives. Jody slept soundly in the bed, so when we could walk without holding onto something, we stoked the fire and left her there.

The men were getting ready to look for us when we pulled up minutes short of midnight. They thought we were dead or maimed, but we were neither. We never told a soul what happened that Monday night, but Jody Richards came to church that next Sunday, one day before Christmas. She was wearing a red dress that she must have bought in New York, thin and kind of see-through, but I didn't say anything about it except what a nice Christmas dress it was.

"How are you feeling, Jody?" I whispered when we found a second's privacy.

"Good, Mrs. Baker," she replied, smiling. "Real good." I looked around the room, and there we were, a bunch of old ladies standing in front of the crèche, grinning at the empty manger. Someone had taken baby Jesus.

Nativity Scenes

RAYMOND ATKINS

And she brought forth her first-born son,
and wrapped him in swaddling clothes, and laid
him in a manger, because there was no room for
them in the inn.

My family is rough on Christmas paraphernalia. I suppose this is due to the gaiety of the season, the fragility of Yuletide ornamentation, and the destructive tendencies of four children and a double-handful of dogs. My wife, Marsha, thinks that the house we live in is the culprit. We live in a very old and very large house—one of the few that the heathen William Tecumseh Sherman did not burn down on his way through Rome back in 1864, curse his black Yankee heart—and her theory is that something about the twelve-foot ceilings just makes children want to run and holler, slash and burn. And she may be right. Over the years, I have seen many children lose all control upon crossing the threshold. But whatever the reason, we have in our time purchased miles of Christmas lights, boxes of ornaments, several tree-toppers, uncounted Santas, five tree stands, four door wreaths, three French hens, two turtle doves, and a partridge in a pear tree. And, we are one of the major southeastern consumers of nativity scenes.

Our first nativity scene was modest, a low-budget affair purchased at Wal-Mart for $9.95. It contained a combination Mary-and-Joseph, a baby Jesus, a cow, a shepherd, an angel, and just one wise man (we never did learn where Gaspar and Balthasar had gotten to). All of these figurines—manufactured from a priceless Hong Kong glass-like shiny substance—were crouched in a ply-wood stable, looking with adoration at the miracle of the birth of Christ. It was a sweet little set, and it lasted two years.

On the fateful Christmas Eve when our first nativity scene took early retirement, it was sitting on the hall table mind-ing its own business, when in rushed our oldest with some rowdy cousins and wiped it out. Sacred figures flew every-where, the stable became kindling as it struck the wall, and when the damage was tallied, what we had left was a cow with one horn, an angel with no wings, and baby Jesus, miraculously unscathed. We carefully wrapped these rem-nants of the catastrophe and placed them out of harm's way.

The following year, early in the Christmas season, we purchased a replacement nativity scene. This one was a bit nicer than the first, with the members of the ensemble formed in porcelain. The stable was made from small planks and looked like a miniature farm building rather than a three-sided plywood box. Mary and Joseph were separate figures—a vast improvement over the Siamese holy parents of last year's model—and baby Jesus had a lit-tle halo over his head. Additionally, there were *three* wise men, two angels, a shepherd with a lamb on his shoulders, a shepherd with a staff, a camel, and the ubiquitous cow. We set them up on the table in the front hall, warned the children that they were just as breakable as the previous occupants of that table had been, and went on about our decorating business. Later in the evening as I was bound for the front door with the wreath, I noticed that some additional figures had somehow made the pilgrimage to the manger. There, amongst the porcelain majesty of our new nativity members, were a shiny cow with one horn, an injured but still game angel, and the unharmed baby Jesus, tucked in next to his brother. I called my wife out to the hall.

"Mary has had twins," I told her.

"And that angel needs a doctor," she replied. The angel did look like she had seen better millennia.

It turned out that our youngest son, then five, had placed the additional visitors at the stable. It was also apparent that he was resistant to the general idea of ringing out the old and ringing in the new.

"Honey, we have the new Mary and Jesus set," his mama told him. "We'll just keep these other pieces wrapped up as keepsakes." She began to reach for the crippled cow.

"Jesus told me that he wanted out of the box," came the boy's stubborn reply. "He said that Mr. Cow and the angel lady wanted to come too." My wife and I exchanged glances. She raised her eyebrow and I shrugged. Who were we to say? Standing before us could have been the Joan of Arc of northwest Georgia. So the additions became permanent, and they were joined the following year by a small Santa Claus candle, which was slid in two days before Christmas by our three-year-old.

"Santa has come to Bethlehem," I noted to my wife. Santa did not look out of place up in the loft of the stable, exactly, but that little wick sticking out of his head was driving me crazy.

"The baby put him there," she replied. "She said that Santa came to all the good children's houses, and that Jesus was a good baby."

"If this keeps up, we're going to need a bigger table," I pointed out, but Santa stayed—minus the wick, which I snipped off with the wire cutters—and we kept that nativity set for another three years. During that time, the assemblage at the manger grew by six. We gained a stegosaurus (his name was Fred, and young Joan of Arc thought a reptile should be present), Frosty the Snowman (because the baby thought Santa was lonesome for someone from home), the *Star Wars* action figure known as Lando Calrissian (because we did not have any black people in our display), and three small owls (I had quit asking by the time they landed on the stable roof. Maybe they belonged to the wise men).

So, it was a rather eclectic group sitting unsuspectingly on the Hall Table of Doom on that cold night in December of 1995 when I—yes, yours truly—backed in the front door with a large cardboard box full of unassembled bicycle. Before I realized it, I had tripped over the table and fallen upon the nativity scene. The response from my family to this tragedy was immediate and heartwarming.

"This is a mess," said my wife.

"Daddy fell on Jesus!" said the baby, now six.

"I hope you didn't kill Fred," said young Joan of Arc, now nine.

"Dad's in *trou*ble," said the oldest daughter, now twelve.

"Whoa, who's the bike for?" said the oldest son, now thirteen.

"Don't worry about me. I'll probably be okay," I said from the rubble.

Once we cleaned up the mess and lined up the survivors, the incident officially qualified as a disaster of biblical proportions. From the porcelain set, Mary and Joseph were broken beyond repair, as were two of the wise men, the shepherd with the lamb, and one of the angels. The list of the wounded included the camel minus his hump, the other shepherd with a broken staff, a wise man missing his gift (and his hands), the cow less one horn (again), and the other angel, short one halo but proud. And the baby Jesus? We found him unscathed among the carnage.

The following year, right after Thanksgiving, my wife and I went out to buy another replacement nativity scene.

"We ought to get one with the figures made of wood," I suggested.

"So you want the house to burn down?" was her reply.

"Stone?" I asked.

"Earthquake," she responded.

I took her cogent points, and we settled on a set made of the new wonder material, resin. This was our most ambitious set yet, and its *official* members included Mary, Joseph, Jesus, the donkey they rode in on, the three wise men, four angels, three lambs, another cow, two shepherds, and the little drummer boy. They all reside in and around a well-made stable complete with a loft, faux straw on the floor, and a roof that looks like it would actually keep the rain out. But what makes this set really special is its unofficial members, and the roots that spread from that hall table down through the history of my family. Without these, this nativity scene would be just another decoration, just a pile of resin waiting for the next shoe to drop.

So there they all stand for a month each year, immobile, silent reminders of the important components of life—love, family, kindness, acceptance, forgiveness, grace. They are Mary, Joseph, three babes wrapped in swaddling clothes, four wise men, six angels, three shepherds, a little drummer boy, Lando Calrissian, Santa, three cows, three lambs, Fred the stegosaurus, Frosty, the humpless camel, the donkey, and three little owls. Have we finished having nativity incidents? I seriously doubt it. The children are older now but still prone to running down that hall, I am still clumsy, and one day there will be grandchildren to contend with. Will the resin baby Jesus emerge unharmed to join his brothers? I refuse to think otherwise. Will the group in attendance to the Virgin birth continue to grow? I am certain that it will. And I am proud to have raised a family that takes all comers at the manger.

A Holliday Tale

JIM HENDRICKS

Christmas, for many, can be a distraction. A store clerk might find some difficulty focusing on the task at hand, adding up the prices of items a customer has placed before him on the counter while he mentally calculates the various lists his own little ones have written to St. Nick in hopeful anticipation. Thoughts of family getting together, concerns over whether a concealed gift will be spotted before it can be properly wrapped, and the general sights, smells and sounds of the season all combine to make for some formidable disruptions to a person's normal routine.

Frank Holliday, however, was a man of unusual clarity when it came to Christmas. To look at him, you would be certain he was the personification of Father Christmas himself. Pudgy and with a red, cherubic face and reading glasses, the bewhiskered old Southern gentleman certainly looked the part, especially when he wore one of the crimson or emerald jackets that had become a Christmas shopping season tradition for him. He greeted his customers by name and, though he was in his late 50s, continually walked his store from one end to the other and then back again. He covered all the areas—groceries, clothing, toys, hardware. People often said that if you couldn't find what you wanted at the Holliday Store, it likely hadn't been manufactured yet. During his walks, though, Frank Holliday was decidedly oblivious to the decorations, lights and piped-in carols that each year turned his store into a child's fantasy land. Mechanical Santas and snowmen waved to children, model trains chugged the inner perimeter of the huge store on an elevated track, a paunchy old fellow in a red suit and white beard listened intently as kids whispered their fondest wishes for Christmas morning and sales clerks cheerfully helped customers pick out the right shirt, dress or toy that would ensure another successful holiday. In the air were the scents of pine and candies and wonderful baked goods. Simply walking through the store was an experience.

But Frank Holliday experienced none of these sensations.

That's because Frank Holliday was not searching for Christmas cheer. Indeed, he purposely did everything he could to avoid stumbling over it. Christmas to him was business, and business was something that needed constant attention and protection. Protection was exactly what he had in mind this night. Frank Holliday was looking for a person, someone in particular. He'd know the person when he spotted him . . . or her. There'd be a peculiar look, an odd glance, a nervous twitch, something that would be a clear giveaway.

Something, for example, like the way Hunter McRae was acting at this exact moment. McRae, his oily hair slicked back and leathered skin lined with worries, was "bad to drink," as the church ladies delicately described it, and rarely showed his angular, stubbled face in any store that didn't sell whiskey. He was a nice enough fellow when he was sober and was known to be a passable piano player, but there were fewer and fewer sober days, especially since his wife died and left him to raise their three children. Ah, Frank thought, those children. Too early they'd learned the facts about gifts and the North Pole and how things really worked. Sad, Frank thought, but that's what happens when your daddy concerns himself more with quenching his thirst than making you happy on Christmas morning. How old were they now? Frank couldn't remember. He suspected the oldest, a girl, was about 10 or 12, but he wasn't sure. He realized his thoughts were drifting, and his mind quickly snapped back to the task at hand—Hunter McRae, who was easing his way toward a door. Frank had never seen Hunter in his store on Christmas Eve, and he'd certainly never seen Hunter, who was known to go barefoot even in the dead of winter, wear an overcoat.

Once outside the Holliday Store, Hunter McRae stood motionless on the sidewalk, lost in the glow of lighted Christmas garlands hanging from the store and holiday displays in the windows. The cold wind, something he rarely noticed, chilled him right through his heavy coat. He hadn't expected to make it out without getting caught. In fact, he hadn't expected to actually have the nerve to go through with what he'd done. But he couldn't bear the thought of the hurt faces he'd see tomorrow morning when his children awoke. A tear welled in his eye and he involuntarily sniffed as he thought of how his children, his precious little children, had awakened too many Christmas mornings to find nothing. Tomorrow was going to be different, he'd seen to that. Oh, he'd had good intentions all along. He'd tried to put back the money needed to pay for the gifts stuffed under his coat, but the pickup truck had to be fixed and the water heater went out and when he figured he didn't have enough left, well, he just went ahead and drank the rest of it . . . for courage.

Funny, he thought as he walked slowly toward his old pickup. He'd pulled it off, but he didn't feel particularly courageous. In fact, he felt a little sick. He'd done some low things over the years, but he'd never out and out stolen anything. Not 'til tonight.

As sick as he felt, however, it was nothing compared to the fiery pang that ripped through his stomach when he felt a hand firmly grasp his left shoulder. He turned slowly and managed a weak smile. "Uh," he said, "h-h-hello, Mr. Holliday. Uh, I mean, good evenin'. Nice evenin', ain't it?"

"I don't know, Hunter," Holliday said, his feigned gaiety vanished. Even in the crisp night air, he was assaulted with heavy whiffs of sale tobacco and bourbon. "I saw you in my store. Kinda odd for a fellow to shop in my store on Christmas Eve and not buy anything at all, not even candy for a stocking. Most folks . . . pick up a little something."

"Well," McRae said, swallowing hard and suddenly feeling flushed and sweaty, "I . . . I didn't really need nothin'. Now, I . . . I really gotta get home. Be seein' you, Mr. Holliday."

McRae turned . . . and bumped into Sheriff Miles Fielding. The sheriff wasn't smiling either.

A short time later, Holliday and Fielding were sitting in the sheriff's office in the red brick courthouse. The only office still open, it was furnished with a gas space heater, a couple of desks, some chairs and a small, plastic Christmas tree on a table near where the sheriff sat. On the walls were assorted notices and posters, many yellowed with age. From a large framed photo, a young Sheriff Miles Fielding, all serious-looking in a khaki uniform, glared out, an obvious warning to troublemakers who might want to cause problems in his county. Near the Christmas tree, a coffee maker permeated the air with a hot aroma that bravely sparred with the smells of Fielding's Lucky Strikes and Old Spice aftershave. Across the street in a concrete and iron building encircled by a high chain-link fence topped with razor wire, a jailer named Chet was processing Hunter McRae on charges of shoplifting. Fielding had on his desk—amid scattered papers, files, lamp, phone and a police radio— the incriminating evidence . . . a baseball and glove, a girl's dress and a chess set. The sheriff leaned back in his chair, which squeaked its protest, drew on his cigarette and ran his fingers through his graying, wavy hair. "Care for some coffee, Frank?" he asked in an exhale of smoke as he reached for the pot by his desk and poured himself a cup.

"No, thanks, Miles," Holliday said. "Gotta get back to my store. Now, you're saying I can't take my merchandise back with me?"

"Evidence, Frank. You'll get it back. 'Course, you could get it back right now if you didn't press charges."

Frank's already ruddy complexion burned scarlet. "Sheriff, I can't believe you'd even suggest such a thing! I got a business to protect. If I let people steal me blind, then I go outa business and if I go out of business, other folks lose their livelihoods, too."

"I know, I know," the sheriff said, stirring some creamer in his coffee. "But it's just ol' Hunter. He was just trying to get his younguns something for Chri . . . ."

"Then he can buy it like anybody else, or get help from the welfare folks. There's places that help people like Hunter McRae and his family. I can't run a charity for every sot that swills away the holidays!"

"I know," the sheriff said, motioning for Holliday to calm down. "You're right, Frank. But what's all this stuff worth, about $120, $130? Seems a pity to lock a daddy up on Christmas Eve over such . . ."

"Miles, you don't know a dadblamed thing about business. It all adds up. I lose $130 here, $50 there and pretty soon I'm out on the street myself. If he's so worried about being a daddy, he ought to be actin' like one instead of drinkin' away his money like a dang fool. My policy is clearly posted all over the store. I prosecute thieves. All thieves. That is a firm policy and it's a fair policy. I treat everybody the same. Hunter McRae is a thief, Christmas Eve or no Christmas Eve. Now, if you'll excuse me, I gotta get back to my store. Might be another sticky-finger out there before we close up." He slammed the door on the way out.

He drove the couple of blocks back to his store, which continued to bustle with last-minute buyers. Frank was still fuming as he pulled into the parking spot out front that bore his name. The very idea of that sheriff, he thought as he locked his car and walked toward the store. Drop the charges, indeed! You catch a common thief red-handed as he's trying to steal food out of your mouth, and the very man who was elected by the people and entrusted with the sacred duty of putting criminals behind bars was suggesting that you let the rascal go scot-free. Well, I ought to . . .

His thought stopped right about there, mostly because he had bumped into a customer coming out of his store. "Excuse me," Frank said, "I didn't . . ."

He didn't finish what he was saying. He looked at the man he'd bumped into, an older fellow, shabbily dressed in a manner that couldn't hope to thwart a winter wind and emitting what could only charitably be described as a distinctly unappealing stench. The man, his chin speckled with graying stubble, looked down and looked back at Frank, who then looked down. Several cans of food had fallen from beneath the stranger's jacket. "You just stand right there," Frank said, holding the man by the arm as he leaned his head toward the store. "Joyce, call Fielding and tell him to get right over here! I caught another one!"

Back in the sheriff's office, Holliday decided to take the lawman up on his second offer of coffee. It was an awfully cold night, at least by south Georgia standards, and Frank, who was feeling unusually cold, needed a little warming up. "You need anything else from me, Miles?"

"Nope," the sheriff said. "I think we've about got it. You know, Frank, if you ever decide to retire from the business world, I could find a place for you so you wouldn't get too bored. You sure seem to have a knack for spotting crooks."

Frank took a sip of coffee from the plastic foam cup and checked his statement through his reading glasses one last time. "Think I'll pass," he said with a chuckle as he handed the papers back to Fielding. "I'm way too old for all that. Let me guess . . . those cans of food are evidence?"

"You expecting a run on Spam tonight, are ya?" Fielding asked, smiling.

"You never can tell," Holliday responded. "Well, it's getting close to closing time. Maybe I can lock my store up before another shoplifter shows up. By the way, who was that feller? I've never seen him 'round here before."

"Ain't sure," Fielding said. "Drifter, I guess. All he's told us is his name is Luke. Won't say where he's from or nothing. We took fingerprints, so we should get him identified sooner or later." The phone rang. The sheriff mumbled into it, then covered the mouthpiece with his hand. "Frank," he said, "that guy you caught . . . Luke . . . he wants to talk to you."

Holliday started to decline. There was, in fact, no reason for him not to decline. Later, when he would rethink the events of the night, he would say his curiosity had merely gotten the best of him. But the truth is, Frank could never quite put his finger on the exact reason why he called his employees and told them to start preparing to close, saying he'd be there before time to lock the doors. He made that call, however, and then he walked across the street to the jail, where Chet, the deputy, led him to the area where—except for the main door he passed through and a fire escape door at the other end—stark, recessed overhead lights and six doors with black, steel bars were the only breaks in the grim hallway of grayish concrete. "I'll be right outside if you need me," Chet said, closing the door behind him.

Luke walked up to the bars in the second cell. He was stooped a bit as he walked, his eyes toward the floor, partially covered by long, stringy locks of brown and gray hair. He took a deep breath and looked up, catching Frank with his eyes. His tattered clothes hung loosely. "I just wanted you to know, sir, that I'm terribly sorry for stealing from you," Luke said. "Hunger's a powerful strong thing, makes a man do things he'd never think 'bout doing otherwise."

"Maybe so," Holliday said, "I guess I just ain't ever been that hungry, not hungry enough to steal from honest folks. Is that what you wanted to tell me?"

"No, sir," the old man said. "I done what I done and I'm willing to deal with what comes next. But this feller in this cell next to me, this Mr. Hunter. I'm a little worried about his younguns."

Frank looked at the adjacent cell where Hunter McRae lay under a thin, blue blanket on a hard, wooden cot. Apparently passed out from his drinking, his snores and snorts rattled around. "What about them?" Frank said.

"Jus' 'fore he went to sleep," the stranger said, "he said he stole some clothes and toys so they'd have presents for Christmas morning."

"Well, if they're his children I'm sure they're used to disappointment," Frank observed. "I'm disappointed when two people try to steal from me on Christmas Eve of all days!"

"I don' blame you, sir, don' blame you a bit for feelin' thataway. I was jus' wond'rin' though, Mr. Holliday. Was you always rich?"

"No," Frank said, his arms behind his back as pride filled him. "My family worked hard just to make ends meet. I worked my way through college, then I came back and opened my store. There were a lot of times when I was on the brink of disaster, but I managed to get by. And today, I'm the most successful businessman in town, all because I stayed focused and persevered."

"That's great, jus' great." Luke said, looking Frank up and down. "Just outa curiosity, Mr. Holliday, how come you never got married?"

"How did you know I was never married?"

"Oh," Luke said, "just a guess. Didn't see no weddin' ring. Guess you jus' didn't have no time for somebody else, what with makin' your store a big success an' all."

"Something like that," Holliday said. "Is that what you asked me over here for, to delve into my personal history? I'm a busy man and I have lots of things to do tonight."

"No, sir," Luke said. "I know it don' excuse nuthin', but I wanted to face the man I stole from and tell him I'm sorry as I can be. It don' change nothin', but I couldn't bear goin' to my grave knowin' I hadn't at least tried to make it right. I'm alone here, too, Mr. Holliday. You know, bein' alone can be awful hard on a man, keeps him from seein' things real clear. You jus' worry 'bout yourself and what you want and you don't see nuthin' 'cept what's right there in front of you. You forget 'bout everybody and ever'thin' else. An' you jus' don' think 'bout what yore doin' is gonna do to them."

"An' I suppose that can make a man steal from a honest businessman?" Holliday asked.

"Oh, it can do a heap worse'n that," Luke said. "It can even make you forget about the teachin's of the feller whose birthday's comin' up tomorrow."

"Perhaps so," Holliday said. "Your apology is noted . . . Mr. Luke. I'm sorry I cannot help you further, but my store's policy is to prosecute shoplifters—all shoplifters—so, you see, my hands are tied."

"I understan', Mr. Holliday. I wouldn't want you to break no policy on my account. What I done was wrong and I'm willin' to face what I gotta face now. But could I jus' ask you one more thing?"

Holliday had already turned toward the steel door at the end of the hallway, but stopped. He turned his head over his shoulder, giving Luke little more than a glance out of the corner of his eye. "Yes, Mr. Luke. Please. By all means, please ask me your final question."

"I only been in this town a few days, but talkin' to Hunter here a while ago, it sounds like you hafta go right by his place to get to yours."

"And your point is . . . ?" Frank inquired.

"I'm jus' curious," Luke said. "Didya ever notice it when you rode by?"

Frank did not answer.

Later that night, Holliday had closed up, wished his employees a happy Christmas and was driving home. He hadn't been able to get the old guy, Luke, out of his mind. It was almost like he was some kind of hobo philosopher. And his words, no matter how badly they mangled the language, were strangely compelling. Holliday had always been proud of his ability to shut out those things that diverted him from his well mapped goals, but tonight he caught himself doing something he'd never done before. He wasn't going straight home. Caught up in his thoughts, he was somewhat shocked to find he was actually driving around town, taking in, perhaps for the first time ever, the lighted displays townsfolk had on their homes and lawns. Many of the displays had been purchased from his store, he happily noted. Even the smallest and most modest of homes had at least a lighted tree, proudly shining from a front window for passersby to see. Some homes had more cars than parking space, with happy sounds slipping somewhat muffled, but thoroughly genuine, through the walls and windows, indications that family and friends were together for an evening of celebration. He felt the weak tug of a memory, one from the distant past when Frank Holliday decorated his store mostly to bring joy to shoppers. Now, it was simply a mindless tradition designed to put people in a frame of mind to spend money.

He stopped at an intersection and watched another happy couple, arm in arm, walk to a house, where they were warmly greeted and beckoned in by another young couple. For the first time in many, many years, Frank Holliday felt envy. And he felt terribly alone.

When he decided he'd seen most of what there was to see, Holliday returned to his normal route home.

The stranger's words continued to resound in his head, especially when he passed Hunter McRae's home, a clapboard shack that was dark and cold. Holliday thought about the three children in there and grew angry. How could their father let them down like this? he asked himself. Hunter is a no-good thief and a sorry, sorry excuse for a father. If I'd ever had children, Holliday affirmed to himself, they'd never have gone wanting like those three. Never!

As he pulled into his driveway, it occurred to Holliday that his own house might well be the only one in town that was as dark and as cold in appearance as McRae's. He'd never strung Christmas lights up outside, and he'd quit decorating a tree years ago. It was a waste of resources. Christmas didn't mean much to a single man who had no one to share it with, he'd decided. And that was when the thought, a peculiar one for him that deftly slipped past his usual mental barriers that held such thoughts in check, suddenly struck him. Luke had told him hunger was a powerful force, one that could make a man do things he'd never do otherwise. Frank was suddenly aware, and more suddenly concerned, that the old fellow hadn't had a chance to eat any of the canned food he'd stolen from the store. Frank also was pretty sure the man had been jailed well after the evening meal was served there. The image of the old man standing weakly, his old clothes hanging so loosely from his dirty, gaunt body was indelibly engraved in Frank's brain. Oddly, he found himself concerned, even worried, that Luke, who was hungry enough to steal, had missed supper . . . and here it was nearly Christmas. He thought about an old Sunday school lesson he'd learned as a child . . . but forgotten as an adult. He couldn't remember the exact words, but it went along the lines that anybody should be able to be kind to his friends, but it was a special person who could be kind to someone who had treated him badly.

Holliday unlocked his back door and went straight into his kitchen. In the refrigerator, he found some beef stew his housekeeper had made for him. He took it out and reached for his red jacket.

On the way back to the jail, he again passed by the McRae house. Still dark, still cold, so silent. Children should be playing, dancing around a Christmas tree and jabbering endlessly about a pending visit from Santa Claus, he thought. And those gifts, the ones McRae tried to steal. What were they? A dress, a ball and glove . . . and a chess set? Hunter McRae, the town drunk, had a child who knew how to play chess? Frank thought hard about that one. He'd been quite a chess player himself in high school, a member of the chess club, in fact. It'd been years since he'd played. Years.

When he arrived at the jail, he saw instantly something was wrong. Instead of the night air being illuminated by the soft glow of the town's Christmas lights, there were piercing, bright flashes of red, making it difficult to see clearly what was happening. As he got closer, he saw the ambulance parked outside the jail compound. And he could see paramedics loading a covered gurney into the orange and white vehicle. Holliday could make out the form of a body under the sheet. He leaped from his car and ran up to the sheriff, who stood by puffing on a cigarette as the paramedics worked.

"My God, Miles, what happened?" he asked.

"Looks like one o' your cases got solved real quick like," Fielding said, taking a drag from his cigarette. The smoke mixed with the usual vapor that wisps from the mouth on cold nights when he spoke. "That's the old feller, Luke."

"He died?" Frank couldn't believe it, and he grasped even more tightly the plastic bowl containing the stew. "How? When? What happened?"

"Probably just natural causes," the sheriff said. "He was old, didn't weigh much more'n my Lab Shelby. Looks like he just didn't take care of himself. Least he went peacefully. Don't look like he suffered none at all. Chet said Hunter'd woke up and him and Luke was back there in the cells talking. Hunter was all cryin' over how he'd messed up again and his children were alone and cold and probably ain't had no supper—you know how Hunter gets when he comes down offa one o' his drunks. Chet said Luke told Hunter to calm down, said he was pretty sure everything'd work out all right. They got to talkin' about Christmas and Jesus and Chet said they even went to singing Christmas songs. Musta been quite a duet, them two croonin', don'tcha think? Then, the old guy just quit singing, Hunter went to hollerin' something was wrong, Chet called the ambulance and, well, here we are."

"What happens now?" Holliday asked.

"Luke's headin' to the hospital morgue," Fielding said. "I reckon he'll end up in a pauper's grave. And, if what Chet heard Hunter saying's the truth, his kids have got to be just about freezin' out there in his ol' shack. I guess I'm gonna have to call welfare and get them to go out and do something with them. Gonna be a downright lousy Christmas for them poor younguns," Fielding said.

Holliday watched as the ambulance pulled away. Funny, he thought, it's not heading toward the hospital. Guess the driver's got something to see about on the way. After all, Luke sure wasn't in a hurry now.

Frank looked down, deep in thought. He kicked a pebble or two as he tried to make some sense of it. He'd wanted to help that old man, but he was too late. He kicked another pebble, and something he hadn't remembered for decades unexpectedly worked its way to the front of his mind. He noticed what he was doing—kicking a pebble—and remembered a kicking game he used to play at recess, back when he was a child, when times were hard, but he still had his family and his friends. He got through some mighty tough times thanks to those family and friends, mighty rough ones.

He looked up, turned sharply and headed toward the sheriff's office.

"You know, Miles, sometimes you just don't stop and look around," he said, blustering through the door.

Miles, who had picked up the phone and was about to make a call regarding the McRae children, was dumbfounded. "You OK, Frank?" he asked, pulling the receiver from his ear. "You sound kinda funny."

"Maybe so, Miles," Holliday said. "But tell me, is it wrong to want to stop and smell the roses every now and then? Is it wrong to not want to spend Christmas Day alone? Is it wrong to play one more game of chess?"

"Not wrong, but I have to say that comin' from you it sounds a little nutty," Fielding said tentatively.

"If that's so, my friend," Frank said, "then what I'm fixing to say is probably gonna get me sent right to the crazy house. But I'm gonna do it anyway. After all, it's Christmas Eve and everybody knows that old fat men in red jackets have important business to take care of on Christmas Eve. Now, here's what I need you to do . . ."

Some time later, twelve-year old Nancy McRae awakened in her cold, dark bedroom with a start. She heard a noise. Was it daddy? When he hadn't made it home by dark, she figured he'd gotten into some kind of trouble up town. He'd been acting funny for a couple of days, like he did when he was on his binges and was about to get fired from his job or something else bad was about to happen. She pulled the covers tighter around her neck to fight the chilly night air. She could see a shadow through her door, created by a dim light and cast against the living room wall . . . but it wasn't shaped exactly right. Then she saw the person making the shadow approach her bedroom door. He was too wide to be her daddy, and he was dressed in a red coat! As he walked up to her bed, she uttered the only word that made any sense.

"Santa?"

Frank Holliday's heart, for the first time in decades, melted a little bit. "No, child," he said, stroking her hair. "I'm not Santa. Not by a long shot. I'm Frank Holliday. And guess what! I've just tonight discovered something rather amazing. I discovered my house is simply too big for just one person. So, I was hoping you could help me. I've invited your father and your brothers to visit with me a while. Would you like to come, too?"

"Is your house warm?" Nancy asked.

"I believe," Frank said, "that when you get there, it will be warmer than it ever has been."

About two o'clock Christmas morning, the McRaes were asleep in the upstairs bedrooms. Frank, however, couldn't settle down. His mind was racing along paths that had long been dormant. He'd promised McRae a job, but only if he'd get help for his alcohol addiction. Clearly it was too early to tell how that was going to work out, but Frank chose to be optimistic. At the very least, he was giving the man a chance to succeed.

He chuckled when he thought of how eager his employees had been to give up some of their own Christmas Eve activities to go to the store and pick up gifts for the McRae children. And when he remarked that Christmas gifts were out of place without a tree over them, they went back to the store and got one—then stayed and helped him trim it! The only payment they would accept was homemade hot chocolate that Nancy—little Nancy!—made with great skill.

Frank knew he'd missed the chance to help a poor stranger, but maybe he could make it up by helping this struggling family that had lived so close by, yet so far away from him. He turned out the lights in the living room, except for those on the tree, and, under its warm glow, felt more at peace than he had in years. He relaxed in his chair, sipped on the last of the hot chocolate and smiled. He was expecting a fine chess game in the morning. Yes, it would be a mighty fine chess game.

As Frank Holliday sat with a renewed spirit and four tired souls slept soundly, knowing tomorrow would bring, for the first time in their memory, hope with its sunlight, an elderly man in a shabby jacket peered undetected through Frank's living room window and smiled. Then he gently whispered a prayer and melted away into air that could only be described as magical.

Gone With the Wind

MARGARET MITCHELL

CHAPTER FIFTEEN

The army, driven back into Virginia, went into winter quarters on the Rapidan—a tired, depleted army since the defeat at Gettysburg—and as the Christmas season approached, Ashley came home on furlough. Scarlett, seeing him for the first time in more than two years, was frightened by the violence of her feelings. When she had stood in the parlor at Twelve Oaks and seen him married to Melanie, she had thought she could never love him with a more heartbreaking intensity than she did at that moment. But now she knew her feelings of that long-past night were those of a spoiled child thwarted of a toy. Now, her emotions were sharpened by her long dreams of him, heightened by the repression she had been forced to put on her tongue.

This Ashley Wilkes in his faded, patched uniform, his blond hair bleached tow by summer suns, was a different man from the easy-going, drowsy-eyed boy she had loved to desperation before the war. And he was a thousand times more thrilling. He was bronzed and lean now, where he had once been fair and slender, and the long golden mustache drooping about his mouth, cavalry style, was the last touch needed to make him the perfect picture of a soldier.

He stood with military straightness in his old uniform, his pistol in its worn holster, his battered scabbard smartly slapping his high boots, his tarnished spurs dully gleaming— Major Ashley Wilkes, C.S.A. The habit of command sat upon him now, a quiet air of self-reliance and authority, and grim lines were beginning to emerge about his mouth. There was something new and strange about the square set of his shoulders and the cool bright gleam of his eyes. Where he had once been lounging and indolent, he was now as alert as a prowling cat, with the tense alertness of one whose nerves are perpetually drawn as tight as the strings of a violin. In his eyes, there was a fagged, haunted look, and the sunburned skin was tight across the fine bones of his face—her same handsome Ashley, yet so very different.

Scarlett had made her plans to spend Christmas at Tara, but after Ashley's telegram came no power on earth, not even a direct command from the disappointed Ellen, could drag her away from Atlanta. Had Ashley intended going to Twelve Oaks, she would have hastened to Tara to be near him; but he had written his family to join him in Atlanta, and Mr. Wilkes and Honey and India were already in town. Go home to Tara and miss seeing him, after two long years? Miss the heart-quickening sound of his voice, miss reading in his eyes that he had not forgotten her? Never! Not for all the mothers in the world.

Ashley came home four days before Christmas, with a group of the County boys also on furlough, a sadly diminished group since Gettysburg. Cade Calvert was among them, a thin, gaunt Cade, who coughed continually, two of the Munroe boys, bubbling with the excitement of their first leave since 1861, and Alex and Tony Fontaine, splendidly drunk, boisterous and quarrelsome. The group had two hours to wait between trains and, as it was taxing the diplomacy of the sober members of the party to keep the Fontaines from fighting each other and perfect strangers in the depot, Ashley brought them all home to Aunt Pittypat's.

"You'd think they'd had enough fighting in Virginia," said Cade bitterly, as he watched the two bristle like gamecocks over who should be the first to kiss the fluttering and flattered Aunt Pitty. "But no. They've been drunk and picking fights ever since we got to Richmond. The provost guard took them up there and if it hadn't been for Ashley's slick tongue, they'd have spent Christmas in jail."

But Scarlett hardly heard a word he said, so enraptured was she at being in the same room with Ashley again. How could she have thought during these two years that other men were nice or handsome or exciting? How could she have even endured hearing them make love to her when Ashley was in the world? He was home again, separated from her only by the width of the parlor rug, and it took all her strength not to dissolve in happy tears every time she looked at him sitting there on the sofa with Melly on one side and India on the other and Honey hanging over his shoulder. If only she had the right to sit there beside him, her arm through his! If only she could pat his sleeve every few minutes to make sure he was really there, hold his hand and use his handkerchief to wipe away her tears of joy. For Melanie was doing all these things, unashamedly. Too happy to be shy and reserved, she hung on her husband's arm and adored him openly with her eyes, with her smiles, her tears. And Scarlett was too happy to resent this, too glad to be jealous. Ashley was home at last!

Now and then she put her hand up to her cheek where he had kissed her and felt again the thrill of his lips and smiled at him. He had not kissed her first, of course. Melly had hurled herself into his arms, crying incoherently, holding him as though she would never let him go. And then, India and Honey had hugged him, fairly tearing him from Melanie's arms. Then he had kissed his father, with a dignified affectionate embrace that showed the strong quiet feeling that lay between them. And then Aunt Pitty, who was jumping up and down on her inadequate little feet with excitement. Finally he turned to her, surrounded by all the boys who were claiming their kisses, and said: "Oh, Scarlett! You pretty, pretty thing!" and kissed her on the cheek.

With that kiss, everything she had intended to say in welcome took wings. Not until hours later did she recall that he had not kissed her on the lips. Then she wondered feverishly if he would have done it had she met him alone, bending his tall body over hers, pulling her up on tiptoe, holding her for a long, long time. And because it made her happy to think so, she believed that he would. But there would be time for all things, a whole week! Surely she could maneuver to get him alone and say: "Do you remember those rides we used to take down our secret bridle paths?" "Do you remember how the moon looked that night when we sat on the steps at Tara and you quoted that poem?" (Good Heavens! What was the name of that poem, anyway?) "Do you remember that afternoon when I sprained my ankle and you carried me home in your arms in the twilight?"

Oh, there were so many things she would preface with "Do you remember?" So many dear memories that would bring back to him those lovely days when they roamed the County like care-free children, so many things that would call to mind the days before Melanie Hamilton entered on the scene. And while they talked she could perhaps read in his eyes some quickening of emotion, some hint that behind the barrier of husbandly affection for Melanie he still cared, cared as passionately as on the day of the barbecue when he burst forth with the truth. It did not occur to her to plan just what they would do if Ashley should declare his love for her in unmistakable words. It would be enough to know that he did care. . . . Yes, she could wait, could let Melanie have her happy hour of squeezing his arm and crying. Her time would come. After all, what did a girl like Melanie know of love?

"Darling, you look like a ragamuffin," said Melanie when the first excitement of homecoming was over. "Who did mend your uniform and why did they use blue patches?"

"I thought I looked perfectly dashing," said Ashley, considering his appearance. "Just compare me with those ragtags over there and you'll appreciate me more. Mose mended the uniform and I thought he did very well, considering that he'd never had a needle in his hand before the war. About the blue cloth, when it comes to a choice between having holes in your britches or patching them with pieces of a captured Yankee uniform—well, there just isn't any choice. And as for looking like a ragamuffin, you should thank your stars your husband didn't come home barefooted. Last week my old boots wore completely out, and I would have come home with sack tied on my feet if we hadn't had the good luck to shoot two Yankee scouts. The boots of one of them fitted me perfectly."

He stretched out his long legs in their scarred high boots for them to admire.

"And the boots of the other scout didn't fit me," said Cade. "They're two sizes too small and they're killing me this minute. But I'm going home in style just the same."

"And the selfish swine won't give them to either of us," said Tony. "And they'd fit our small, aristocratic Fontaine feet perfectly. Hell's afire, I'm ashamed to face Mother in these brogans. Before the war she wouldn't have let one of our darkies wear them."

"Don't worry," said Alex, eyeing Cade's boots. "We'll take them off of him on the train going home. I don't mind facing Mother but I'm da—I mean I don't intend for Dimity Munroe to see my toes sticking out."

"Why, they're my boots. I claimed them first," said Tony, beginning to scowl at his brother; and Melanie, fluttering with fear at the possibility of one of the famous Fontaine quarrels, interposed and made peace.

"I had a full beard to show you girls," said Ashley, ruefully rubbing his face where half-healed razor nicks showed. "It was a beautiful beard and if I do say it myself, neither Jeb Stuart nor Nathan Bedford Forrest had a handsomer one. But when we got to Richmond, those two scoundrels," indicating the Fontaines, "decided that as they were shaving their beards, mine should come off too. They got me down and shaved me, and it's a wonder my head didn't come off along with the beard. It was only by the intervention of Evan and Cade that my mustache was saved."

"Snakes, Mrs. Wilkes! You ought to thank me. You'd never have recognized him and wouldn't have let him in the door," said Alex. "We did it to show our appreciation of his talking the provost guard out of putting us in jail. If you say the word, we'll take the mustache off for you, right now."

"Oh, no, thank you!" said Melanie hastily, clutching Ashley in a frightened way, for the two swarthy little men looked capable of any violence. "I think it's perfectly lovely."

"That's love," said the Fontaines, nodding gravely at each other.

When Ashley went into the cold to see the boys off to the depot in Aunt Pitty's carriage, Melanie caught Scarlett's arm.

"Isn't his uniform dreadful? Won't my coat be a surprise? Oh, if I only had enough cloth for britches too!"

That coat for Ashley was a sore subject with Scarlett, for she wished so ardently that she and not Melanie were bestowing it as a Christmas gift. Gray wool for uniforms was now almost literally more priceless than rubies, and Ashley was wearing the familiar homespun. Even butternut was now none too plentiful, and many of the soldiers were dressed in captured Yankee uniforms which had been turned a dark-brown color with walnut-shell dye. But Melanie, by rare luck, had come into possession of enough gray broadcloth to make a coat—a rather short coat but a coat just the same. She had nursed a Charleston boy in the hospital and when he died had clipped a lock of his hair and sent it to his mother, along with the scant contents of his pockets and a comforting account of his last hours which made no mention of the torment in which he died. A correspondence had sprung up between them and, learning that Melanie had a husband at the front, the mother had sent her the length of gray cloth and brass buttons which she had bought for her dead son. It was a beautiful piece of material, thick and warm and with a dull sheen to it, undoubtedly blockade goods and undoubtedly very expensive. It was now in the hands of the tailor and Melanie was hurrying him to have it ready by Christmas morning. Scarlett would have given anything to be able to provide the rest of the uniform, but the necessary materials were simply not to be had in Atlanta.

She had a Christmas present for Ashley, but it paled in insignificance beside the glory of Melanie's gray coat. It was a small "housewife," made of flannel, containing the whole precious pack of needles Rhett had brought her from Nassau, three of her linen handkerchiefs, obtained from the same source, two spools of thread and a small pair of scissors. But she wanted to give him something more personal, something a wife could give a husband, a shirt, a pair of gauntlets, a hat. Oh, yes, a hat by all means. That little flat-topped forage cap Ashley was wearing looked ridiculous. Scarlett had always hated them. What if Stonewall Jackson had worn one in preference to a slouch felt? That didn't make them any more dignified looking. But the only hats obtainable in Atlanta were crudely made wool hats, and they were tackier than the monkey-hat forage caps.

When she thought of hats, she thought of Rhett Butler. He had so many hats, wide Panamas for summer, tall beavers for formal occasions, hunting hats, slouch hats of tan and black and blue. What need had he for so many when her darling Ashley rode in the rain with moisture dripping down his collar from the back of his cap?

"I'll make Rhett give me that new black felt of his," she decided. "And I'll put a gray ribbon around the brim and sew Ashley's wreath on it and it will look lovely."

She paused and thought it might be difficult to get the hat without some explanation. She simply could not tell Rhett she wanted it for Ashley. He would raise his brows in that nasty way he always had when she even mentioned Ashley's name and, like as not, would refuse to give her the hat. Well, she'd make up some pitiful story about a soldier in the hospital who needed it and Rhett need never know the truth.

All that afternoon, she maneuvered to be alone with Ashley, even for a few minutes, but Melanie was beside him constantly, and India and Honey, their pale, lashless eyes glowing, followed him about the house. Even John Wilkes, visibly proud of his son, had no opportunity for quiet conversation with him.

It was the same at supper where they all plied him with questions about the war. The war! Who cared about the war? Scarlett didn't think Ashley cared very much for that subject either. He talked at length, laughed frequently and dominated the conversation more completely than she had ever seen him do before, but he seemed to say very little. He told them jokes and funny stories about friends, talked gaily about makeshifts, making light of hunger and long marches in the rain, and described in detail how General Lee had looked when he rode by on the retreat from Gettysburg and questioned: "Gentlemen, are you Georgia troops? Well, we can't get along without you Georgians!"

It seemed to Scarlett that he was talking feverishly to keep them from asking questions he did not want to answer. When she saw his eyes falter and drop before the long, troubled gaze of his father, a faint worry and bewilderment rose in her as to what was hidden in Ashley's heart. But it soon passed, for there was no room in her mind for anything except a radiant happiness and a driving desire to be alone with him.

That radiance lasted until everyone in the circle about the open fire began to yawn, and Mr. Wilkes and the girls took their departure for the hotel. Then as Ashley and Melanie and Pittypat and Scarlett mounted the stairs, lighted by Uncle Peter, a chill fell on her spirit. Until that moment when they stood in the upstairs hall, Ashley had been hers, only hers, even if she had not had a private word with him that whole afternoon. But now, as she said good night, she saw that Melanie's cheeks were suddenly crimson and she was trembling. Her eyes were on the carpet and, though she seemed overcome with some frightening emotion, she seemed shyly happy. Melanie did not even look up when Ashley opened the bedroom door, but sped inside. Ashley said good night abruptly, and he did not meet Scarlett's eyes either.

The door closed behind them, leaving Scarlett open mouthed and suddenly desolate. Ashley was no longer hers. He was Melanie's. And as long as Melanie lived, she could go into rooms with Ashley and close the door—and close out the rest of the world.

Now Ashley was going away, back to Virginia, back to the long marches in the sleet, to hungry bivouacs in the snow, to pain and hardship and to the risk of all the bright beauty of his golden head and proud slender body being blotted out in an instant, like an ant beneath a careless heel. The past week with its shimmering, dreamlike beauty, its crowded hours of happiness, was gone.

The week had passed swiftly, like a dream, a dream fragrant with the smell of pine boughs and Christmas trees, bright with little candles and home-made tinsel, a dream where minutes flew as rapidly as heartbeats. Such a breathless week when something within her drove Scarlett with mingled pain and pleasure to pack and cram every minute with incidents to remember after he was gone, happenings which she could examine at leisure in the long months ahead, extracting every morsel of comfort from them—dance, sing, laugh, fetch and carry for Ashley, anticipate his wants, smile when he smiles, be silent when he talks, follow him with your eyes so that each line of his erect body, each lift of his eyebrows, each quirk of his mouth, will be indelibly printed on your mind—for a week goes by so fast and the war goes on forever.

She sat on the divan in the parlor, holding her going-away gift for him in her lap, waiting while he said good-by to Melanie, praying that when he did come down the stairs he would be alone and she might be granted by Heaven a few moments alone with him. Her ears strained for sounds from upstairs, but the house was oddly still, so still that even the sound of her breathing seemed loud. Aunt Pittypat was crying into her pillows in her room, for Ashley had told her good-by half an hour before. No sounds of murmuring voices or of tears came from behind the closed door of Melanie's bedroom. It seemed to Scarlett that he had been in that room for hours, and she resented bitterly each moment that he stayed, saying good-by to his wife, for the moments were slipping by so fast and his time was so short.

She thought of all the things she had intended to say to him during this week. But there had been no opportunity to say them, and she knew now that perhaps she would never have the chance to say them.

Such foolish little things, some of them: "Ashley, you will be careful, won't you?" "Please don't get your feet wet. You take cold so easily." "Don't forget to put a newspaper across your chest under your shirt. It keeps the wind out so well." But there were other things, more important things she had wanted to say, much more important things she had wanted to hear him say, things she had wanted to read in his eyes, even if he did not speak them.

So many things to say and now there was no time! Even the few minutes that remained might be snatched away from her if Melanie followed him to the door, to the carriage block. Why hadn't she made the opportunity during this last week? But always, Melanie was at his side, her eyes caressing him adoringly, always friends and neighbors and relatives were in the house and, from morning till night, Ashley was never alone. Then, at night, the door of the bedroom closed and he was alone with Melanie. Never once during these last days had he betrayed to Scarlett by one look, one word, anything but the affection a brother might show a sister or a friend, a lifelong friend. She could not let him go away, perhaps forever, without knowing whether he still loved her. Then, even if he died, she could nurse the warm comfort of his secret love to the end of her days.

After what seemed an eternity of waiting, she heard the sound of his boots in the bedroom above and the door opening and closing. She heard him coming down the steps. Alone! Thank God for that! Melanie must be too overcome by grief of parting to leave her room. Now she would have him for herself for a few precious minutes.

He came down the steps slowly, his spurs clinking, and she could hear the faint slap-slap of his saber against his high boots. When he came into the parlor, his eyes were somber. He was trying to smile but his face was as white and drawn as a man bleeding from an internal wound. She rose as he entered, thinking with proprietary pride that he was the handsomest soldier she had ever seen. His long holster and belt glistened and his silver spurs and scabbard gleamed, from the industrious polishing Uncle Peter had given them. His new coat did not fit very well, for the tailor had been hurried and some of the seams were awry. The bright new sheen of the gray coat was sadly at variance with the worn and patched butternut trousers and the scarred boots, but if he had been clothed in silver armor he could not have looked more the shining knight to her.

"Ashley," she begged abruptly, "may I go to the train with you?"

"Please don't. Father and the girls will be there. And anyway, I'd rather remember you saying good-by to me here than shivering at the depot. There's so much to memories."

Instantly she abandoned her plan. If India and Honey who disliked her so much were to be present at the leave taking, she would have no chance for a private word.

"Then I won't go," she said. "See, Ashley! I've another present for you."

A little shy, now that the time had come to give it to him, she unrolled the package. It was a long yellow sash, made of thick China silk and edged with heavy fringe. Rhett Butler had brought her a yellow shawl from Havana several months before, a shawl gaudily embroidered with birds and flowers in magenta and blue. During this last week, she had patiently picked out all the embroidery and cut up the square of silk and stitched it into a sash length.

"Scarlett, it's beautiful! Did you make it yourself? Then I'll value it all the more. Put it on me, my dear. The boys will be green with envy when they see me in the glory of my new coat and sash."

She wrapped the bright lengths about his slender waist, above his belt, and tied the ends in a lover's knot. Melanie might have given him his new coat but this sash was her gift, her own secret guerdon for him to wear into battle, something that would make him remember her every time he looked at it. She stood back and viewed him with pride, thinking that even Jeb Stuart with his flaunting sash and plume could not look so dashing as her cavalier.

"It's beautiful," he repeated, fingering the fringe. "But I know you've cut up a dress or a shawl to make it. You shouldn't have done it, Scarlett. Pretty things are too hard to get these days."

"Oh, Ashley, I'd—"

She had started to say: "I'd cut up my heart for you to wear if you wanted it," but she finished, "I'd do anything for you!"

"Would you?" he questioned and some of the somberness lifted from his face. "Then, there's something you can do for me, Scarlett, something that will make my mind easier when I'm away."

"What is it?" she asked joyfully, ready to promise prodigies.

"Scarlett, will you look after Melanie for me?"

"Look after Melly?"

Her heart sank with bitter disappointment. So this was his last request of her, when she so yearned to promise something beautiful, something spectacular! And then anger flared. This moment was her moment with Ashley, hers alone. And yet, though Melanie was absent, her pale shadow lay between them. How could he bring up her name in their moment of farewell? How could he ask such a thing of her?

He did not notice the disappointment on her face. As of old, his eyes were looking through her and beyond her, at something else, not seeing her at all.

"Yes, keep an eye on her, take care of her. She's so frail and she doesn't realize it. She'll wear herself out nursing and sewing. And she's so gentle and timid. Except for Aunt Pittypat and Uncle Henry and you, she hasn't a close relative in the world, except the Burrs in Macon and they're third cousins. And Aunt Pitty—Scarlett, you know she's like a child. And Uncle Henry is an old man. Melanie loves you so much, not just because you were Charlie's wife, but because—well, because you're you and she loves you like a sister. Scarlett, I have nightmares when I think what might happen to her if I were killed and she had no one to turn to. Will you promise?"

She did not even hear his last request, so terrified was she by those ill-omened words, "if I were killed."

Every day she had read the casualty lists, read them with her heart in her throat, knowing that the world would end if anything should happen to him. But always, always, she had an inner feeling that even if the Confederate Army were entirely wiped out, Ashley would be spared. And now he had spoken the frightful words! Goose bumps came out all over her and fear swamped her, a superstitious fear she could not combat with reason. She was Irish enough to believe in second sight, especially where death premonitions were concerned, and in his wide gray eyes she saw some deep sadness which she could only interpret as that of a man who has felt the cold finger on his shoulder, has heard the wail of the Banshee.

"You mustn't say it! You mustn't even think it. It's bad luck to speak of death! Oh, say a prayer, quickly."

"You say it for me and light some candles, too," he said, smiling at the frightened urgency in her voice.

But she could not answer, so stricken was she by the pictures her mind was drawing, Ashley lying dead in the snows of Virginia, so far away from her. He went on speaking and there was a quality in his voice, a sadness, a resignation, that increased her fear until every vestige of anger and disappointment was blotted out.

"I'm asking you for this reason, Scarlett. I cannot tell what will happen to me or what will happen to any of us. But when the end comes, I shall be far away from here, even if I am alive, too far away to look out for Melanie."

"The—the end?"

"The end of the war—and the end of the world."

"But Ashley, surely you can't think the Yankees will beat us? All this week you've talked about how strong General Lee—"

"All this week I've talked lies, like all men talk when they're on furlough. Why should I frighten Melanie and Aunt Pitty before there's any need for them to be frightened? Yes, Scarlett, I think the Yankees have us. Gettysburg was the beginning of the end. The people back home don't know it yet. They can't realize how things stand with us, but—Scarlett, some of my men are barefooted now and the snow is deep in Virginia. And when I see their poor frozen feet, wrapped in rags and old sacks, and see the blood prints they leave in the snow, and know that I've got a whole pair of boots—well, I feel like I should give mine away and be barefooted too."

"Oh, Ashley, promise me you won't give them away!"

"When I see things like that and then look at the Yankees—then I see the end of everything. Why, Scarlett, the Yankees are buying soldiers from Europe by the thousands! Most of the prisoners we've taken recently can't even speak English. They're Germans and Poles and wild Irishmen who talk Gaelic. But when we lose a man, he can't be replaced. When our shoes wear out, there are no more shoes. We're bottled up, Scarlett. And we can't fight the whole world."

She thought wildly: Let the whole Confederacy crumble in the dust. Let the world end, but you must not die! I couldn't live if you were dead!

"I hope you will not repeat what I have said, Scarlett. I do not want to alarm the others. And, my dear, I would not have alarmed you by saying these things, were it not that I had to explain why I ask you to look after Melanie. She's so frail and weak and you're so strong, Scarlett. It will be a comfort to me to know that you two are together if anything happens to me. You will promise, won't you?"

"Oh, yes!" she cried, for at that moment, seeing death at his elbow, she would have promised anything. "Ashley, Ashley! I can't let you go away! I simply can't be brave about it!"

"You must be brave," he said, and his voice changed subtly. It was resonant, deeper, and his words fell swiftly as though hurried with some inner urgency. "You must be brave. For how else can I stand it?"

Her eyes sought his face quickly and with joy, wondering if he meant that leaving her was breaking his heart, even as it was breaking hers. His face was as drawn as when he came down from bidding Melanie good-by, but she could read nothing in his eyes. He leaned down, took her face in his hands, and kissed her lightly on the forehead.

"Scarlett! Scarlett! You are so fine and strong and good. So beautiful, not just your sweet face, my dear, but all of you, your body and your mind and your soul."

"Oh, Ashley," she whispered happily, thrilling at his words and his touch on her face. "Nobody else but you ever—"

"I like to think that perhaps I know you better than most people and that I can see beautiful things buried deep in you that others are too careless and too hurried to notice."

He stopped speaking and his hands dropped from her face, but his eyes still clung to her eyes. She waited a moment, breathless for him to continue, a-tiptoe to hear him say the magic three words. But they did not come. She searched his face frantically, her lips quivering, for she saw he had finished speaking.

This second blighting of her hopes was more than heart could bear and she cried "Oh!" in a childish whisper and sat down, tears stinging her eyes. Then she heard an ominous sound in the driveway, outside the window, a sound that brought home to her even more sharply the imminence of Ashley's departure. A pagan hearing the lapping of the waters around Charon's boat could not have felt more desolate. Uncle Peter, muffled in a quilt, was bringing out the carriage to take Ashley to the train.

Ashley said "Good-by," very softly, caught up from the table the wide felt hat she had inveigled from Rhett and

225

walked into the dark front hall. His hand on the door knob, he turned and looked at her, a long, desperate look, as if he wanted to carry away with him every detail of her face and figure. Through a blinding mist of tears she saw his face and with a strangling pain in her throat she knew that he was going away, away from her care, away from the safe haven of this house, out of her life, perhaps forever, without having spoken the words she yearned to hear. Time was going by like a mill race, and now it was too late. She ran stumbling across the parlor and into the hall and clutched the ends of his sash.

"Kiss me," she whispered. "Kiss me good-by."

His arms went around her gently, and he bent his head to her face. At the first touch of his lips on hers, her arms were about his neck in a strangling grip. For a fleeting immeasurable instant, he pressed her body close to his. Then she felt a sudden tensing of all his muscles. Swiftly, he dropped the hat to the floor and, reaching up, detached her arms from his neck.

"No, Scarlett, no," he said in a low voice, holding her crossed wrists in a grip that hurt.

"I love you," she said, choking. "I've always loved you. I've never loved anybody else. I just married Charlie to—to try to hurt you. Oh, Ashley, I love you so much I'd walk every step of the way to Virginia just to be near you! And I'd cook for you and polish your boots and groom your horse—Ashley, say you love me! I'll live on it for the rest of my life!"

He bent suddenly to retrieve his hat and she had one glimpse of his face. It was the unhappiest face she was ever to see, a face from which all aloofness had fled. Written on it were his love for her and joy that she loved him, but battling them both were shame and despair.

"Good-by," he said hoarsely.

The door clicked open and a gust of cold wind swept the house, fluttering the curtains. Scarlett shivered as she watched him run down the walk to the carriage, his saber glinting in the feeble winter sunlight, the fringe of his sash dancing jauntily.

Contributors

RAYMOND ATKINS resides in northwest Georgia with his wife, his dog, and between one and four children, depending on the season. His stories have appeared in *The Old Red Kimono*, *The Blood and Fire Review*, and *The Lavender Mountain Anthology*. He is currently working on his second novel.

TONI CADE BAMBARA was a native of New York who moved to Atlanta in the late 1970s to teach at Spelman College. She won the National Book Award for her novel *The Salt Eaters*. A prolific writer, she authored works for page, stage, and screen. She died in 1995.

ERSKINE CALDWELL published twenty-six novels, sixteen collections of stories, fifteen books of nonfiction, two children's books, and a collection of poetry in the years between 1929 and 1984. Two of his novels, *Tobacco Road* and *God's Little Acre*, are among the best-known works of twentieth-century America. *Tobacco Road* and its hero, Jeeter Lester, rose to cult status due in part to the novel's successful adaptation to the stage. Caldwell died in 1987.

LAURA DABUNDO chairs the Department of English at Kennesaw State University, Kennesaw, Georgia. She has published critical essays related to her research interest, English Romanticism. In addition she has authored several general-interest essays in *The Department Chair*.

JANICE DAUGHARTY hales from Valdosta, Georgia, where she lives, works, and studies. She has published a succession of novels beginning with *Dark of the Moon* in 1994 and including *Necessary Lies, Pawpaw Patch, Earl in the Yellow Shirt, Whistle,* and *Like a Sister.* In addition she has published a collection of short stories called *Going Through the Change.*

LEWIS GRIZZARD was born in 1947 in Moreland, Georgia, the birthplace of another famous Georgia author, Erskine Caldwell. Grizzard was a columnist for the *Atlanta Journal Constitution* and published such national best sellers as *Chili Dawgs Always Bark at Night, Don't Bend Over in the Garden, Granny, You Know Them Taters Got Eyes,* and *I Haven't Understood Anything Since 1962.* He died in 1994.

JOEL CHANDLER HARRIS was born in Eatonton, Georgia, in 1848, and died in Atlanta in 1908. During his lifetime he held editorial positions on papers in Forsyth, Savannah, and Atlanta. At the *Atlanta Constitution* Harris began writing local color sketches in a rendition of African American dialect from which came "Uncle Remus," the character with which he is popularly associated. A prolific writer, he produced six novels, a biography, a history of Georgia, a translation of French folktales, six volumes of children's stories, and seven volumes of short stories for adults.

JIM HENDRICKS is the managing editor of the *Albany (Georgia) Herald* and writes a humor column for the newspaper. A graduate of Valdosta State University, he has won a number of writing awards in his twenty-year career. He and his wife, Cheryl, have two sons, Steven and Justin.

MARGARET MITCHELL was born in Atlanta in 1900 and died in 1949. *Gone With the Wind,* published in 1936, has proven to be one of the most enduring works of fiction in

American literature, with the film version, released in 1939, propelling the novel's heroine, Scarlett O'Hara, into the realm of cultural icon. Ms. Mitchell received both the Pulitzer Prize and the National Book Award.

DOROTHY DODGE ROBBINS teaches in the Department of English at Louisiana Tech University. Her essays and reviews have appeared in *The Centennial Review*, *Critique*, *The Midwest Quarterly*, *The Southern Quarterly*, and *The Texas Review*. She is the coeditor of *Christmas Stories from Louisiana* (University Press of Mississippi, 2003) and *Christmas on the Great Plains* (University of Iowa Press, 2004).

KENNETH ROBBINS serves as director, School of the Performing Arts, Louisiana Tech University. His short stories have been published in *The Briar Cliff Review*, *Heritage of the Great Plains*, *The North Dakota Quarterly*, *St. Andrews Review*, and *The Southern Quarterly*, among others. His novel, *Buttermilk Bottoms*, received the Toni Morrison Prize for Fiction and the Associated Writing Programs Novel Award. Robbins's stage plays have been performed throughout the United States, Canada, Denmark, Ireland, and Japan. He was born in 1944 in Douglasville, Georgia, and holds degrees from Young Harris College, Georgia Southern University, and the University of Georgia.

FERROL SAMS is a lifelong resident of Fayetteville, Georgia, where he continues his work as a medical doctor. His Porter Osbourne trilogy (*Run with the Horsemen*, *The Whisper of the River*, and *When All the World Was Young*) firmly establishes him as an American author of note. In addition, he has published *The Widow's Mite and Other Stories* and *Epiphany*.

KAREN SCHWIND currently teaches in the Department of English at the University of Georgia. Prior to this appointment, she was assistant department chair of modern languages at Truett-McConnell College's Watkinsville campus. She has published in *Athens Magazine* and *The Conspirator.*

JACK SLAY, JR., has published stories in *Realms of Fantasy*, *Talebones*, *The Habersham Review*, *Scouting*, *Mississippi*, *Cemetery Dance*, and *Snake River Review*. He resides in LaGrange, Georgia, where he teaches in the Department of English at LaGrange College.

LILLIAN SMITH, born in Jasper, Florida, is a leading figure in Georgia letters. Her fame was established with *Strange Fruit*, a novel that stirred a national controversy with its truthful depiction of the segregated South. *Killers of the Dream* confirmed her international status as a writer of social criticism. She died in 1966.

JASON TAYLOR is a graduate student in the Master of Arts in Professional Writing program at Kennesaw State University in Kennesaw, Georgia. He freelances while working as a full-time writer for two magazines.

PHILIP LEE WILLIAMS is the author of eight novels and two works of creative nonfiction. Among his publications are *In the Heart of a Distant Forest* (for which he won the Townsend Award for Fiction, Georgia's highest award for a fiction writer), *The Song of Daniel*, and *Crossing Wildcat Ridge: A Memoir of Nature and Healing*. He is the public relations writer for the Franklin College of Arts and Sciences at the University of Georgia.